FRANCES MURRAY

The Burning Lamp

ST. MARTIN'S   NEW YORK

To my colleagues in the LSA who were so helpful
in the matter of useless objects.

AFFILIATED PUBLISHERS: Macmillan Limited, London
—also at Bombay, Calcutta, Madras and Melbourne

The Burning Lamp

1

"YOU LOOK EXTREMELY YOUNG," said Miss Nightingale.

"I will be twenty in November," stated Phemie.

"I prefer my nurses to be older," Miss Nightingale said severely. "Twenty-five is as young as . . ."

"Age isn't really a matter of years, I find," returned Phemie. "I know people twice my age who will never be as old as I am now."

Miss Nightingale, thus countered, gave Phemie her full attention. Phemie, subjected to this ordeal, sat calmly, her hands in her lap and her eyes upon Miss Nightingale's face: after a moment the somewhat frosty expression upon that face relaxed into a rueful smile.

"My dear, this is lamentably true, as I know well. But I was really thinking of physical maturity. You are undergrown and shockingly slender. You look as if a puff of wind would blow you away."

"It's this black," explained Phemie. "I'm really very strong, Miss Nightingale . . . and I'm never ill."

Miss Nightingale made a note.

"You say you have nursed," she resumed. "Surely you are too young to have had much experience of the sickroom?"

Phemie frowned and considered for a second.

"I don't know quite what you would regard as experience, ma'am. My father was a doctor . . ."

Miss Nightingale indicated Phemie's black garments with a gesture of her neat hands.

"These . . . they are for your father?"

1

Phemie nodded.

"He died a month ago after a long illness. I nursed him for eighteen months. My mother was ill for a year before she died and I helped my sister care for her. I learned about illness and sick people from my father and read a number of his books."

Miss Nightingale looked slightly disapproving at this.

"I wonder at his permitting you."

Phemie looked down her nose and said nothing.

"However," continued Miss Nightingale, "your information alters the situation somewhat. I would certainly say that you had had some experience though I could wish for your sake that it had been in less tragic circumstances. And despite this you still want to train in my school?"

"Yes," said Phemie calmly.

"You don't consider, perhaps, that we can teach you very little?"

Phemie glanced up at this and considered Miss Nightingale's bland expression.

"I hope I know better than that," she responded drily.

Miss Nightingale smiled and made another note.

"Why do you want to train for a nurse?" she enquired.

"Because I want to earn a living and I feel that this is one way in which I can."

Miss Nightingale's delicate eyebrows rose at this bluntness.

"You are left poorly provided for?"

"No," said Phemie, "not precisely. But there are conditions attached to the enjoyment of my inheritance which I find myself unable to observe."

"Indeed."

Miss Nightingale's voice was icy.

"I trust you may not feel similarly about the rules which govern probation in my school."

"No," said Phemie again, "I may prefer to choose my disciplines but I promise you I will comply with whatever I choose."

Miss Nightingale laid down her pen and looked more closely at the diminutive figure before her; what she saw was unim-

2

pressive. Phemie was a tiny person, her pale and plain face redeemed only by a well-shaped mouth, small and firm. Her eyes were a good grey-blue but not large and her eyelashes long but light in colour. Her one beauty was a mane of pale, red-gold silky hair and this was screwed back into an unbecoming chignon which looked too heavy for her slender neck. From this one tendril had escaped and lay on the black velvet collar of her jacket.

"I think," said Miss Nightingale, "that you had better tell me the whole story. I can have no place in this scheme of mine for runaway schoolgirls or refugees from imaginary wrongs. They cause me trouble and waste time which I can ill spare and what is worst they make poor nurses. If I am to consider your application I must know the truth."

Phemie in her turn studied the face in front of her, sighed and answered in a kind of non-sequitur.

"It is all so much easier for boys," she said with a shade of resentment. "If things don't suit them they can join the army or run away to sea or do a dozen things and no one says any the worse of them . . . their reputation isn't ruined . . ."

Miss Nightingale didn't smile at this outburst. A slight frown appeared between her brows and she nodded agreement.

"My father had a partner," Phemie went on, "he was an assistant really. He came when my father fell ill and before long, of course, he had the whole practice on his shoulders. And he brought in new patients . . ." She paused and went slightly pink.

"A personable young man evidently?" remarked Miss Nightingale drily.

Phemie nodded.

"He wanted a partnership but he didn't have a penny, and father . . ." She frowned and swallowed.

"He knew fine by then he wasn't to get better and he'd me and Jean to see after. This way he couldn't just give Neil . . . Doctor Linklater the practice. So . . . they made an agreement. Doctor Linklater was to pay Jean—she's my elder sister and married on a doer in Glasgow—a certain sum out of the practice for the next ten years . . ."

"And you?"

"I was to marry Doctor Linklater."

"I see."

"He left me Blackburn Riggs, a wee farm which was my grandfather's. That was to be my tocher."

Miss Nightingale looked enquiringly.

"My portion . . . my dowry. It was just a token really, the rent's only twenty pounds a year . . ."

"Am I to understand that you were not much consulted in the matter, Miss Witherspoon?"

Phemie didn't answer at once.

"Father wouldn't have *made* me marry him," she replied at last, "not if I'd said I didn't want to. He'd no opinion of women but he wasn't a bully in that way. He just didn't think we were people like men are. We were creatures to be looked after . . . like horses. As he saw it, an arrangement like that looked after me and I . . ."

Once again she went pink.

"I made no objections . . ."

"How old were you at this time?"

Miss Nightingale's voice was expressionless.

"Old enough to know better," returned Phemie energetically, "I was nearly eighteen."

She looked up from the contemplation of her black-gloved hands, her face scornful.

"I doubt I'd not be handed over now as the make-weight in the purchase of a practice," she added.

Miss Nightingale smiled. "I feel sure you would not. I take it the marriage did not take place?"

"No," said Phemie. "The engagement was announced and then my father fell really ill so that I was needed all the time . . . and Neil . . . Doctor Linklater . . . was in no hurry."

Her face expressed a certain wry amusement.

"We agreed to wait until after the death of my father."

She paused again, evidently finding it a little difficult to tell the rest of the story. Her listener said nothing but waited.

"The day after the funeral," Phemie continued at last,

"Doctor Linklater informed me that after all he would prefer to marry Mary Deuchar and that he had made other arrangements for me. She was pretty, you see, and her parents were very well to do . . ."

A touch of acid informed the quiet voice.

". . . her father's business is the manufacture of earthenware sanitary appliances . . ."

Miss Nightingale permitted herself another smile.

"I have supervised the fitting-out of too many hospitals not to be familiar with the name, Miss Witherspoon," she observed. "And what were these 'other arrangements'?"

Phemie's lips tightened.

"I was to live with my married sister Jean and he would pay a little extra to cover my food and keep until another husband could be found for me."

She swallowed hard.

"He didn't explain how anyone was to be found to take me, *me*, shilpit and as plain as a plate of brose on a tocher of a hundred and fifty acres of poor, sour land."

She looked Miss Nightingale in the eye.

"What they'd really done was to hand over the practice to Linklater half-price and in return for the service Jean and her man got a free housekeeper and nursery-maid for as long as they needed one. I'm not quite a fool and I knew that fine. I asked if I could look for a post as a governess; with the salary from that and the income of Blackburn . . . when Eck Miller could pay his rent which wasn't always . . . I could keep myself and not want money from anyone."

"And what did they say to this proposal?"

"Did I mention that my father had made Linklater one of my trustees? He said he could not reconcile it with his conscience to let me go out to work."

"And the other trustee?"

Phemie gave her a scornful look.

"Frank Dinwoodie, my brother-in-law. He agreed with Linklater. And when Jean heard of the scheme she just laughed and said I couldn't play on the piano to save my life, I sang like a

5

crow and knew never a word of the French or the Italian and a fine kind of governess I would make.''

Miss Nightingale again permitted herself a smile.

''Disabilities certainly in a family of fashion.''

''I didn't want to become a lady's-maid or to sew for a dressmaker, that's slavery to my mind, and slavery without purpose. I came to the conclusion that the only thing I knew more than a little about was nursing the sick. So, I decided to come here.''

''And they permitted this?''

Phemie looked scornfully at her questioner.

''I didn't ask for permission. I came.''

For the first time during the interview Miss Nightingale looked disconcerted.

''Am I to understand that your people have no notion of your present whereabouts?''

''None,'' said Phemie.

''And you have travelled from Glasgow to London in the train unescorted?''

Phemie nodded.

''I came to no harm. Everyone was most civil and helpful.''

''And if they had not been?'' demanded Miss Nightingale. ''You are by far too young to travel alone. I suppose you are now penniless?''

''I have enough for a night's lodging.''

''When did you eat last?''

''I had breakfast this morning.''

Miss Nightingale rang a bell on her desk.

''Suppose I were not to accept you, what would you do?''

''There are a number of hospitals in London,'' returned Phemie. ''One of them will accept me as a practical nurse. It is not what I want but it will do until I am old enough to apply to you again.''

''And if I do accept you, what will your family have to say?''

''Oh, they'll agree to a fait accompli,'' Phemie told her. ''Doctor Linklater will be pleased to have the skeleton removed from his wedding-feast and my brother-in-law will agree for the

6

sake of peace. And you have made nursing respectable, ma'am
. . . Jean need not blush for a sister who is training with the
great Miss Nightingale's school in London as she would have
blushed for the underpaid governess on the other side of Glasgow."

A maid answered the bell.

"If you please, Cooper, bring Miss Witherspoon a bowl of
broth and some bread and butter. I find she has had no
luncheon."

Cooper regarded Phemie's small frame with concern, tut-
tutted disapprovingly and departed.

Phemie rose to her feet.

"Really, ma'am, I assure you . . . it is quite unnecessary."

"Be seated," said Miss Nightingale sharply. "Don't be
foolish. If you are to look after others, you must first look after
yourself. If you do not, you are a fool."

"I have heard," observed Phemie as she sat down again, I
have heard that you do not suffer fools gladly."

Miss Nightingale looked amused.

"There are innumerable fools in the medical profession,"
she told Phemie, who opened her eyes widely. "And if you are
to become a nurse suffer them you must, gladly or no. Tell me,
how did you come by the notion to apply to Mrs Wardroper?"

Phemie opened her reticule and pulled out a letter.

"For the last fortnight of my father's life he was very helpless
and I needed some assistance in caring for him. Doctor Linklater
arranged for one of your nurses to come from the hospital in
Glasgow. Her name was Miss Merriwether."

"Eleanor Merriwether?"

"Yes."

"She impressed you?"

"Very much. She impressed my father too. In fact he
mentioned her in his will."

Miss Nightingale's face froze with distaste but Phemie continued smoothly:

"He left her a small sum on condition she spent it wholly on
female frivolities."

7

There was a tiny silence and Miss Nightingale began to laugh once more.

"That will puzzle her, poor child."

"She was kind enough to write this letter about me to Mrs Wardroper."

Miss Nightingale held out her hand.

"As you know already Mrs Wardroper is out of London . . . or you would not be here. She will not object if I read it."

She broke the seal and unfolded the sheet just as Cooper entered with a tray, exquisitely set, which she put in front of Phemie who began upon its contents at once.

"Do you know what she wrote?"

"No."

When she had finished Miss Nightingale laid the note on her desk.

"You appear to have impressed my serious Merriwether as much as she impressed your father. She remarks on your courage and your independent and powerful mind."

"I am not certain," commented Phemie ruefully, "whether she regarded the latter attribute as a virtue. In fact I am convinced she did not."

"It was certainly not an attribute which she shared with you," Miss Nightingale said rather acidly and then looked kindly at Phemie as she finished the broth and laid the napkin upon the tray. "Nor is it one which will make your chosen career an easy one."

"I have already discovered that its possession makes being any kind of female sufficiently burdensome," said Phemie wryly. "I don't despair of learning to dissemble in time and appearing as mawkish as the lave."

Miss Nightingale laughed aloud and rang her bell again.

"It is a weapon to be used with discretion," she agreed, "but let me entreat you not to let it rust in disuse."

After Cooper had gone away with the tray Miss Nightingale looked over at her guest and frowned.

"I would like to enrol you," she said, "I want people of your calibre and education, but at your age you must have the consent of your guardians."

"They will sign a consent," Phemie affirmed confidently.

"You are sure?"

She nodded.

"It is most irregular, but . . ." Miss Nightingale hesitated, "but I will give you a note to the staff at the hospital and they will accommodate you until we have sorted out this matter of consent. No, don't thank me. I would feel uncomfortably thinking of you alone in this city."

She looked up from the note she was scribbling, and smiled. "And somehow I feel sure you will have your way with your trustees, Miss Witherspoon."

When Phemie had gone her way, Miss Nightingale looked at Doctor Sutherland who was finishing a cup of tea. He had been summoned to meet a countrywoman and a new recruit. His relationship with Miss Nightingale was a curious one. Invalidish as she was she depended upon him to intervene between her and those aspects of the outside world she preferred to keep at a distance. He was a bobbing-block for the political world's impatience and exasperation with Miss Nightingale and for Miss Nightingale's irritation and impatience with a male-dominated political world. He was her amanuensis, her collector of information, her digester of statistics, her messenger and her spokesman. In return she abused him heartily and continually and trusted him absolutely. Despite his Turkish treatment he continued to love and admire her without illusion: he had a dour common sense and strength of character which caused him to refuse her the self-immolation in a cause which Miss Nightingale demanded of less stable characters. Though she would never have admitted it to him Miss Nightingale depended more on him than upon anyone: nor would she need to admit it, for the knowledge of her dependence made part of their vast store of mutual understanding of which the impatience and the abuse was no more than a surface phenomenon.

"Promising child, don't you agreed, Scottie?" she said, "I feel she has that blend of qualities which will make a matron one of these days."

Doctor Sutherland took the remaining scone from the dish and chewed it thoughtfully.

"Ye'll have trouble with that one," he commented at last.

"Why, in heaven's name?"

"Instinct, woman . . . intuition, call it what ye like, but ye will have trouble . . . or other folk will. She's too like yersel'."

He went out and Miss Nightingale defiantly dipped her pen in the standish to begin her dossier on WITHERSPOON Euphemia Dorcas.

". . . entered as Lady Nurse subject to guardians' consent. On first interview," wrote Miss Nightingale, "she made a favourable impression upon me. She seemed truthful, intelligent, unaffected . . ." She paused and frowned at the door through which Dr Sutherland had passed. "There is, however," she added, "a certain independence of mind . . ." She paused again ". . . which however admirable in itself . . ." The pen dipped and dried and dipped again. ". . . might in some circumstances involve her in difficulty . . ."

Three days later, Phemie and the eight other newly entered Lady Nurses were being fitted for uniform dresses. She regarded the brown stuff bodices and skirts without great interest until she noticed a surprising feature of the skirt she was about to put on.

"That's never a train?" she exclaimed.

Miss Allonby who was supervising the operation explained.

"All Lady Nurses have trains to their dresses, Miss Witherspoon."

"Why?"

Miss Allonby turned her back and bent solicitously over an imaginary bed.

"Even in this position my ankles are completely covered," she pointed out. "You may carry out quite energetic duties in

10

the open ward without danger of exposing yourself unduly to
. . . er, male patients.''

Phemie eyed the not inconsiderable area thus unexposed but
kept her unladylike reflections to herself. Miss Allonby
resumed the vertical.

''And, ladies, when these trains wear out with brushing upon
the wooden floors of the wards, they are to be replaced and not
removed. You understand?''

Her charges chorused, ''Yes, Miss Allonby.''

And for the fifth time that afternoon she told them, ''You call
me Sister.''

And for the fifth time that afternoon someone responded to
that statement with, ''Yes, Miss Allonby.''

Later that same day in their brown dresses, white aprons and
starched caps the latest recruits to the new profession filed into
the lecture room where the Matron of St Thomas's, Mrs
Wardroper, was to address them. Phemie by this time had
acquired a companion. Adela Wedmore was almost exactly the
opposite of Phemie in every way, tall, decidedly plump, dark
haired, highly coloured, emotional and, Phemie decided after a
few minutes' conversation, not endowed with more than common sense. She had been allocated the cubicle next to Phemie's
and seemed to regard this circumstance as a foundation for a
firm and lasting friendship. Phemie, ruefully conscious of the
ludicrous study in extremes they made together, was quite
unable to repulse her clumsy overtures. This afternoon her
inability had involved her in a certain amount of discomfort for
sharing a bench with Probationer Wedmore was an obliterating
experience.

Mrs Wardroper, tall, imposing and bespectacled, came into
the room, put up her hand for silence and began to speak
forcibly. She welcomed them to the hospital, warned them of
the rules they must obey and the sights they must be able to face
and the tasks they must not flinch from accomplishing. She went
on:

". . . upon you, young ladies, will rest the reputation of the Nightingale School. When you consider the type of female formerly employed to nurse the unfortunate sick you will realise that even a breath of malicious talk can damage the profession in a disastrous manner . . ."

Phemie remembered how Miss Nightingale's face had frozen at the mention of her father's will. She remembered, too, the unkempt and unwashed creature sent by the doctor to nurse her mother who had been thrust forth from 'Rosebank' by Jean.

Miss Wardroper enlarged on this moral theme for a few minutes: flirtation would entail immediate expulsion from the School; Probationers must never leave the doors of the Home unescorted: untoward passages between patient and nurse would result in immediate dismissal. They must be nuns in all but name. She looked around the circle of faces to make sure they had all understood what she had said and then began to outline the year's work. At this point Phemie began to take notes on the paper she had brought. Her time was to be divided between the wards and lectures in the room they were in. Ward duties were to include: checking and replenishing stores, cleaning the ward and the lavatories, blanket-bathing patients without exposing them either to cold or to any lascivious gaze, the prevention of bedsores, the making of beds, the making and application of dressings, the correct application of 'friction', the measurement of temperatures, simple treatments and the administration of drugs as part of them, sick cookery, observation of symptoms and the keeping of charts, the prevention of infection, the management of convalescents, the laying out of corpses, and finally, methods of instructing others in these skills.

". . . because your turn to stand here will come, young ladies, and come soon. You are the pioneers and your task will be to pass on what we teach you wherever you go. You must take careful and detailed notes on your cases, taking especial care to list their symptoms and describe their treatment. You will also be expected to keep a meticulous diary of your work on the wards which will be submitted at intervals either to me or to Miss Nightingale . . .''

She then outlined their course of study which was to include the study of nourishment, medical terms and their abbreviations, classification of drugs and medicines, their origins and their uses, elementary physiology . . .

Adela Wedmore turned her head to look at Phemie, her eyes round with alarm.

''Whatever can that be?''

''How the body works,'' whispered Phemie.

''. . . elementary anatomy . . .'' continued Mrs Wardroper.

Adela looked again and Phemie smiled reassuringly. ''How the body's made.''

''Oh, dear me,'' whispered Adela miserably, ''I could never learn a tenth of that.''

''. . . poisons and their antidotes . . .'' Miss Wardroper was well into her stride and did not even pause as she frowned on the two whisperers. ''. . . elementary chemistry, the symptoms of common fevers, weights and measures and the interpretation of prescriptions, the treatment of burns and scalds . . .''

The list lengthened inexorably under Phemie's pencil and Adela's face gradually assumed an expression of utter despair.

''I thought we'd be in the wards all the time, *doing* things,'' she mourned breathily against Phemie's ear, ''I was never bookish . . . I'll never be able to learn any of that . . .'' She planted a finger as thick and blunt as the handle of a broom on Phemie's list. ''. . . I haven't even *heard* of half of them . . .''

''. . . and before I conclude, let me emphasise once more that upon the behaviour and deportment of each one of you depends the reputation of the whole profession. Good afternoon to you.''

Mrs. Wardroper waited until the Probationers rose from their seats, smiled grimly upon them and swept out.

 . . . we are to begin in the wards tomorrow and I am to go to Elizabeth Ward where there are women who have had operations or accidents or sores which must be dressed every day. Tell Jean I have a little cubicle all to myself. The Home would be drab were it not for the flowers sent up from Lea Hurst by Miss Nightingale. There is often fruit and game from the same source of the dinner-table. Nothing is too good for 'her girls' as she calls us.

Our hours are very long but we have a great deal to learn in our Probation Year and I can hardly see how we can cram it all in in the time. We are released from our duties on the wards two days a week for two hours to hear lectures on medical topics from various doctors; which reminds me, please, Frank, would you send me my father's medical books. They will be of the greatest assistance. Linklater has no claim on them . . . they are part of the house-furnishings, not of the practice and so you may tell him . . .

It must have been over three months later that Phemie was sitting at a table in the cubicle on the top floor of St Thomas's writing up her ward journal. Summer had come and it was stiflingly hot under the roof. She had removed the heavy stuff gown and was sitting before the open window in her cotton petticoat. A knock fell upon the door and she sighed. She had hoped that Adela might be resting her feet and she would be free of her company for an hour or so.

"Come in!" she called and wrote busily on.

The door was opened, there was a brief pause and then a shocked, "Witherspoon! What are you about? Please make yourself decent this instant. I will wait outside until you are fit to be seen. I have something of a very particular nature I wish to tell you." She turned her back. "Miss Nightingale will certainly hear of this."

The door snapped shut and Phemie, her lips pressed tightly together, scrambled into the brown stuff gown and tidied herself with a speed born of practice. In just over two minutes she presented herself at the doorway to meet the comminatory glare of the Wardroper spectacles.

"Miss Witherspoon, permit me to tell you, that while you may dress as you please in your room according to the

14

exigencies of the season or of your toilet you must not on any account admit anyone while you are in a state of such disarray."

"No, Matron."

"I should think not indeed. Not but what it is extremely hot up here, I have remarked it often. However, you must recall the dignity of the profession of which you are to be a member."

"Yes, Matron."

"I came to tell you that you have a visitor."

Phemie stared, for she knew of no one who might be liable to visit her unless it were Frank or Jean and neither of them were able to leave Glasgow at that time as Jean was hourly expecting her second child.

"It is your brother," Mrs Wardroper kindly informed her, "I have asked him to wait in the visiting room."

Phemie's face rarely expressed her emotions and it did not now.

"Yes, Matron," she said. "How kind of you. I'll come at once."

She went downstairs in Mrs Wardroper's wake, her train hushing after her on the treads of the staircase, wondering who her 'brother' might turn out to be. The tall figure looking out of the window at the dusty summer street was unmistakable.

"Good afternoon, Neil," said Phemie. "Won't you sit down?"

"Phemie!" Neil turned round as she spoke. "You look as if you had grown two inches. It must be that singularly unbecoming garment."

He waited until she sat down at one of the small tables in the room and then joined her. Phemie considered him dispassionately.

"Why have you come?" she asked politely.

He hesitated for a second, looking at her unresponsive face.

"As a matter of fact I came to see whether you'd got tired of all this . . . ." He gestured distastefully around the rather dreary room. "I thought you might be ready to come home and I could be your escort back to the North."

15

"No. I don't want to come," she responded calmly. "I like my work here."

"The sheerest drudgery. I've watched nurses."

He picked up one of her hands. "Look at it! Rough as a scullery-maid's and for the same reason. Be sensible, girl. Surely anything would be better than slaving away here for a tiny pittance?"

Phemie pulled her hand away.

"And just what might you mean by 'anything'?" she demanded. "Slaving away for Jean for nothing at all?"

"No," said Neil, "as a matter of fact I thought we might go back to the original arrangement and get married."

Phemie stared at him quizzically. "And Mary Deuchar?" she asked.

"She doesn't come into this."

"Turned you down, has she?"

Neil flushed.

"As a matter of face she has not. Not yet. It was on my conscience that I'd treated you shabbily . . . I found I couldn't go on with it."

Phemie laughed in his face.

"On your conscience, Neil! Stuff! You haven't one!"

"I am speaking nothing but the truth," retorted Neil stiffly. "If I could be sure you were safe in the care of your sister and leading the kind of life for which your sheltered upbringing had prepared you . . . then perhaps, knowing you were in good hands and that your prospects were in no way impaired, then I might have been able . . . to follow the dictates of my heart and . . ."

"Stuff!" said Phemie again, but failed to put her suitor out of his stride.

"But as things are I find I cannot reconcile it with my sense of what is proper to enjoy the comforts of matrimony and a well-appointed home knowing that you are alone here and leading such an uncomfortable and unnatural existence."

Phemie opened her eyes widely.

"You did not appear to suffer these pangs when you signed

the consent for my entering here," she remarked. "In fact there was a distinct flavour of 'good riddance' about your letter."

Neil merely shook his head at this challenge with an air of understanding forgiveness.

"In fact," Phemie went on, "I'd give a good deal to know what's brought this change of heart about. Either Mary has turned you down like a sensible creature . . . though I must say this is not the impression of her that I received . . . or more likely her parents have, Johnnie Deuchar is no fool . . ."

"I promise you this is not the case."

"Perhaps a fairy godmother has left me a fortune bigger than Mary's or . . . I have it . . . my father has appeared to you at midnight in the surgery and shaken his hoary locks at you . . ."

Neil was stung into reproof.

"You ought not to speak lightly of the dead," he told her.

"I doubt he'd not take the trouble to return for my sake anyway," reflected Phemie and got up.

"Where are you going?"

"Back to my room. I have work to finish."

He looked confounded.

"Aren't you going to give me an answer?"

"Just as you like," said Phemie. "It is 'no'."

"No?"

"No," agreed Phemie. "Thank you for the offer but I prefer to pursue my course of training."

"But," protested Neil and his face reddened again, "I thought . . . I had reason to suppose that such a proposition might not be unacceptable to you."

"Had you indeed?" returned Phemie. "Well, I have an unworthy pleasure in informing you that this is no longer the case. If it ever was."

"You had better think carefully," he advised her. "I may not renew this proposal, Phemie . . . remember your . . . your disadvantages in this respect. Consider before it is too late whether it is likely that you will receive further opportunities to enter into the matrimonial estate."

"Plain and penniless as I am," said Phemie serenely, "I am quite sure that I must prefer single blessedness to being yoked to a pompous hypocrite."

She curtseyed in the grand manner and made for the door. Neil intercepted her.

"If I were to tell you that only the basest and most mercenary of motives which I regret more deeply than I can express tempted me into breaking a solemn undertaking made to your dying father," he declared, "and that that undertaking agreed with all the impulses of my heart and nature . . ."

"If you did I wouldn't understand you," observed Phemie trying to dodge round him, "and if I did work out your meaning I wouldn't believe a word of it."

"I implore you to believe the truth of what I say," Neil went on earnestly. "Only give me an opportunity to prove how sincerely I regret the way I treated you."

"Oh, Neil, for pity sake," she exclaimed in exasperation, "this isn't Drury Lane. Let me go upstairs and let you go and marry your Mary with a clear conscience. I relinquish all claim. And if father's ghost troubles you, refer him to me."

"I don't *want* to marry Mary," stated her suitor irritably. "I want to marry you."

"Stuff!" said Phemie for the third time. "I cannot believe that you are serious. Let me pass if you please . . ."

She moved forwards to where he stood in front of the door.

"I'll prove how serious I am!" he exclaimed and before she could dodge him, picked her up bodily and kissed her on the mouth. Phemie flushed hotly with anger and revulsion. She wriggled and kicked and pushed until he put her back on her feet.

"What a termagant!" he laughed at her, "I can see I am going to have trouble with you."

Phemie pulled away wiping her mouth with her hand and considered his handsome complacent face. She hit it with all the strength she possessed. After three strenuous months of lifting patients, carrying trays and making beds it hurt him enough to remove the smile. He put his hand to his cheek and stared at her, hurt and angry.

"There was a time, miss," he snapped, "when you would not have done that."

"I can't recall, sir, that you ever made use of the opportunities thus afforded you. And I will make sure that you never have others! Good day to you."

She stormed upstairs, leaving him to find his own way out which he did uncomfortably conscious of the red weals now beginning to show on his cheek.

Upstairs Phemie shut her door with what might be called a slam, sat down again at the table which doubled for desk and dressing-table and dipped her pen ready to continue writing up her journal. The last entry stared up at her . . .

"8-9: After prayers washed 15's hands and face and brushed her hair. Sister showed me how to prepare and apply the belladonna plaster to her neck . . ."

An open cancer of the neck . . . Phemie stared out of the window but she didn't see the sickening sore which was dressed every day, she saw 15's patient face and remembered her five children . . . Her pen began to travel over the paper.

. . . Attended various calls from patients. Prepared screen, oil, lint, etc. for dressing number 18 and watched Sister clean and dress the burn. 18 is much weaker today and has some fever. There is a smell of pus. Sister fears that the burn is beginning to mortify. Got lotion to syringe 24's knee and redressed that as I have been doing for the past week. Removed all utensils afterwards.

9-10.15: Attended Sister and Mr Parry the surgeon in the small ward with cancer patient. Removed and replaced her dressings under supervision and watched Sister measure out her laudanum. Washed all the lockers on my side. Collected and washed all the basins, soup-plates, flower-pot stands, porringers, wound-trays etc., etc. Brought them back into the ward. Washed the basins and stone tops

in the lavatories and tidied them. Attended to calls from
patients . . .

Phemie considered the beginning of her day and contrasted it
with her life if she were to become Neil's wife. There would be
comfort, a degree of elegance . . . money to spend on clothes . . .
she had always had a suspicion that clothes might make a
considerable difference to the way she looked. Music, books
. . . as many as she wanted, he could hardly refuse her those.
There might be children and she liked children. There would
also be Neil . . . she considered this and flushed. His kiss had not
left her unmoved, in fact the violence of her reaction to it was a
measure of how much she had been affected. But . . . would
there always be Neil? It seemed less than likely. She had no
desire to play the injured wife in a melodrama however luxurious the setting; and there would be those long spaces of the day
to be got through with no occupation worth the doing that she
could not hire someone to do better. No . . . she had made the
right decision. She dipped the pen and continued her entry.
"10.15-10.45: Changed the ice bags in the small ward. Got
number 10 up and into a chair. She is better but still very weak.
Attended to various calls . . ."
She had finished her entries and was just beginning to expand
the notes she had taken from Doctor Orde's lecture on the
Alimentary Canal into a section of her lecture book when Adela
Wedmore rapped on her door, came in and sat down on the bed
which sagged and creaked in protest.
"Wouldn't you care to come for a walk before tea, Phemie?"
she asked plaintively. "It's too hot to stay up here till then."
Phemie, conscious of the sweat trickling down her spine,
nodded.
"I'd like that," she agreed. "I'll finish this tonight before
bed. It'll be cooler then."
"I hear your brother came to see you today," Adela
mentioned, as Phemie replaced her white cap with the regulation straw bonnet. Her pale narrow face peered from its depths
like a little animal in a burrow.

20

"In fact," said Phemie, and burned her boats, "Neil is not my brother."

Adela digested this face as she tied the strings of her bonnet under one of her chins. On her the regulation bonnet looked like a rim of pastry round a cheesecake.

"He looked fearfully handsome," she observed wistfully as they made their way downstairs.

"Did you think so?" said Phemie politely but unresponsively. "Would you object if we paid a visit to the bookshop?"

Adela sighed. She had spent many hours during the past months waiting in the dark little shop while Phemie turned over the grimy stock in search of textbooks.

"Very well," she said patiently, "but you study too much, Phemie. You'll addle your brain. Females aren't meant to study like men."

"Haivers," said Phemie.

It was an expression she used frequently in conversation with Adela.

As usual Phemie made straight for the old bakers' tray in the middle of the shop which held the battered fifth and sixth-hand copies of medical textbooks sold off by the impoverished students at St Thomas's. There were cleaner copies ranged on the rickety shelves but Phemie could not afford to patronise them very often. Today she examined the much-thumbed derelicts in the tray and found a treasure. She put out a gloved hand and picked it up a fraction of a second before a large, somewhat hairy hand, the fingers stained with chemicals seized it from the other side of the tray. The owner of the hand was as large and hairy as his hand suggested and loomed up into the gloom of the shop, his head disputing space with the dangling cobwebbed objects which hung from hooks in the ceiling beams.

"I beg your pardon," said Phemie politely and her fingers tightened on the book.

"I beg yours, ma'am," responded the large and hairy figure and his fingers also tightened. Phemie gave a tiny jerk and pulled the letter-press away, leaving the back board and tattered spine in her rival's possession.

"Oh, dear!" she exclaimed and held out her other hand for the rest of the book. Reluctantly he handed it over and she took her find to the proprietor who was engrossed in a copy of the *Illustrated London News* from the heaps of periodicals which lay about him like autumn leaves.

"Fourpence," he said without taking the pipe from his mouth and holding out a palm encased in a grimy mitten. Phemie put the coins in his hand, the book in her reticule and rejoined Adela who was waiting on the pavement outside, considering the rather doubtful collection of objects jumbled behind the greenish panes of the window. They moved off to return to the hospital but had not gone more than a few hundred yards when Phemie noticed they were being followed. She tugged at Adela's arm and they stopped to gaze into a baker's shop. Their shadow came up and stopped behind them.

"Ma'am . . . ." said a rather husky voice. "Excuse me . . . ma'am!"

Adela made to beat a retreat but Phemie stood her ground so that Adela had to lumber back and stand beside her.

"Yes?" Phemie enquired.

"That book, ma'am . . ."

"Yes," said Phemie.

"It is *Murchison on Fevers* is it not, ma'am?"

"Yes," agreed Phemie.

Now he was in the sunlight her rival could be seen to be a very large young man with a mane of fair hair and sidewhiskers which gave him the look of a gentle and rather uncertain lion.

"I am a medical student, ma'am," he announced.

"Indeed," said Phemie.

"I find I have great need of that book . . . Perhaps you would be kind enough to sell it to me?"

"No," said Phemie and smiled sweetly, "I am sorry to disoblige you, sir, but I too have need of it. Come, Adela."

They moved away again but the student moved with them and walked alongside to plead his case. He, it appeared, had

22

neglected fevers and now he was faced by imminent examination. Wouldn't she take pity on his ignorance . . . please.

By this time they had turned into the street which was dominated by the block of the hospital and Adela was showing signs of acute discomfort. She tugged at Phemie's arm and pulled her to a halt.

"If Mrs W. was to see us . . ." she wailed. "Tell him to go away or we'll both be dismissed."

Phemie turned to their follower.

"We are nurses from the Nightingale home," she explained. "If we are as much as seen with a medical student we will not be allowed to finish our training. Please go away."

His eyes gleamed at this information.

"Sell me that book and I'll vanish like the morning mist." he promised poetically, "and if you don't I'll stick closer than a poultice right up to the door of the Home."

Phemie turned on him.

"That is nothing but blackmail," she declared.

"Lady," pleaded the student, "my case is desperate."

Phemie pulled the book out of her reticule. "I won't sell, Mr er . . . er . . ."

"Parsons . . . Evan Parsons, *very* much at your service . . ."

"I won't sell it, Mr Parsons, but I will lend it to you for as long as you have need of it."

"Angel!" he exclaimed. "Even fourpence is a consideration at this present."

"But I must have it back," said Phemie firmly . . . and an inspiration came to her. "And I would like, in return, to read your case notes on some surgical patients."

He stared.

"What! Gruesome drawings and all?"

She nodded.

"Just as you wish . . . though it's an odd wish in all conscience. Meet me a week on Monday. The worst will be over by then. Where?"

"At the bookshop," said Phemie. "Promise?"

"On my faith and honour as I hope to heal suffering humanity,'' declared Mr Parsons with his hand upon his heart. ''When?''

''Half past three.''

''I'll fail thee not.''

He bowed with a flourish, kissed his hand to both of them, stuffed the book in his pocket and strode across the street.

''Well . . .'' said Adela, uncertain whether to be shocked or gratified, ''of all things! Well, I never did! What a bold creature! Whatever do you want with his notes, Phemie? You know Miss Nightingale is fearfully against us setting ourselves up to be like doctors.''

''I wish I could *be* a doctor,'' said Phemie. ''My father was, you know.''

''But women aren't doctors!'' said Adela faintly. ''I mean, nobody ever heard of such a thing.''

''I know,'' said Phemie. ''They'd never let me within a mile of medical school. But I tell you this, Adela, I intend to learn as much as I can. One of these days I'll know as much as any ignorant sawbones of the lot!''

Adela speechless (for once) with disapproval, looked reproachfully at her companion and hurried towards the hospital gates.

On the dressing-chest Phemie found a letter. The postmark was Glasgow and it was directed to her in Frank's handwriting. She snatched it up, eager to know what had occurred to bring Neil to London. Had Mary Deuchar found a more eligible *parti*?

The explanation was quite unexpected but none-the-less convincing:

> . . . have some surprising news for you, [wrote Frank]. You may remember that Blackburn Riggs was the freehold property of your father and he left it to you to make up your tocher. It has recently been proved to overlie a rich deposit of coal. As all the rights are vested in yourself it begins to look as if you might become a wealthy woman . . . after you marry of course . . . for the property may not be

touched before that. Doctor Linklater and I discussed the situation and we are agreed that the sums at present accruing must be treated as your portion according to the will and consequently I have invested the first returns in the company, a very excellent and reliable concern to whom we have entrusted the exploitation of the mineral . . .

"*We* are agreed, are we?" Phemie muttered scornfully. "I know whose notion, that was."

I hope [Frank continued] the receipt of this news will decide you to return to Jean and me and to take up a life more consonant with your means. Perhaps once you are safely back in Glasgow we can find some way to make you a small allowance. You may have a visit from Linklater who thinks with me that with this improvement in your prospects you should leave this nursing nonsense and come home . . .

"Easier for him to lay siege in Glasgow," commented Phemie. "Well . . . he'll have to watch the money mounting up in the bank and not be able to touch a penny, and it'll be all his own doing."

Adela came in to find Phemie busily writing a letter and chuckling from time to time.

"Whatever are you about?"

Phemie looked up.

"I'm writing to tell my fairy godmother to put the pumpkin back where she found it," she said. "I find I don't care for balls . . . especially with chains attached."

2

Mrs Wardroper picked up a letter from her desk and looked at Phemie over the top of her spectacles.

"I have had a most perturbing communication from one Doctor Linklater . . ."

Phemie's hands gripped together in her lap.

". . . from an address in Scotland."

"Indeed, ma'am," murmured Phemie, her face expressionless.

Mrs Wardroper gave her a sharp look.

"He claims to be some connection of yours."

"He was, at one time, my father's assistant and was made my trustee. He is no relation."

"Indeed."

Mrs Wardroper ran her eye down the single sheet.

"He claims to have your welfare very close to his heart."

Phemie smiled faintly.

"But," added the Matron acidly, "in view of what he has to say I take leave to doubt that assertion. He claims that you have been . . . ahem . . . frequently in the company of a student at this hospital, one Evan Parsons. Is this correct?"

"I have met him from time to time this past year," admitted Phemie, her heart pounding. "We patronise the same bookshop."

Mrs Wardroper looked distressed.

"So it is true! He says that your relationship with this man is the talk of the whole hospital."

Phemie flushed.

"If that is the case they must have very little to talk about. He is merely a casual acquaintance."

The Matron put the tips of her fingers together and looked severely.

"You must realise Miss Witherspoon that this is a very serious allegation. In fact if it is true, you would have to leave St Thomas's immediately."

"And that would be just what Doctor Linklater wants."

"Would you care to explain that statement?"

Phemie gave a brief explanation of the situation and added:

"Miss Nightingale is aware of the circumstances."

She had been unable to resist sharing the humour of the visit from her repentant suitor with her patron. Mrs Wardroper did not laugh as Miss Nightingale had done but she was suitably shocked and her attitude was decidedly mollified.

"Well, this must certainly alter my view of this news. I must admit I would be sorry to see you go. Your work in the wards and out of them has been admirable and your conduct, as far as I have been able to observe it, exemplary. I do not scruple to tell you that Miss Nightingale and I had hoped that you might accept the post of a Sister after your training is completed."

She fell silent for a moment and flicked the letter with her fingernail.

"I had hoped," she observed with a note of petulance in her voice, "that you would be able to tell me that this was all a spiteful invention."

"I could have told you that," said Phemie, "but it would not have been true and you would have been able to find that out. Doctor Linklater knew that by exaggerating a story with a germ of truth in it he might be able to force your hand . . ."

"Force my hand!"

Mrs Wardroper swelled with indignation.

"Scheming creature!" she added and then remembered that the scheme had still to be sifted. "Just how much truth, Nurse?"

"I have met Mr Parsons on about six occasions . . ."

"Six!"

27

Mrs Wardroper's spectacles fell to the length of their black ribbon.

"Six or seven," said Phemie. "You might ask Miss Wedmore. She was with me on each occasion."

The spectacles were replaced and Phemie was considered through them.

"This letter was at pains to imply some form of . . . amorous . . . er . . . intrigue. It did not mention Miss Wedmore."

"No," said Phemie, "I don't suppose it did. And yet Miss Wedmore is not easy to overlook, I imagine. In fact an onlooker would be more likely to suppose that she was the object of such attentions than that I was."

"True," agreed the Matron with a certain disregard for Phemie's *amour-propre*.

"In fact we have all three been sharing a library," explained Phemie. "I have some medical books of my father's and Parsons has others which were recommended during our lectures and we met occasionally to exchange these. I do not suppose that the letter mentioned the books either."

The Matron shook her head.

"I must see Miss Wedmore and put the whole affair before Miss Nightingale. It must rest with her how we regard this . . . missive."

Phemie then returned to Elizabeth Ward and resumed her morning's duties. The last of these was to attend a call from the cancer patient in the small ward. It was one of her 'good' days. Phemie gave her a bedpan and waited at her side.

"You're Nurse Witherspoon, ain't you?"

Phemie nodded.

"Got summat for you I 'ave."

She produced a note folded into a cocked hat from the folds of the bandage round her chest.

"Young whippersnapper with the whiskers, 'e gave it me. On no 'count to let that Sister see, 'e said."

Phemie took it and thanked her, tucking it into the pocket of her gown while she made the woman comfortable again. There was no time to read it until she left the ward to eat her dinner and

28

even then she could do more than glance at it surrepetitiously. Fortunately it was not long.

"Got what you want. Old Wiseman's at 4. Must talk. Important. Someone's tipped the cole to Harry Tyler. E.P."

Adela was, for once, unhelpful. She had the headache, she said, and she was tired of those poky, dirty streets. She was going to lie down upon her bed. Phemie did not argue. Adela did not look well; her normally high colour had faded to an unbecoming sallow grey and her eyes looked dull and sore. Phemie reached for her hand and found it hot and dry.

"Your pulse is racing, Adela . . . you could be in a fever. Better see Mrs Wardroper and see will she give you a cachet."

Adela nodded wearily and continued to push the food about on her plate.

At ten to four Phemie put on her old black bonnet and pulled down the veil and looked out the heavy serge travelling cloak which she had brought from Glasgow. Such a garb might disguise who she was but in such weather it made her conspicuous. The summer, heedless of the calendar, had burned on into September and it was extremely hot. The sky was brassy and London, not to put too fine a point upon it, stank like a midden. The Thames, low with the summer's drought, festered between its banks and forced the staff at St Thomas's to close the long windows in the wards despite the stifling heat.

Phemie slipped down the backstair without meeting anyone and went out into Hospital Lane. A narrow alley took her towards the square where Wiseman had his shop. As she hurried along she noticed an air of lethargy among the people who sat about their doorways in the hope of an evening breeze. 'We need rain,' said the countrywoman in her, 'please God, send us a good thunderplump, we're all wilting.' There was a queue at the pump on the corner, dishevelled women holding chipped ewers, and dirty, listless children with buckets and jugs. A dismal, discoloured trickle of water dripped from the spout. The well was low.

At Wiseman's Parsons could scarcely wait for her to get inside the door. He did not notice Adela's absence.

"Look, Miss Phemie, there's trouble. I'd a jaw today from the Prof about tampering with the affections, etc., etc. He'd had a note from your dragon."

"I know. My trustee wrote to her."

"However did *he* hear about it? And what a low-down trick!"

"He has his reasons," said Phemie grimly, "and he'd like to see me packed home in disgrace."

"Light dawns upon the unenlightened. I take it you don't want to go back to the family bosom."

"No," said Phemie, "I do not."

"But if you are cast out from those chaste walls, what can you do?"

"I don't know," Phemie answered, "but I'll not go home."

He swallowed.

"Look, you'll have to let me help you. It's my fault you're in trouble."

"Haivers," Phemie disagreed, "I needn't have come here."

"I'll be qualified soon . . . I hope . . . and actually you know, that's much better than likely now . . . you've got a sort of knack of explaining things. I'm not the brightest of prospects I know, but there's m'father's practice and he's taking me in as a partner and you could stay with mother till I was finished here."

He stared at her earnestly like a worried lion.

"You're more than kind . . . but I assure you there's no need . . ."

"I mean you could . . . I'd esteem it an honour and all that . . . marriage, I mean. Can't think of a better wife for someone like me. You've the brains for both of us."

Phemie felt a lump in her throat.

"I am more grateful than I can say, Mr Parsons, for your concern. And I thank you for such a generous offer . . . but I cannot let you make such a sacrifice . . . and I cannot think your parents would approve."

Even in the dimness of the shop she could see him colour.

"Not a sacrifice," he mumbled unevenly, "a pleasure . . .

30

want to marry you. Just that I hadn't much to offer and all that. This business sort of gave me a chance, don't you know . . ."

Phemie knew a desire, which would have shocked Mrs Wardroper to the core, to hug him fiercely, but instead she took his hand and said:

"Evan Parsons, you're that rare creature a gentleman. I won't forget this. I don't think I'll come to harm but I'll certainly come to you for help if I do. Thank you . . . thank you very much, my friend."

He gripped her hand agonisingly, cleared his throat and then picked up the parcel he had brought.

"Some notes on amputations and the treatment of wounds. The lecturer chap was out in the Crimea so he should know about things. Hasn't much time for your Miss Nightingale, I must say."

"I don't suppose she has much for him. Thank you. If I send them to the porter's lodge would you be able to get them?"

He sighed.

"I don't suppose we'll be able to go over things any more. Pity. Always made them sort of clearer for me when I had to explain them to you . . . not just a mass of things to learn . . . started to hang together . . . if you know what I mean. You know, an odd thing came into my head when I was waiting for you . . . you should really be the doctor, not me . . . I mean you've got the headpiece . . ."

It was a pity that Phemie did not hear this ultimate accolade. She was peering into the gloom at the back of the shop where Ezra Wiseman lurked among his periodicals.

"Did you hear something?" she asked.

"No, actually . . ."

"I thought I heard a groan . . ."

She moved among the clutter of broken furniture until she found the owner.

"Evan . . . come here, do!"

There was a note of alarm in her voice.

"Ezra's ill," she said. "Really ill. Light the gas."

31

Parsons obliged with a lucifer and the pale light revealed Wiseman slumped in his chair with his eyes shut.

"He's burning with fever," said Phemie and made to open the neck of his filthy shirt.

"Don't touch him!" exclaimed Parsons sharply and pulled her away. "We've had over fifty cases of contagious fever this last week. It's this sickly weather. I shouldn't have asked you to come here. I'm a fool."

He bent over the sick man, looked at his chest and tested the heat of the dry skin.

"It's the same, I think," he said at last. "You'd better go. Don't forget your notes."

"Nonsense," said Phemie. "Do you suppose he has anyone to look after him?"

"Does he look like it? No . . . he'll have to come in . . . for what that's worth. He's pretty far gone. I wonder how long he's been like this. For any favour, girl, keep away from him!"

He pulled her away from the chair and pushed her out of the door.

"Send the porter to fetch him," he instructed her. "I'll stay till he comes."

"But couldn't we make him more comfortable?"

"Not in there," said Parsons, looking into the dingy interior, "not if his living quarters are anything like the shop."

Once at the hospital Phemie informed the porter, told him the address and helped him wheel out the ambulance, a long flat board, mounted on two big wheels and fitted with two sets of straps, a straw pillow and a blanket. She saw him wheel it off towards Wiseman's and then walked into the main hall. It seemed pointless to try to creep in unseen. She was met almost at once by two other nurses looking anxious and upset.

"Witherspoon!" they greeted her with relief, "wherever have you been? We thought you might be ill."

"Ill?" said Phemie, bewildered. "Why should I be ill?"

"Your friend Wedmore's sick. They've taken her into the wards."

"Adela? What is the matter with her?"

"She's got this fever . . . the contagious fever."

"No . . . . oh, no!"

They both nodded like Chinese mandarins.

"But all she had was a headache," protested Phemie. "And that was at dinner time."

"She went to Mrs W. for a cachet after dinner," explained Fulton. "She took one look and sent for Doctor Orde."

"Poor girl."

"That's not all," said Fulton's friend, "there's been more than fifty cases reported and probably more never notified . . . Mrs W. says we've got an epidemic on our hands. The porters are pulling out all the extra cots and blankets and we're to be prepared for the suspension of ordinary routine . . . that means no more lectures for a bit, thank goodness."

Mrs Wardroper's room was on the landing and she must have heard the voices for she came out and sent Fulton and her friends scuttling back to their rooms to rest.

"Miss Witherspoon, I wish to see you. I sent for you earlier but you were not to be found. Where were you?"

"I went for a walk. It was so hot."

Too late she remembered her heavy cloak and veiled bonnet. Mrs Wardroper raised her eyebrows.

"No one wanted to go with me so I thought these would cover my uniform."

It was a fairly lame explanation but the Matron appeared to be ready to accept it. Phemie's heart beat fast, for all that, as she followed her into the stuffy overcrowded little room.

"You have heard, no doubt, that your friend Miss Wedmore has fallen victim to a fever?"

"Yes, ma'am. I trust she does not have it in a severe form."

"Only time will tell us that. She is very sick. You are frequently in her company. Do you feel quite the thing yourself?"

"I am perfectly well."

"You may also have heard that we may have an outbreak of fever upon our hands. The weather is very sickly and the wells are low."

33

"Yes, ma'am."

"Before I sent for Doctor Orde your friend was able to confirm that you had been all the time in her company when you met this young man. I feel . . ."

She paused and looked uncomfortable.

"I feel in view of what she said that I am justified in doing . . . this."

She tore the letter into little pieces and dropped it into the wastepaper basket.

"Thank you, ma'am," said Phemie, relief flooding through her, "I promise that you'll have no cause to regret that decision."

"I trust not," said the Matron and smiled. "Now run along and take your tea . . . and remember please that during the coming weeks you must pay careful attention to both ventilation and exercise if you are to avoid infection."

The following weeks were a chaos of days and nights; of carrying trays and bowls, washing delirious and abusive patients, scrubbing endlessly at implements, dishes, clothes, furniture and the lavatories. The heat continued so that exhausted as they were the nurses found it hard to sleep high and hot under the roof. The huge number of restless and often delirious patients in the hospital involved a constant hum of noise which penetrated even there. Phemie lay one baking hot night, staring at the ceiling and seeing there a procession of faces, men, women and children, distorted by delirium, quiet in coma, stiff in death. Her feet throbbed and her hands still stung from the harsh soap used in the wards. Sleep held off from her in the same way that the rain held off from London though thunder muttered and grumbled along the line of hills to the north. After five weeks her world had become limited to the hospital and the people, well and ill who were in it. The rest of the world seemed like a dream. She could see Wedmore, her moon face fallen in, her clothes loose upon her, walk unsteadily across the courtyard to the cab which would take her on the first stage of a journey to Lea Hurst where the Nightingale servants would coddle her back to health. She saw Mrs Wardroper, her dignity forgotten, kneeling beside an improvised bed on the floor of a corridor taking down a letter from a dying woman to her mother 'somewhere near Coventry'. She heard of the death of the bookseller and the collapse and death of one of the porters who had penetrated the stinking alleys and the ghastly courtyards not a hundred yards from the hospital to bring in the sick. Two nurses had slipped away secretly at night leaving notes of apology, saying they were too afraid to continue. Phemie felt only sympathy. It was a virulent fever, not unlike jail fever, and an unpleasant death. For herself, she was too tired to be afraid. She reached for a drink. The waterbottle on her table was filled with mineral water, supplied by Miss Nightingale. Water from the pipes and wells was cloudy and smelt. It was fit only to wash the piles and piles of fouled linen which had exhausted the resources of the laundry-maids scrubbing away in the steam of the basement.

As Phemie sat up to reach for the bottle the tiny window of the cubicle was lit unbearably brightly by a blue flash and she winced from it, shading her eyes with her hand. There came another flash and another and then a colossal clap of thunder shook and rattled the windows. A gust of wind sucked the muslin curtains out through the open casement and then with a suddenness which seemed frightening and unnatural the rain began. It was as if the gods had emptied the bowl of the sky over the stinking city. Phemie leaped out of bed to close her window and protect the notebooks and papers piled upon the table beneath. She saw in the light of another blue flash the wildernesses of roof outside, gleaming in the rain, while below the sill the gutter hissed and gurgled as it filled and ran, brimful, to the downpipes. Almost at once the air cooled. Phemie back in bed pulled up a blanket unused for weeks and slept as if someone had hit her on the head with a hammer.

A fortnight later the epidemic had burnt itself out and the great hospital slowly and painfully began to restore the normal routine. Gaps, temporary and permanent, had appeared in the nursing staff and those who remained were driven to the limit to care for the still-swollen numbers of sick and the usual quota of sick, injured and dying who were brought to the door every day. By the beginning of November Phemie, who had been made acting Sister in Elizabeth, looked more fragile than ever. Her eyes had sunk in her head and she drove her nurses as hard as she drove herself. Miss Nightingale made one of her sudden visitations at the dinner hour on Friday, took a hard look at her and swept her off for a 'Saturday to Monday in bed' at South Street. During this blessed respite Phemie slept for twenty hours and woke up hungry for the first time in months.

While she did justice to the delicious meal which was sent up to her room Miss Nightingale came to share her coffee.

"Yes, you look very much more the thing, my dear," she remarked. "I am very glad to see it. A week at Lea Hurst and you shall do."

Phemie thanked her.

"And after that . . ." said Miss Nightingale, "I think, perhaps, a slightly less arduous position for a while."

She pulled a letter out of her belt, a letter written on hot-pressed scented paper in a sprawling hand.

"This letter is from a friend of mine who asks me if I will be good enough to find her a suitable person to attend upon the daughter of a friend of hers. This daughter she describes as an 'invalid of some kind'."

Phemie looked up at the slightly tart inflection on the last words and Miss Nightingale raised her eyebrows in reply.

"I must explain that had my friend really expected me to oblige her in this matter she would have been more . . . forthcoming. I collect that there is very little wrong with this Mrs Manners and that the letter is written in fulfillment of a promise made to an importunate acquaintance. I am not expected to be able to find anyone."

Phemie looked enquiringly.

"I note that Mrs Manners intends to spend the winter in Town principally to be near her medical man, Sir Aloysius Roebuck. One of St Thomas's consultant staff, as you may know."

Phemie did know. He had set the Nurses' Home all on end in the summer by writing a letter to the *Morning Post* deploring the introduction of 'Lady Nurses' and the end of the 'excellent creatures who have more than adequately, nay devotedly, served us and our patients until this time . . .' It was evident from Miss Nightingale's expression that she had not missed this epistle.

"Mrs Manners' attendant would thus not be far from the hospital should she wish to return . . . nor would she be far from what London has to offer. I understand, Miss Witherspoon that you have a weakness for bookshops?"

Phemie coloured faintly.

"And when you return to us . . ." Miss Nightingale went on smoothly.

"When would that be?"

Miss Nightingale considered the letter.

"Mrs Manners hopes to spend the spring travelling on the Continent to see whether the spas can effect an improvement. She may have found that she can do without your attendance by then . . . or you may have become indispensable to her comfort. Only time will tell."

Her voice was cool and amused.

"However, if after a few weeks when you are more rested you find the position not wholly to your taste . . . no doubt we will be able to find a place for you. I feel . . ."

There was no doubt now about the amusement in her voice.

". . . I feel that this experience may make a valuable part of your training. It will certainly provide a contrast."

"Thank you, ma'am."

"And Miss Witherspoon . . ." Miss Nightingale rose to her feet. ". . . while I have to agree with you that the ignorance and arrogance of many males is hard to bear and that doctors as a race appear to include a disproportionate number of muddleheaded asses . . ."

"I have never expressed such opinions, ma'am," protested Phemie.

"Not to me. But did you not inform Doctor Bristowe's new young man that he was a blundering ignoramus and tell him to take his clumsy hands off one of your patients?"

Phemie coloured again.

"Quite," said Miss Nightingale. "And while I would hesitate to say this to everyone . . . I sympathise, but, I cannot condone. We cannot afford to offend the medical profession, Miss Witherspoon, because we are as yet too dependent upon their goodwill. The time may come, indeed I am sure it will, when the boot will be on the other foot but for the present, suffer their inanities in silence, correct their mistakes unobtrusively and tactfully, and interfere with their actions only when you know that they are doing active damage. And when you are tried very high—as I have been, Phemie—recall that there are good and learned and devoted men among them."

"Yes, Miss Nightingale."

"Regard your next position in the light of an exercise in the suffering of fools."

Mr and Mrs Manners occupied a handsome town house not far from Bruton Square. Mr Manners was undistinguished in appearance and rather ineffectual in character. He had a rosy face surrounded by fair though scanty hair and whiskers and watery blue eyes which peered short-sightedly at the world. His plump hand hovered constantly over the pince-nez in his pocket. He was too myopic to dispense with these and too vain to wear them constantly. His father had left him a large fortune, his widowed mother a larger and his bankers and men of business were now busily employed in increasing both. His wife had been chosen by his mother from an equally wealthy family. As he was totally without interests or occupation he turned (naturally) to politics. He was asked to stand in the Liberal interest for a remote and undemanding constituency and by mounting a lavish campaign succeeded in becoming their Member. Before long he found that it was as easy to slumber on the back benches as it was in his own book free study, and he learned in time to ignore the uproars created by the ineffable Irish as easily as he ignored the plaints of his wife.

Mrs Manners was pretty in a commonplace way, plump, and quite unbelievably ignorant, having been spoiled by doting parents beyond the influence of a score of governesses. She obediently married Mr Manners when she was told because he had a large fortune and a house in Town. She had spent all her life in a small provincial town. She bore him one child, and decided that the process of gestation and birth was painful and undignified besides inhibiting her social debut. To prevent a recurrence of this situation she hit upon the notion of becoming an interesting semi-invalid. She emerged from the lying-in period with the symptoms of a weak spine and a heart subject to irregularities. This established, she retired to her luxurious rooms to eat sweets, design over-trimmed peignoirs and read novels. From here she would emerge wiltingly to receive her dressmaker, preside over dinner-parties or grace gatherings elswhere attended by carrying chair and smelling salts. Mr Manners connived at this because he had revived an old ac quaintance of whom his mother had been ignorant. Now in possession of his inheritance he had installed her in the odour of utter respectability in an Italianate little villa in St John's Wood and was thus able to bear his wife's indispostion with complaisance.

However, in time, certain difficulties had presented themselves. Mr Manners in consequence of his unswerving obedience to the Party Whip (and a large donation to their funds) was in daily expectation of being created a peer; there being a need for such somnambulant Members in the Lords and his seat being required for a protégé of the Leader. But of what use was it to become a peer of the realm if the title could not be imparted to a dynasty. Their only child was a mere girl. Mr Manners approached his wife in the matter but found her impervious to hints and unresponsive to coaxing. In fact, she took again to her bed and surrounded herself with all the appurtenances of the sickroom: batteries of bottles, burning pastilles, tisanes and

39

lowered blinds. In fact all she lacked was the now fashionable attendance of a 'trained nurse'.

Through a friend of her mother who was an acquaintance of Miss Nightingale the application was made, despite the pooh-poohing of her medical man, Sir Aloysius Roebuck. Old Nanny who had sufficed to nurse until this time was banished to the nursery. Mrs Manners lay among her pillows looking pale (from lack of exercise and fresh air) sending away her meals (because she was more than adequately sustained by a diet of fruit and sweets between them) and resenting the fact that her robust physique would prevent her ever from presenting the picture of fragility and suffering bravely borne after which she strove. It would be (she hoped) not only unchivalrous but downright inhumane to ask someone in such a condition to face the ordeals and discomforts of childbearing. Phemie duly arrived to lend further colour to this affecting picture after a week at Lea Hurst where her nightly dreams of the fever victims began to fade with rest and fresh air.

Her advent was not an unqualified success. For a start she misunderstood her function and made a determined effort to improve her patient's condition which was not at all the idea. Mrs Manners found a gust of fresh air blowing through her rooms, her boxes of comfits removed, her meals made more wholesome and less lavish, and her back subjected to energetic and occasionally even painful 'friction'. These measures effected no improvement in Mrs Manners's condition, which was scarcely surprising, but they did serve to exasperate her. Nor was this exasperation lessened by the fact that it was quite impossible to spell out to Phemie just what was expected of her.

In the event she complained gently to Sir Aloysius who shook her finger at her, reminded her that he had opposed the idea from the very beginning and then patted her hand paternally and promised to 'have a word with the girl'. Before he left he summoned Phemie to the boudoir. When she came in she had to suppress a smile for he looked singularly out of place in that smother of pink and white brocade, being small, thin and grizzled like a pensioned fox-terrier. He did not rise at her

40

entrance but fixed her with what was intended for a piercing gaze.

"Miss Widderspin," he began abruptly, his accent declaring his Welsh origins, "do sit down . . . sit down do."

Phemie obeyed warily.

"I thought it might be advantageous to discuss the welfare of my . . . our . . . patient," he announced. "As you must know it is ab-so-lutely essential that there should be total co-operation between us . . . tot-tal."

Phemie inclined her head.

"No one . . . no one," said Sir Aloysius, emphasising his point with a long bony forefinger, "appreciates more than do I the excellence of Miss Nightingale's training in hospital work. I may have had doubts at one time, nay, I may have cast contumely on the whole scheme, but up to a point I have to admit that within the walls of a hospital her training has its uses . . . indeed yes."

He paused.

"But . . . but . . . Miss Nighingale has not really considered the different conditions which must obtain when nursing superior females in their own homes . . . no indeed."

Phemie looked down her nose.

"The discipline so necessary for the lower orders, so essent-essential in the very full hospital day . . . here . . ."

He gestured around the welter of pink and white *bijouterie*.

"Here . . . my good woman, it is not the same at all . . . not at all. Do you not agree?"

Phemie smiled agreeably, fixing her mind as firmly as she could upon the words of her mentor, 'when tried very high . . .'

"My patient must not be made to feel like the inmate of a charity ward, the poor lady," he insisted. "It is most deleterious to her already fragile health . . . you must see that."

Phemie regarded her folded hands . . . 'good, learned and devoted men among them . . .'

"Perhaps if you were to consider this, Miss Wedderspan," he continued acidly, "before you subject my patient to a regime to which she is not accustomed and to which there is no need that

41

she should become accustomed and which merely accentuates her suffering.''

Phemie rose and stood demurely in front of him, her hands clasped in front of her and her attitude copied exactly from that of Mrs Wardroper.

"I will bear in mind all you say, Sir Aloysius, and your directions will be carried out.''

He rubbed his hands and grimaced in her direction.

"Good . . . good . . . very good! That is what you are here for after all . . . to obey the doctor's instructions. Here are my directions for medicines. These prescriptions must be made up . . .''

He handed her a sheaf of prescriptions for the druggest. Sir Aloysius never dispensed his own medicines. Phemie considered them: a sleeping potion . . . necessary for a person who sleeps away much of the day, bismuth for the indigestion which followed an indiscreet and ample diet, an aperient . . . she smiled faintly and Sir Aloysius took instant exception.

"May I enquire what you find amusing?'' he demanded huffily. ''And bear in mind that she must have plenty of port wine . . . this is necessary as a tonic and to build up her strength.''

"Was I smiling?'' she asked in shocked accents. ''I humbly beg your pardon, Sir Aloysius. Such a list is no smiling matter.''

There was an uncertain pause, he grunted irritably and strode to the door where he turned.

"Mind what I say now,'' he jerked out, and shook his finger at her. ''None of your charity ward notions here.''

Phemie bobbed a curtsey for good measure and he went away.

The sickroom regime was relaxed, the comfits reappeared the windows were closed and the friction reduced to a comforting half-hour. Phemie, now fully conversant with her role, stood about to 'dress the set', in the theatrical phrase, whenever it was required and for the rest of the time pursued her own interests.

It was not long before the inwardness of the situation was made clear to her. One afternoon Mr Manners beckoned Phemie into the barren study where he begged her to be seated and then fell unhappily silent standing straddled before the fire, his hands under his coat-tails. Twice he cleared his throat and twice the observation he intended to make failed to come to birth. Phemie at last took pity on him.

"You wish to speak to me, Mr Manners?"

"Yes . . . er . . . we . . . that is I . . . a delicate matter . . ." he stammered. "Unwilling to bring a blush . . . what?"

Phemie felt more inclination to laugh than blush.

"Does it concern my patient?" she enquired.

Mr Manners nodded.

"Then I'll answer you if I can. And please don't be too solicitous of my sensibilities, Mr Manners. You must understand that our training informs us to some degree on matters which might otherwise be considered only the province of married ladies."

Thus encouraged, Mr Manners became completely dumb, his mouth opening and shutting like a goldfish as Phemie waited with an air of polite attention. Words came at length.

"My wife . . . is she . . . can she . . . are there signs of improvement?"

This question put Phemie in something of a dilemma: in view of her growing conviction that there was nothing at all the matter with her patient a truthful answer would give rise to untoward alarm, and Phemie had a dislike of playing with the truth.

"Quite as much as can be expected," she parried.

Mr Manners kicked at the fender.

"Will she . . . I mean . . . her indisposition would not . . . that is the expectation would not be impaired so to speak?"

Phemie opened her eyes very wide.

"The expectation of what?"

Mr Manners gazed imploringly at her, blushed to the roots of his receding hair and gulped.

"Of . . . er . . . that is of . . . offspring."

Suddenly Phemie saw the whole situation as if she had been handed a key to a puzzle.

"Her Majesty . . ." Mr Manners was still mumbling on, ". . .

recognition of political services . . . Baron Manners of Mottwood.''

Phemie stared.

"What I want to know is,'' he finished in a hurry, "whether there is any chance of an heir to the title?''

He turned his back upon her and looked into the fire as if he expected an oracle there but when she did not reply at once he turned back and gazed earnestly at her.

"Am I to understand . . . no hope of . . .''

"No such thing!'' she replied roundly. "In my opinion your wife is perfectly capable of bearing healthy children. Her indisposition . . .''

She paused, uncertain where that sentence was going to end. Mr Manners jumped eagerly into the gap.

"Her indisposition?'' he prompted.

"I feel certain,'' Phemie chose her words carefully, "that it will yield to the correct treatment.''

But all the care in the world did not avert the next question.

"Ah!'' said Manners. "In your opinion, is she receiving the correct treatment?''

Once again Phemie cursed her predilection for the truth.

"That, Mr Manners, is not my province,'' she said firmly. "My task is to carry out Sir Aloysius's instructions to the best of my ability. I am not qualified to evaluate those instructions. I suggest you should apply to Sir Aloysius himself.''

"I have done,'' said Mr Manners petulantly, "more than once. All I got was 'Wait a little, my dear sir, wait a little. We must be patient.' All very well for him to be patient at three guineas a call. She seems worse now than she did when all this started.''

Phemie looked sympathetically at the plump figure before the fire.

"I expect you have shown your wife the utmost consideration since this indisposition showed itself, have you not?''

"Yes,'' he said sulkily. "Had no choice.''

"I wonder if this was, in fact, the best course?'' reflected Phemie demurely.

44

"Do you, b'George!" exclaimed her employer.

"But of course I would be obliged if you kept my doubts on this score secret from Sir Aloysius . . ."

"Yes . . . 'pon m'soul . . . yes, indeed."

"I would not dream of challenging his opinions on a purely medical matter, you understand, but when it comes to matters which are more personal and feminine than medical perhaps I may be permitted to hold an opinion of my own?"

She looked at him with an air of deprecation.

"Of course, of course . . ." he responded eagerly.

"I feel Mrs Manners ought to have something to take her out of herself . . . to be given a new interest in life. Perhaps a determined assault, Mr Manners . . ."

His eyes bulged slightly.

". . . flowers of course," Phemie continued dreamily, "presents, admiration, jewels and trinkets . . . poems?"

She looked enquiringly. Mr Manners blew slightly and was heard to mutter his determination, to try his hand at a verse or so.

"Perhaps a new carriage might encourage Mrs Manners to take the air a little more . . . and this cannot but be beneficial you know. It strikes me that Mrs Manners would appear to advantage in one of the new open Victorias. You could suggest this to her."

"Yes . . . yes . . ."

"And then . . . perhaps a little holiday? I believe that Italy is very popular in the world of fashion, just now. The stimulus of new surroundings might turn the scale. Venice might be more to her taste than Spa. More romantic."

She smiled at her employer, rose and straightened her cap.

"Most grateful, most . . . pon m'soul I am!"

Mr Manners spluttered slightly in his gratification.

"One other thing, Mr Manners," Phemie turned at the door to make the suggestion, "be masterful. At an appropriate moment, of course, but remember . . . be masterful."

She slipped away and left him practising a masterful attitude in front of the fire. 'That's put a spoke in Sir A's wheel, I wouldn't wonder," she thought.

During the following weeks she was amused to see that her advice was being followed to the letter. Flowers embowered the bedroom and each day brought its delightful surprise: trinkets, ornaments, scent from Paris, jewels from Rundells, all showered upon the satin coverlet, each accompanied by a folded note in which Phemie, shamelessly peeping, could see the uneven lines of verse. Tea-time brought the sender of these offerings to court the invalid with pretty speeches and boxes of almond comfits. The patient thrived on such attentions, was heard to declare that he was not nearly such an old bear as she had thought, quite gallant, upon her word . . . and she was more exigent than ever about the brushing of her hair and the choosing of her lacy bedjackets.

With more cunning than Phemie had believed him to possess, Mr Manners at length presented his wife with a superb sable cape and muff. At this she sat bolt upright without any evident difficulty, kissed the donor enthusiastically and at once determined to find an opportunity to wear them. It was this offering which precipitated an event which was to have far-reaching repercussions.

3

PHEMIE WAS SPENDING A studious half-hour in her bedroom in the Manners' house, reading and making notes on a manual rather formidably entitled, *Difficulties and Untoward Conditions Frequently Attending the Process of Parturition* by a Well-known Accoucheur at Present Practising in the Metropolis. She was considering a nightmarish section called 'Malpresentations' when a tap fell on her door and Mrs Manners' personal maid came fluttering in. Esther was not unlike the women she served, fair, fat and rather feathery.

"Oh, Nurse!" she exclaimed before she was well into the room, "you are wanted in the Mistress's room. The Master's there and in a rare taking and Sir Aloysius is fit to be tied and the Mistress crying like a crazy thing, the poor soul . . ."

Phemie sighed, closed her book and put on her cap. On the way downstairs Esther gave her some notion of what was afoot.

"Was the carriage ride not a success?" Phemie enquired.

"Oh, yes, miss. Madam looked a picture in her new furs and the new carriage was very comfortable and they met any number of their acquaintances in the Park . . . Madam came back with quite a colour and walked up the stair just the thing and went back to the bedroom. Then I helped her to bed and brought in the tea-tray and when I went away they were talking about who they'd spoken to . . ."

"What do you think happened?"

"I dunno, miss, I'm sure. But the Master's real put out about something and Mistress crying and calling him a brute and Sir Aloysius came in not ten minutes since and now he's standing by the bed and shouting that matters have been set back by months and abusing the Master like you never heard in all your life . . .''

From which account Phemie could collect that her employer had pushed matters to a crisis rather sooner than was advisable. She collected sponge, towel, basin and a ewer of cold water from the dressing-room and made her entrance while the dispute was reaching its climax. Mrs Manners was half-buried in her pillows, her face red and damp and mopping at her tears with a corner of the sheet. Her husband was standing at the window looking mutinous and Sir Aloysius at the bedside was spluttering like a firework.

"Ah, Nurse!" he snapped, "please attend to your patient. She has been grievously overset . . . and by the person who should have her welfare most at heart! Her husband!"

He cast a glance of contumely and scorn at that unfortunate. Phemie poured water into the basin, wrung out the sponge in the icy liquid and began ruthlessly to sponge the flushed face among the pillows. Mrs Manners gave a muffled protest which drew Sir Aloysius's attention.

"Surely," he enquired awfully, "for a patient so indisposed some restorative is desirable? Cold water may be efficacious in some cases of hysteria but it is not appropriate here!"

"As you say, Sir Aloysius," agreed Phemie and continued to mop.

"And have you no restoratives?" he demanded peevishly. "No sal volatile, no brandy?"

"At once, Sir Aloysius."

Phemie finished drying her victim, raised her from the tumbled pillows, rearranged them with an expert touch and lowered her back on to them. The sal volatile was in the dressing room. She replaced the ewer and basin and poured out a dose of the medicine. Back in the bedroom she found Mr Manners had turned at bay.

"Her back was strong enough to jaunt round the Park in the carriage most of the afternoon . . ." he was saying sulkily, "and I don't see that it's any of your business what I say to my wife."

"Your wife," returned the doctor, swelling until he looked like an aggressive pigeon, "is *my patient*! As such I must deplore any action which may retard her progress. You, sir, by your unmanly attentions have undone months of care!"

Phemie administered the sal volatile and Mrs Manners spluttered and choked over the pungent fumes.

"Nurse! How often must I tell you that your charity ward notions are out of place here? A glass of port wine or weak brandy-and-water would have met the case perfectly!"

"I beg your pardon, Sir Aloysius."

Phemie removed the offending remedy and returned with a glass of the sweet Malaga favoured by Mrs Manners, who accepted it and sipped languidly.

"How can you expect improvement . . ." Sir Aloysius returned to the attack, "when you consistently flout my instructions . . . insist on the employment of somebody who continually departs from my prescribed regime . . . how, I ask again, can you expect to see improvement?"

Mr Manners stood his ground sulkily.

"There certainly hasn't been any. If anything she's got worse."

"Pre-cisely, my dear sir, indisputably . . ." Sir Aloysius wagged a finger at him. "And you know why!"

Mr Manners summoned up the blood and giving a rather unconvincing imitation of the tiger said:

"Do I? Do I, b'George? . . . I believe I do! I believe we need another doctor!"

Sir Aloysius went scarlet and his bushy hair and terrier eyebrows bristled like a dog's hackles: before he could explode into speech his patient intervened with an energy unexpected in one who, a second before, had been reclining limply among her pillows.

"You brute!" she shouted with surprising shrillness and volume. "You absolute thoughtless inconsiderate brute! You shan't send my dear Sir Ally away. I won't have it—do you hear? I won't have another doctor, he understands me . . ."

Sir Aloysius, a trifle disconcerted by this energetic championing turned to his patient, pressed her back against the pillows, and took her wrist. Hauling forth a vast hunter watch he counted her pulse. At length he replaced her hand on the coverlet, patted it comfortingly and returned the watch to its ambush in his waistcoat.

"I must prescribe a composer," he announced in doomladen tones, "the pulse is tumultuous!"

He turned majestically to Phemie.

"My good woman, bring me the laudanum. I will administer it myself."

"Well . . ." Mr Manners had stiffened his sinews again, "I'll tell you what *I* think—I think there's nothing the matter with her at all! *I* think it's all a sham! Anything she wants to do she can do perfectly well."

This speech counteracted the laudanum in no uncertain fashion. Mrs Manners sat up and pushed Sir Aloysius's restraining arm unceremoniously away.

"I *am* ill!" she shouted in tones which made this statement rather unconvincing. "I'm much sicker than you think! You've no idea how I suffer!"

"Stuff and nonsense! Moonshine!" her husband retorted. "You only suffer when you don't get your own way! You're no more ill than I am, and your precious Sir Aloysius knows it!"

"Sir! I must protest at such an aspersion upon . . ."

Sir Aloysius's protest was drowned in his patient's shrill outcry.

"You're cruel . . . unfeeling . . . insensitive! My mother warned me that men were all brutes and she was right! I *am* ill! I *am*! I *am*!"

She pounded her fists energetically on the coverlet.

"You ask Nurse. She knows. You ask her."

"Very well I will!" bellowed her husband.

"She knows how weak I am. You ask her. You ask her how my poor back aches! Ask her about my spasms!"

"Very well then, I will, if you'll only hold your tongue for a few minutes," shouted Mr Manners. "Nurse! What is your honest opinion of my wife's condition?"

Out of the corner of her eye Phemie could see Sir Aloysius's scarlet face and knew what it would mean to offend him.

"I am not qualified to give an opinion," she parried, "that is no part of my responsibility."

Sir Aloysius exploded at last on this easiest of victims.

"I am glad to hear you admit that, Nurse," he shouted, "it is time and high time that you recalled that your place in this establishment is that of a hired servant . . . and you are not hired to think or to have opinions. Quite unheard of! And what possible value could such opinions have, I ask you . . . the maunderings of an uneducated and ignorant woman. To set up your ideas against mine! *Mine!* After thirty years' experience of human suffering and service . . ."

"However," said Phemie as if he had not spoken, and she could feel the blood beating in her ears, "my personal opinion, not as a nurse, or a hired servant, but as a personal acquaintance is at your disposal, Mr Manners."

"Hold your tongue . . . insolent and impertinent hussy!"

"And it is this. Mrs Manners has a sore back . . ."

"There!" This was a shrilly triumphant cry from the patient.

". . . which is caused by spending too much time in a bed which is far too soft."

The silence was intense.

"She has occasional palpitations," Phemie continued calmly, "and in my view these are caused by bouts of indigestion which is the result of taking no exercise whatsoever and eating too much rich food."

She paused and looked at her spell-bound audience.

"In fact, Mrs Manners is as healthy as a coach-horse and would benefit from resuming a normal existence and finding some sensible occupation such as housekeeping or the care of a child . . ."

Mr Manners brightened perceptibly.

"She needs fresh air, exercise, a sensible diet . . ." Phemie smiled sweetly at Sir Aloysius. ". . . a sound spanking. What she does *not* need is rest and cosseting and medicine. And, if she has much more of this sort of treatment she will really become ill. My post here is a useless sinecure and I propose to relinquish it without delay. In fact from this very instant . . .''

An hour later she was recounting the story to Miss Nightingale who was watching and listening with an expressionless face.

''. . . before I left Sir Aloysius stamped out declaring that nothing would bring him beneath the roof again. Then Mr Manners called me into the study and gave me my salary and this . . .''

She placed a bill for twenty pounds on Miss Nightingale's desk.

''I would like it to go into the fund for the Crimean soldiers if you please.''

Miss Nightingale picked it up and considered it.

''And then?'' she said gently.

''He said he would lose no time in following my advice. I packed my bag then and left at once. Mrs Manners was bellowing so that she could be heard all over the house and her maid was whimpering up and down the stairs calling me cruel and heartless—she'd been listening at the door—and all the rest of the servants were laughing in corners . . . it was very distressing . . .''

Phemie's voice died away and she looked at her mentor. Miss Nightingale's expression was hard to read, half-amused, half-stern.

''My dear girl,'' she began at last, ''this is rather a coil. But I do not really think that I can blame you for it . . . it's really my own fault.''

''That's haivers, Miss Nightingale,'' said Phemie bluntly.

Miss Nightingale's eyebrows rose.

''Thanks to my long acquaintanceship with Doctor Sutherland I have learned to translate that as nonsense. That is uncivil, girl.''

Phemie went scarlet.

''I did not mean to be uncivil . . . I just meant that it wasn't your fault that I lost my temper.''

"I meant that I should never have let you go to a post in which your inability to tolerate fools would be so severely tried. I ought to have realised that something like this was bound to occur."

"I should have kept my mouth shut," admitted Phemie, repentantly, "and tried to pretend that it was a comedy I was watching. That was how I managed before. But yon hypocritical old humbug got my dander up. And the silly female quacking herself into an early grave . . . leaving her wee lass to the servants . . . it scunnered me and that's the truth. But there's no denying I shouldn't have said what I did."

"As far as the Manners are concerned," said Miss Nightingale drily, "you have probably done them a kindness. It's yourself you have injured."

There was a tap on the door and the maid handed in a note on a silver salver. It was folded awry and the wax splashed wildly over the back.

"This was delivered by hand two mintues since, ma'am."

"Is the messenger waiting?"

"Yes, ma'am."

Miss Nightingale slit open the note and read it. She sighed and handed it over to Phemie.

"You have certainly got under Sir Aloysius's thick hide, my dear. I congratulate you. I had thought his vast complacency impervious."

The note had obviously been composed in a tearing rage for the pen had spluttered ink in three places and little or no regard had been paid to the formalities . . . or the courtesies.

Tuesday.

Ma'am,

You will instantly dismiss from your school the Nurse Witherspoon. She has behaved in a grossly insolent, arrogant and unprofessional manner and caused infinite distress to a lady once a patient of mine. She is a disgrace to the practice of medicine. If she sets foot in St. Thomas's again I will instantly commend to the Board of Governors

53

that they do away with your so-called School of Nursing
and return to the perfectly satisfactory system of *Practical*
Nurses which we employed before you brought in this
gaggle of 'superior' women . . . incompetents rather, who
set themselves up against their betters.

sgd. A. Roebuck.

"Can he do that?"

"No. We are too well established for that. But he has a
following on the Board and could make it a little uncomfortable
for us."

"I am truly sorry."

Miss Nightingale pulled a piece of paper towards her and
picked up her silver pen.

"Ring the bell, my dear."

She wrote for a second or two and then passed the sheet over
to Phemie while she wrote the direction on an envelope.

Tuesday. South Street.

Sir,

I am investigating your allegation.

F.N.

"Let him chew that over," said Miss Nightingale and handed
it to a maid with instructions to give it to the waiting messenger.

"Now. We must consider what is to be done," she said when
the door was closed again. "I fear you cannot go back to St
Thomas's. That would be provocation and at this point we can't
afford that. I can give you shelter here for a space but you must
decide what you want to do. Do you want to nurse in Scotland?"

Phemie thought of Neil and shook her head.

"You do want to continue nursing?"

"Very much," said Phemie.

"You know that people are beginning to write to me asking
for my nurses to start similar training schools in other hospitals.

Already there are one or two up and down the country. Would you consider a post like that?''

''Willingly.''

''Unfortunately the only post I have at the moment is one in London and I feel that this is a little too near Sir Aloysius.''

Phemie considered also that it was a little too near Sir Aloysius.

''Just a moment, though . . . there was a letter from America . . .''

Miss Nightingale pulled open a drawer and produced a large sheet of paper covered with a sprawling and—at first glance—rather illiterate handwriting.

''It is from a place called Argentana in . . . Colorado Territory.'' Miss Nightingale looked up. ''I am never very clear about the geography of the United States. It will not stay the same long enough to establish itself in my mind. I think that this is somewhere in the south-west near the mountains. See what you think of the letter.''

The letter was dated over a month ago from the Town Hall of Argentana, the 'Silver Capital of Colorado Territory'. It made frequent reference to Miss Nightingale's enduring fame, the bloody Crimea, the healing lamp and the lack felt during 'our war' of similar ministering angels as those who had alleviated the suffering of the brave Britishers in the land of the Turk. However, under the verbiage the message was clear. Argentana enjoying a silver bonanza had decided to erect a civic hospital as a memorial to that apostle of freedom President Lincoln lately tragically slain in his hour of triumph by the forces of oppression. The citizens of Argentana were anxious, nay they were eager, to adopt the most forward-looking methods in this hospital and appealed to Miss Nightingale, that paragon of her sex, to assist them in this object. The writer subscribed himself her very devoted servant to command, Malachi Jackson McDowall, one-time captain in the Union Army and now Mayor of Argentana by popular vote whatever the other party might make it their business to say.

"I haven't replied. I had meant to send them a civil refusal because I could not think that it would interest any of my girls. But perhaps it will interest you?"

It did. Phemie took a day and a night to consider and at the end of that time decided to accept the challenge of such a propostion. Miss Nightingale, either the victim of second thoughts or in an attempt to test the strength of Phemie's resolution, tried hard to argue her out of her decision.

To this end she introduced Phemie to a man in the American Embassy who was acquainted with the Frontier, as he termed it. His brief was to tell her about the difficulties and dangers she was likely to meet. It was, from Miss Nightingale's point of view, a disappointing encounter. Phineas Marlowe was a Bostonian but he had escaped from his birthplace to the West in his younger days, made a vast fortune there, and only returned to fight for the Union during the Civil War, at which time he had been married and reclaimed for civilisation by his wife. He retained a love for the West, the wild country as he called it, and was well able to express it. In the incongruous setting of Miss Nightingale's white-painted drawing-room with its elegant furniture, Phemie listened to his description of the endless plains, the vast forests, the majestic mountains and the great bowl of the sky. She heard of the titanic weather, the treacherous rivers and the mushroom towns like Argentana growing up in a few days beside a find of gold or silver. She listened to stories of the Indians, of buffalo, of the railroads creeping five miles a day across the plains, tales of hardship and endurance, tragedy and comedy. When he left, Phemie's mind was more firmly set than ever. There was only one problem: who would be willing to go with her. Miss Nightingale was doubtful if volunteers could be found and if they were not Phemie could hardly be permitted to travel alone.

In the event the problem was solved easily if not wholly satisfactorily. Adela Wedmore in floods of tears declared that she would follow Phemie to exile, as she put it, casting Sir Aloysius in the role of the villain in a melodrama; she had no ties in England as her brother and sister had both emigrated to

Australia and her mother had died just before she began her training.

"She is not an ideal choice," remarked Miss Nightingale, "but she is biddable and good-humoured and will do simple tasks well without supervision . . . which is something. You will have to rely on Forsyth for anything more complicated."

Forsyth had a sister in America and wanted to join her. She signed a contract for three years' service in Argentana with rather a bad grace, murmuring that three years was a long time. With her the little group of 'pioneers', as Miss Nightingale called them, was complete. A letter was despatched to Argentana and an even more rhetorical letter was received which welcomed the 'little ladies of the lamp' to 'God's Own Country' and, what was much more to the point, enclosed a large draft upon an American bank to pay for the long journey. Mr Marlowe was pleased to advise them on their equipment for the overland part, while his wife, an elegant Bostonian who (privately) regarded Phemie and her party as unsexed hoydens, advised about the Atlantic crossing but refused her husband's request to receive them at the Embassy on the grounds that while such people were doubtless admirable they were certainly not socially acceptable.

Miss Nightingale who was far from well and preparing to plunge into what Doctor Sutherland described as another Sisyphean orgy in an attempt to reform the unsanitary conditions in which the majority of Her Majesty's soldiers languished and sickened, still found time to despatch a bundle of letters of introduction to friends and acquaintances in the United States as well as a few 'demi-semi-official' letters (as she termed them) to people and personages with whom she had no acquaintance but on whom she considered her name and fame might exercise a useful influence. Their trunks were packed, their passages were booked and their sailing date settled for March 16th.

Miss Nightingale's health did not permit of her attending the departure of her west-bound fledgelings from Waterloo station to board their ship at Southampton but a carriage-load of flowers, candy and fruit awaited her three 'pioneers' when they eventually boarded the steamer, as well as a warm woollen travelling rug apiece, a considerate gift for an Atlantic crossing so early in the year. But if Miss Nightingale was not at Waterloo except in spirit they did not lack for well-wishers on the platform. Mrs Wardroper had engaged an omnibus for such of her nurses who could be spared from their duties and sent with them a gracious note of good wishes. Miss Forsyth's family were there in force, veiled and dressed in black and weeping profusely. One might have imagined that the SS *Indiana* was bound for the bottom of the ocean and not the other side of it. Wedmore who had never before ventured upon a journey had piled cloaks and shawls upon herself until she resembled nothing so much as an old-clothes barrow. She stood surrounded by her fellow-nurses who clearly considered that she was doomed and were depressingly determined upon giving her a cheerful send-off. Their consolatory pats and surreptitious nose-blowings would have lowered the spirits of a more volatile character than Adela Wedmore who at last sat down on a porter's barrow and wept miserably over the keepsakes they showered upon her, penwipers, hairtidies, bookmarks, pincushions, buttonhooks, etuies and posies of crocheted woollen flowers.

Phemie, not much given to tears at any time, did not find this lachrymose scene to her taste. She had said goodbye to Miss Nightingale and one or two friends the night before and while she was not unpopular among the other nurses there was something about her which prevented their forming fast-friendships with her. Only Wedmore had blundered past this barrier. Phemie stood a little apart from the group looking with interest at the busy scene at this important terminal. Cabs discharged their passengers, porters trotted bawling behind trolleys piled high with baggage.

Suddenly her eye was caught by a stir among the crowd and a man strode along the platform, evidently looking for somebody.

Phemie conquered her desire to hide behind Adela's broad back and stood her ground, reflecting that the train was due to leave in less than ten minutes. It did not take Neil long to see her and he came striding up, scowling.

"What new nonsense is this?" he demanded without preamble. "Just what do you think you are doing? To leave like this without informing your family or your friends. I heard of your intentions only by chance."

"I must say I'd give something to know the name of that 'chance'," said Phemie. "I fail to see what business it is of yours what I do or where I go."

"Don't be such a simpleton!" he said contemptuously, "of course it's my concern. Aren't you my fiancée?"

"That I am not!" flared Phemie.

"This nonsense has gone on far too long," he snapped. "I've been a fool to indulge you. You are coming back to Glasgow with me in the morning."

"Am I indeed?" said Phemie. "And how do you propose to accomplish that?"

"Your father arranged for us to marry. I intend to carry out his wishes. If necessary I'll pick you up and carry you."

Phemie stared at him.

"Blackburn Colliery must be prosperous indeed," she observed.

Neil flushed and seized her arm.

"Are you coming with dignity or are you going to make a spectacle of yourself in public."

"I won't do that, I promise you," said Phemie thinking very quickly.

He pulled her towards the barrier. Phemie went unresistingly. She could see Forsyth and Wedmore pause in their weeping to stare. To her relief she saw the hoped-for figure at the barrier, a comforting sight in his blue frock-coat, metal buttons, dangling truncheon and the new helmet. She began to resist Neil's grasp.

"Constable!" she called out. "Constable, please! This man is molesting me!"

59

Neil's grip tightened painfully but he stopped dragging her along.

"You little vixen!" he said between his teeth.

The constable came through the barrier towards them, pulling rather uncertainly at his superb whiskers. Phemie jerked her arm out of Neil's grasp.

"Will you please tell this man to leave me alone," she demanded.

"I am this young lady's fiancé," Neil declared. "She has run away from home and I wish to restore her to her family."

The constable looked from one to the other, rather bewildered.

"I am one of Miss Nightingale's nurses," announced Phemie, and the constable's expression changed. "I am leaving England to take up a post in America. I am not engaged to marry this person and I do not want to be. Please tell him to leave me along."

"I will do nothing of the kind," snapped Neil.

Forsyth and Wedmore and the others had come up the platform to join them, their tears forgotten and their eyes wide with astonishment. The policeman cleared his throat and addressed Phemie:

"Are you really one of Miss Nightingale's nurses, miss?"

"I tell you she has run away from home," said Neil before Phemie could reply. "Her family has deputed me to bring her back, I have a letter . . ."

"Stuff and nonsense!"

Forsyth's voice came shrilly into the discussion before he could produce it and Adela surged forward to take up her position behind Phemie. Neil looked up from his search for the letter to see two females identically dressed in heavy frieze cloaks and close bonnets glaring belligerently at him.

"You leave our Sister Witherspoon alone, you . . . you . . ."

Wedmore added her powerful contralto. The constable, although a little bewildered by the increase in the number of the cast stuck firmly to his point.

"Is this young lady one of Miss Nightingale's nurses?" he asked again.

"She is still under age and thus subject to the wishes of her family . . ." insisted Neil, "and I intend to take her back to them."

He grasped Phemie by the arm again and waved a letter at the constable. The crowd which had begun to gather around murmured at this, especially when Phemie made an unavailing attempt to pull herself away. The constable's face darkened.

"I was in the Barrack 'Orspital . . ." he growled, "four month I were there. Is this young lady one of that sainted woman's nurses?"

Forsyth and Wedmore answered in confused chorus and were backed up by the farewell-takers. The constable found himself facing a bevy of similarly cloaked and bonneted young ladies who had overcome the discretion so emphatically urged upon them by Mrs Wardroper in order to take part in the debate. Their witness was voluble but unintelligible and the constable, his face now a dusky red, demanded yet again:

"Are you one of . . ."

"Yes, I am," said Phemie. "I told you I was. These ladies are all Nightingale nurses. They have very kindly come from St Thomas's Hospital to see us off on the train. And Miss Wedmore and Miss Forsyth are going with me."

Another shrill and ragged chorus bore witness to the truth of this statement. The constable unbuttoned his pocket to withdraw a notebook and a pencil which he sucked with deliberation.

"If it warn't for that sainted woman and her nurses," he rumbled, "Albert Beckwith would be a cold corp in a furrin land. As far as Albert Beckwith is concerned them young ladies is as near angels as any of you is likely to meet an' he don't take kindly to folk as lays vi'lent hands on them"

He flattened the pages of his notebook until it looked as if it might never close again and glowered down at Neil.

"Was you wishin' to prefer charges, miss?" he enquired.

"No," said Phemie. "I just want him to go away and leave me alone."

The constable buttoned up his notebook and settled his helmet with a practised thump.

61

"Very good, miss."

He gathered up Neil by his collar and one arm.

"Come along o' me, young man . . . an' if you know what's good for you, come quiet."

"This is an outrage!" protested Neil furiously. "Take your hands off me!"

"Don't you go a-wavin' of your fists at me, young feller-me-lad," warned the constable and marched him inexorably through the barrier, propelled him into the heart of an interested (and on the whole hostile) crowd, turned about and saluted Phemie solemnly. "I'll take care he don't try it on again, miss. 'E'll not get by me."

"Thank you very much indeed!" called Phemie.

"A pleasure, miss," returned her champion and eyed the unfortunate Neil with distaste.

During the argument the rest of the passengers had been shepherded into the carriages and the porters came to urge Phemie and her companions to follow their example. As soon as the doors were slammed upon them the whistle blew, the flag waved and the train ground slowly away leaving a flutter of white handkerchiefs on the platform and a perfect flood of tears in the compartment.

At Southampton the trio found grey skies and yeasty seas. The U.S. Mail Steamer *Indiana* was fidgeting ponderously at the quayside. Below, their cabin was found to be compact, not to say cramped, and after having heard the first rumblings of a disagreement between Wedmore and Forsyth over the allocation of lockers Phemie decided to unpack later. She left the combatants as they reached the stage of acidulated politeness and went to explore the other amenities offered by SS *Indiana*. She peeped through the open doors to view the luxuries of the first-class saloon and among the plum-coloured plush and polished brass lamps she saw, to her surprise, a familiar leonine figure chewing reflectively at the brim of his silk-hat.

"Evan Parsons!" she exclaimed. "Whatever are you doing here? Are you travelling to America?"

At the sound of her voice he leaped to his feet and came to the doorway.

"You've got here at last," he said and wrung her hand repeatedly. "I did think of waiting for you at the station but it would have been too easy to miss you there and I knew you must fetch up on the ship. It's easier to talk here too. Come and sit down."

He piloted her among the vast plush chairs and the brass cuspidors and seated her on a settee designed for giants.

"You don't have to go . . ." he told her earnestly, ". . . my offer holds . . . it always will, you know . . . no need for such desperate measures. And Hampshire's miles from London . . . *she* won't hear of it and I don't care a button if she does!"

Phemie stared at him in bewilderment.

"You know . . ." he went on, "I take it very ill that you didn't write me what was going on. You might have known you could rely on me . . ."

"Rely on you for what?"

"To punch old Sir Noisome on the nose!"

He sat down beside her on the settee.

"I tell you, Phemie, if I'd been there, I'd have tapped his claret for him . . . the old scoundrel. I don't care if he was ten times a knight! And as for that old besom Nightingale . . ."

"You will *not* in my presence refer to Miss Nightingale in such terms, Evan. She has been uncommonly kind to me. And I really don't know what you are talking about."

He stared at her puzzled.

"*I* heard that old Noisome had had you turfed out of the Manners house. They said he'd told the Nightingale that you'd accused him of poisoning Mrs Manners with physic and seduced Mr Manners into believing this story and dismissing him and he threatened to take you to court for slander and the Nightingale was forcing you to emigrate to hush the scandal round her precious School. They said you were sailing with this boat so I . . ."

"Just a minute," cried Phemie. "Who told you this . . . this farrago of nonsense?"

"Jackie Bilton wrote to me. He says it's all round the hospital. Isn't it true?"

"Not a word of it."

He looked at her, frowning slightly.

"Then why are you here?" he asked.

She explained in a very few words and he sat for a moment looking chapfallen.

"Ah, well," he sighed at last, "always seem to be bargin' in where I'm not wanted. Just that I thought you'd rather . . . I mean, I'm qualified now . . . let loose upon suffering humanity as the Prof put it. Said he hoped that experience would teach me more than he'd been able to do . . . not that I'm getting much, my father lets me drive the gig and pound the jalap and that's about all. But I thought . . . well, it's a pleasant place enough . . . better than going to the back of beyond . . ."

From which Phemie gathered that he had intended to renew his offer of marriage and she knew a pang of remorse. Silence fell between them for a few uncomfortable seconds and the *Indiana*'s siren erupted into it. Phemie saw Evan's lips move but could not make out what he was saying until the noise stopped.

". . . I'll let you know," he was telling her earnestly, "I mean they might need . . ."

The siren once more informed the world that SS *Indiana* was about to depart.

". . . a better place to get experience," he was saying when it stopped.

"Of course," she said as he seemed to expect some sort of response.

"Then, if you'd just write down your address," he asked.

While she was doing this the cry of "All ashore!" echoed down the companionway.

At the gangway where the leavetakers were pouring ashore they had to wait for a few moments. Phemie put her hand on his arm.

"Evan, just because I didn't need your help doesn't mean I'm not very grateful to you for offering it. You are very good to me."

64

"You won't mind too much if I do, then?" he muttered mysteriously, gave her hand an agonising squeeze, dropped a kiss on her cheek and was gone down the gangway.

Indiana churned her way towards open water and Phemie massaging life back into her fingers saw a rather disconsolate figure waving on the quay. She produced her handkerchief and responded in kind. As the distance between them increased she sighed very slightly.

'Poor old Perseus,' she thought, 'but it wouldn't be right. I'd make him feel . . . unimportant . . . and he'd hate that. And so would I.'

4

IT WAS SOMEHOW CHARACTERISTIC of Phemie that she should prove to be a good sailor. Forsyth and Wedmore turned green almost before *Indiana* pushed her bows out beyond the Solent and by the time she was rising and swooping over the Atlantic rollers marching eternally out of the west towards her they were prostrate in the cabin convinced that the end would come at any second and past caring if it did. Phemie did her duty by them and by any other seriously afflicted passengers introduced to her notice by the stewards and stewardesses. She ate almost in solitude and took exercise round the deck when the ship's motion permitted, which was not often because they made a difficult and stormy passage during which head winds slowed progress and devoured fuel. It was nearly four weeks after leaving Southampton that *Indiana* steamed, very slowly, into New York harbour.

Wedmore and Forsyth revived enough to pack their bags and while *Indiana* laboured towards her berth attended by two noisy tugs and an equally noisy cloud of gulls they remained in the cabin with Phemie preparing for the next stage in their journey. Phemie pruned rigorously the amount they packed in their valises and relegated much that they considered essential for a prolonged journey by train to the trunks which would go in what Phineas Marlowe referred to as a baggage car. She explained that they would need to carry food and washing materials as well as the necessary clothes and underclothes and that porters were an unknown breed in the West; but still they sulked as various items such as gloves, shoes and parasols were thrust into obscurity and replaced by towels, soap, books and materials for sewing and knitting.

"Have you any notion how long it may take us to reach the railhead? We could be more than a week on the journey. You must take something to do," Phemie told them. "Mr Marlowe says the scenery can be pretty monotonous."

She did not add, 'And so can your conversation,' but the unkind thought was in her mind as she added a pharmacopoeia to the already formidable pile of reading-matter in her own valise. That much she had learned from the voyage.

"What are we going to do after we dock?" enquired Adela, and Phemie was conscious of a faint irritation that this should be the first time Adela had thought to ask.

"We must go through the formalities," she told her, "so *don't* put your passport in the very bottom of your bag. After that we'll call a cab and go to some boarding house. I have a list of decent places from Mr Marlowe."

"And what then?"

Phemie could not explain to herself what there was about Forsyth's question to make her feel uncomfortable. There was nothing she could have defined . . . perhaps it was an un-accustomed air of reticence, though on what subject Phemie could not tell. She paused before she answered and looked at Forsyth's narrow olive-skinned face which reddened under her gaze.

"I thought I would try to book our tickets on the train tomorrow. My Marlowe told me where to go. We can write letters home and then we can go out and see something of the city and buy what we need for the journey."

A shudder and a slight jar indicated that *Indiana* had come alongside the quay and the cabin party stopped discussing their plans and began to fasten straps and search the lockers to make sure that they had left nothing behind. No more than a minute or two after the jar there was a tap on the cabin door. Forsyth, who was ready, opened it, gave a little scream, stepped back and fell over her own valise in an undignified flurry of boots and petticoats. Wedmore stared, blenched and gave vent to a squeak of dismay and even Phemie lost something of her usual self-possession.

67

In the half-light of the 'tween-decks their visitor was sufficiently alarming. He was very tall, very black and his eyes and his gleaming beautiful teeth were all that was clearly visible of him.

"Which of you good ladies Mis' Widderspoon?" he enquired in a voice like very dark brown velvet.

Phemie found her own voice.

"That's me . . ." she croaked, ". . . I mean that's I . . . I mean I'm she . . ."

"This note for you. From my lady."

He handed it over with a bow.

"From whom?"

"From my lady. At the British Consulate," he explained paternally. Phemie detected the hand of Miss Nightingale at work and she was quite right. The note was headed 'British Consulate, New York' and was written in a neat clear hand.

> Dear Miss Witherspoon,
>
> Miss Nightingale writes to me by the last steamer to inform me of your arrival by SS *Indiana* and your intended journey to Colorado Territory. I do hope that you and your colleagues will permit my husband and myself to assist you to the best of our ability in arranging this journey and to offer you hospitality as long as you will be in New York. Scipio brings this note to you; please let him help you through the various formalities. He is very good at this as he meets all our visitors. After that I have told him to bring you straight to me where I have ready beds which stay in one plane, fresh milk and bread, and hot fresh water, for all of which I am persuaded you must be longing.
>
> I hope you had a tolerable journey and that you will be able to rest for a space before you set out for the West.
>
> Yours etc.
>
> Elizabeth Lacombe.
>
> PS. May I extend a particular greeting to a fellow-Scot.
>
> E.L.

There was something extraordinarily comforting about such a letter. Phemie's eyes filled as they had not done during the farewell in England. She had been braced for the business of steering herself and her companions through the customs and the immigration office, finding porters and cabs and suitable accommodation in a strange place and then setting about to arrange a journey into what was virtually a wilderness. For a girl only just twenty-one it had been a daunting prospect. To be offered such unexpected help and hospitality was to be spared an ordeal. She aimed a silent and heartfelt shaft of gratitude towards Miss Nightingale, at that moment locked in deadly combat with the War Office, and smiled upon Scipio whose answering smile fairly lit up the dim cabin.

"Lady Lacombe the consul's wife has been kind enough to invite us all to stay," she explained to Wedmore and Forsyth who had picked herself up and was staring at Scipio with a kind of horrified fascination. "She says Scipio will take us through the customs. Are you Scipio?"

The huge negro bowed.

"My name Scipio Africanus Beauregard."

Phemie smiled a greeting.

"How do you do?"

"I do everything, Mis' Widderspoon," said Scipio. "You show me your bags and your boxes then you go topside there and I do it all."

In less than an hour they were bowling in an elegant brougham down a broad street lined with well-built houses made of a brown stone and surrounded by trees which were just beginning to come into leaf. Behind at distance came a cab which bore their baggage. The trio stared about them and marvelled at the height of some of the buildings in the centre of the city.

"I daresay some of them were ten storeys!" said Adela awestruck.

Lady Lacombe was waiting to meet them, a tall graceful woman in her thirties, her dark hair in a coronet of plaits but it was not until they had been allowed to wash in heavenly fresh water that she received them in her own room and offered them tea. She waved Phemie's gratitude aside.

"Nothing of the kind," she told her, "a pleasure, I assure you. We have an enormous respect for Miss Nighingale and what she has achieved. In fact . . ." She smiled rather ruefully. "As you will no doubt discover very soon my eldest daughter has a burning ambition to emulate her and her cross is that she was born too late to go to the Crimea. I hope she may not turn you all inside out with questions . . . Or perhaps it would be more rational to hope that you will not mind too much when she does."

She picked up a sheet of paper from her bureau.

"Now," she went on, "my husband asked his secretary to prepare this for you. Perhaps you would care to consider it. You'll note that he has been told to make sure that you spend at least a week with us . . ."

'This' was a complete itinerary of their journey to Abilene from the point where they would board the 'steam cars' till the eventual arrival. It told them the places where the train would halt, how long each stage would take and how much it would cost. There was also a list of what they would need upon the journey even longer than that which Phineas Marlowe had given her. When she had taken in the contents Phemie looked up at her hostess and smiled.

"He seems to have left me nothing to do but call a cab and go to the . . . depot."

"But Scipio would not hear of that!" said Lady Lacombe in mock dismay. "I'd never hear the end of it." She mimicked the negro's soft voice. "Where I come from, ma'am, the guests do not leave by cab . . ."

The door was flung open and two girls rushed in. The first was a pretty child about sixteen with very fair hair and blue eyes, the other a quiet, dark little person of about eleven who was so like her mother that it was startling.

"Mama! Mama! Are they here yet—oh!"

The older girl put her hand over her mouth and looked

70

embarrassed. Lady Lacombe sighed and put out a restraining hand.

"Yes, Louisa . . . they are here and if you will just calm down a little I'll introduce you. Miss Witherspoon, Miss Forsyth and Miss Wedmore, may I introduce my daughter Louisa."

The child curtseyed. Her sister tugged at Lady Lacombe's hand.

"Me too, Mama, please."

Her mother looked down at her.

"But Miss Lambe will be expecting you."

"She won't mind. Scipio gave her a letter. It's from her lover I expect because she went pink. She'll want to read it by herself and I want to talk to Miss . . . Miss . . ."

She nodded decidedly in Phemie's direction. Lady Lacombe looked slightly helpless and introduced her as well.

"My daughter Joanna."

Joanna curtseyed and walked over to perch on the arm of Phemie's chair.

"Mama says you are from Scotland. I want to go there. What's it like?"

Before Phemie could answer she was overwhelmed by a flood of questions from Louisa and was forced to deny ever having been in the Crimea or even having met a soldier let alone nursed one.

"I was younger even than Joanna during the war," she explained.

Louisa then turned eagerly to Forsyth and Wedmore.

"Were you in the Crimea? Or you?"

Forsyth flushed at this artless implication of a more aged appearance for she was only three years older than Phemie, but Adela smiled.

"I wasn't there," she said. "But my father's sister, she went. That's how I wanted to be a nurse, hearing her tales."

Louisa enthusiastically dragged the details out of Adela but Phemie who had heard them before felt a gentle tug on her

71

sleeve and heard a few words in what she recognised as Gaelic though she did not understand it.

"I beg your pardon?" she said, a little bewildered, and the child's face fell.

"Don't you understand?" she asked. "That's the language they talk in Scotland. Mama taught me and Nanny talked it."

"But I am a Lowlander," said Phemie, "and we don't have the Gaelic as a rule. Your Mama and your Nanny must come from the Highlands."

"From the Isles," corrected Joanna. "Papa says we will all go there for a visit when we go home."

"And when will that be?"

"Oh, very soon. In fact if it hadn't been for that unspeakable war . . ."

Phemie smiled involuntarily to hear this adult echo.

". . . we'd be there already. But they didn't want somebody new while everyone was fighting and then they killed poor Mr Lincoln and made a fearful to do . . . so, we're still here."

"Well," said Phemie, "I'm glad of that, if you're not."

"Where in Scotland do you come from?"

"Near Glasgow . . ." replied Phemie but before she had a chance to expand on this Louisa pounced on her again.

"Miss Witherspoon! Miss Wedmore says that you are a Sister! Is that right?"

Phemie nodded.

"But you don't look much older than me."

Lady Lacombe intervened.

"Louisa, please!"

Her daughter made an apologetic face.

"Sorry, Mama," she said perfunctorily. "Miss Witherspoon, I *so* want to be a nurse. How old must I be?"

"At least five and twenty," said Phemie in her flattest tones.

"Five and twenty! Oh, no!" Louisa's vivid face was a mask of despair. "But I'm only sixteen—that's nine whole *years*!"

"I fear so," said Phemie.

Louisa's attention fixed on her. "You're not five and twenty,'' she accused, ''nor anything like. And you're a Sister!''

Lady Lacombe intervened again. ''Louisa . . . will you please try to be a little more temperate in your speech or I will have to send you upstairs to Miss Lambe.''

''Oh, please no, Mama. I want to know how to set about being a nurse . . . Surely I won't have to wait for nine years, Miss Witherspoon . . . not nine years!''

Phemie relented slightly. ''Of course, Miss Nighingale is not absolutely rigid about age,'' she admitted, ''she's too sensible for that . . .''

''Of course she is . . . Isn't she the most wonderful woman who ever lived?''

''. . . But she does insist on some previous experience of nursing if she makes an exception,'' Phemie continued, ignoring this encomium.

''What sort of experience had you had?''

''I nursed both my father and my mother.''

''Oh,'' said Louisa, dashed.

''I feel it is only fair to warn you, Louisa,'' Lady Lacombe put in, ''that both your father and myself have remarkably robust constitutions . . .''

''Oh, Mama!''

''. . . and neither your brother Hector nor Joanna show any symptoms of chronic illness.''

Louisa hunched an impatient shoulder.

''Was that all?'' she demanded of Phemie, who hesitated.

Adela flung herself into the gap. ''Sister Witherspoon is very bookish too,'' she told Louisa, ''perhaps if you were to apply yourself to your studies . . .''

Louisa's eyes widened in dismay. ''Studies!'' she exclaimed. ''What sort of studies?''

''Chemistry, anatomy, physiology . . . such stuff,'' sighed Forsyth, ''you've no idea . . .''

''Can I get the right books here?'' Louisa demanded heroically.

''Oh, I expect we can order them from London if necessary,'' said Lady Lacombe. "In the mean time, dare I suggest that a little more attention to your ordinary lessons would get you into the habit."

Louisa made a face. "Music and German and French!" she said scornfully. "What use would they be for nursing?"

"I have often wished I could read French more easily," said Phemie. "There is some important work going on in France just now and as I know not one word of German I must depend for my knowledge of Kaiserwerth on the impressions of other people. You are lucky, Miss Louisa."

Louisa looked less than convinced.

"But why should all these things be necessary to nurse sick people and wounded soldiers?" she protested. "Surely it's what you do, not what you know, that really matters?"

"It's necessary to know what to do," said Phemie drily, and why you do it. Otherwise you'll be in sore danger of doing the wrong thing."

"Oh," responded Louisa, "I see."

"My poor lamb," said her mother, "it is a rather grim prospect, nine years to wait before you can apply for training and all that hard study . . . perhaps you won't object if we lighten it with a party or so and some pretty clothes?"

"Oh, you don't *want* me to be a nurse!" Louisa flung at her tearfully. "You want me to be presented to that dreary old queen and be paraded like a horse and marry someone *suitable*. I'd rather die. I want to *do* something and now there's something girls can do you're going to do everything you can to stop me. Well, you won't, do you hear? You won't! I'll *be* a nurse—I will! I will!"

She rushed out of the room leaving her mother's guests open-mouthed and staring. Lady Lacombe closed the door calmly and surveyed the company.

"It would, I hope, be superfluous to tell you that I would not dream of preventing Louisa's becoming a nurse. If that is what she wants she may do it with our good will. But I doubt of her being suitable material for Miss Nightingale . . . at the moment at all events."

74

"In the summer," Joanna put in from her place beside Phemie, "Mama took us to see *Hamlet*—the play, you know—and after that Louisa wanted to be an actress. It wasn't till she heard the lecture about the Crimea in the Fall that she changed her mind."

"Joanna . . ." warned her mother.

"Though I must say," said Joanna unregarding, "the nurse-thing has lasted longer than the Ophelia-thing . . ."

"That will *do*, Joanna!" said her mother and sighed. "I seem to spend my life saying those words."

"And what do you want to do?" asked Phemie.

Joanna considered for a second.

"To be captain of a steamship."

Their next encounter with this rather disconcerting pair was on the following day. Sir Hector, anxious to trace their journey for them upon the map, found that his newest map had gone up to the schoolroom.

"Joanna," he explained philosophically. "That child has a passion for maps."

He led the way up to a cheerful room on the second floor. Here they found Lady Lacombe and Joanna conducting a conversation in slow and stilted German while Louisa stared dramatically out of the window, a book open and ignored on the table in front of her.

"Ah, Liz . . . have you seen my new map?" asked Sir Hector, and then looked about. "Where's Miss Lambe?"

Lady Lacombe did not reply at once but Joanna answered for her.

"Her lover has come back from the army."

"Ah!" said her father.

"Nothing of the sort," said Lady Lacombe rather tartly. "It isn't in the least Ah. He has married some predatory Southern belle and poor Miss Lambe is laid down upon her bed with the headache."

"Oh!"

"Yes. It is much more Oh than Ah."

"Her Hopes are dashed for Ever," said Louisa, her eyes still fixed on the world outside. "She has made up her mind that as her Life has been Blighted she will Devote it to the Betterment of Mankind by means of Education."

This depressingly worthy resolution silenced the company if only momentarily.

"I thought," said Joanna dragging a rolled-up map taller than herself out of the cupboard, "that actually Miss Lambe was getting rather friendly with Captain Wolfe . . ."

"Hardly an appropriate friendship, I feel," put in her father. "Have they met frequently?"

"Oh, yes," said Joanna, "in the morning, you know, on the staircase, she says 'Good Morning, Captain.' "

The mimicry was startling.

". . . And he says, 'Yes . . . yes, rather . . .' and twirls his moustache."

To do them credit neither parent laughed at this description of the courtship though there was a charged silence for a few seconds. Lady Lacombe's face assumed the slightly helpless expression which her younger daughter could so easily call forth and Sir Hector pulled thoughtfully at one luxuriant sidewhisker.

"Well, yes," he said at last, "it hardly seems enough on which to base a permanent relationship, does it?"

"Of course not," agreed Louisa scornfully, "the merest commonplace."

Joanna held down one end of the map while her father unrolled it on the inkstained schoolroom table.

"You wait," she assured him.

It took some time to find Argentana on the map and it was Phemie who located it at last. Sir Hector regarded the dot with evident misgiving.

"It seems to me," he said, "that you will be in the heart of the Comanche country. If you will just excuse me a moment I'll ask the military attaché."

"That's Captain Wolfe," confided Joanna. "I think he's much nicer than Miss Lambe's other lover . . ."

"Joanna, that will do," said her mother.

76

However, when he did arrive it was plain to be seen that Captain Wolfe might well be able to tempt Miss Lambe from her dedication to Education . . . should he so desire. He nodded to Lady Lacombe, warded off the clamorous greeting of her younger daughter and bowed politely to Louisa and the three guests. His information was full and up-to-date. Yes, there had been some trouble with the Comanche even before the war but a fort had been established not far from the town and a cavalry unit posted there in the fall of 1865. He had met the commanding officer . . .

"A rattling good soldier," he said enthusiastically, "he served with Grant."

He seemed to think that this circumstance would remove most of the hazard from the long stage journey, though not the discomfort.

"Regular bounders, those stages," he declared, "jolt the teeth out of your head . . . and bundles of mail fallin' all over you . . ."

Phemie, rather daunted by this description, peeped at her companions to see who they had reacted and realised that Adela was too lost in admiration of the speaker to have heard a word he said, while Forsyth was still poring over the map and paying no attention. However, her interest did not appear to be in the West. It was now centred in New England. She glanced up to find Phemie looking at her and unaccountably went scarlet.

"So strange . . ." she said hastily, "all those familiar names in such a setting. Plymouth . . . Peterborough . . . Manchester . . ."

Once again Phemie felt uneasy about her without quite understanding why.

The reason was made plain some two days later when Lady Lacombe tapped on Phemie's door soon after it was light.

"Miss Witherspoon . . . Phemie . . . Oh, you're awake."

Phemie laid aside her book and sat up. Her hostess with two plaits down her back looked little older than Louisa and quite uncharacteristically agitated.

"What's the matter?" Phemie asked. "Is someone ill?"

It seemed the only possible reason for such a visit.

"No," said Lady Lacombe and thrust a letter at her. "I don't know whether it's an irretrievable disaster or an unforeseen mercy for you but Miss Forsyth is gone. She left the house last night some time. Scipio found this letter in the hall and Marcia brought it up for me."

While she unfolded the note Phemie realised that Lady Lacombe had not liked Forsyth. The letter was addressed to Lady Lacombe thanked her for her kindness and asked that Sister Witherspoon be informed that the writer had changed her mind about going to Argentana as the project seemed hare-brained in the extreme. She had instead gone to her married sister in New England. Miss Witherspoon would no doubt defray the cost of sending her baggage on to the address which she would send later.

Phemie refolded the graceless little letter.

"And then there were two . . ." she commented. "I suppose I should have been expecting something like this for I don't suppose she ever had the remotest intention of coming with us. It was to be a free passage to America. I will have to tell Miss Nightingale and she will be angry and disappointed."

Lady Lacombe sat on the edge of the bed.

"Will this make things very difficult for you?"

"Not really."

Phemie considered the matter.

"I suppose I could hold her to the contract but really I'd rather have someone who wanted to come and someone who really wanted to nurse."

"I must entreat," sighed her hostess, "that you avoid saying such things in Louisa's hearing."

Phemie laughed.

"No. I promise you, I shan't do that."

"In some ways it would be easier if she would fall in love with someone wildly unsuitable. I could deal with that."

"I'll be as discreet and discouraging as I can."

"Seriously, what will you do?"

78

"What we always meant to do," said Phemie. "Find suitable women there and train them. It's a set-back, I don't deny, but we'll contrive."

"There's one thing," remarked her hostess and got to her feet, "it would take much more than a married sister in New England to tear the faithful Wedmore from your side."

It was a prophetic remark.

Forsyth's going was not to be the only set-back. Spring apparently brought problems to American railroads. Ground thawed under the track and the rails vanished under mud; floods washed the line away altogether, landslides blocked it and each week brought with it families clamouring to travel West while the trains stood unmoving in the sheds. More than a fortnight went past before Phemie and Adela were able to board the train and move out of the depot towards Trenton. Phemie had insisted that no one except Scipio come with them to the train, so early was the departure but at the Consulate everyone had turned out to give them a send off, even Miss Lambe and Captain Wolfe: everyone except one.

Louisa had greeted the news of Forsyth's defection as a Providential Intervention intended to provide her with the necessary experience to appease Miss Nightingale. She at once announced her intention of making one of the Argentana party. First her mother told her gently that such a plan was out of the question, and when this was ill-received Phemie told her bluntly that she was not to come. At this Louisa perceived the Hand of her Mother at Work and refused to believe that Sister Witherspoon would not want the assistance of one who was so obviously a Born Nurse. There followed some days of constant and wearing argument which terminated in scenes and tears. Sir Hector, the final court of appeal, stared when he heard his daughter's request and gave a blunt and none too tactful refusal.

"For Heaven's sake," he adjured her, "have a little sense. Phemie and Adela will have quite enough to do without looking after children."

Which remark might have been guaranteed to result in a

monumental fit of the sulks . . . and did. Louisa emerged from this only two days before they were due to leave, restored, or so it seemed to an angelic good nature but almost immediately succumbed to a feverish cold and had to go to her bed where, on the morning of their departure she still was, although she had sent a very civil message of farewell the night before. The storm and stress of this situation had served to put Phemie on very intimate terms with the Lacombes. They regarded her with a mixture of admiration and amusement and saw her go with regret, making her promise to send them news and rely on them for any assistnace in their power.

The train was unlike any that either Phemie or Adela had ever seen. The carriages (the 'conductor' called them cars) were not divided into compartments but were built with rows of seats on either side and a narrow passage between them up the centre and a door at either end. A small iron stove at each end warmed the car and served as water-heater, cooking-stove and social centre for the travellers in that and other cars . . . for it was perfectly possible, though horribly dangerous, to pass from car to car the whole length of the train. The seats could be converted to sleeping places by the ingenious use of boards which were stowed beneath them during the day and cushions supplied by the travellers themselves. Phemie and Adela had found themselves overwhelmed by presents of cushions 'for your journey' from the people they met at the Lacombes but they were soon to understand how necessary they were. The train stopped twice in the day so that the passengers might get out for fifteen minutes during which time they were expected to swallow a hot meal and buy necessities from the pedlars who haunted the depots. For the rest they depended on their own stores and the coffee which brewed endlessly upon the stove under the care of a kindly woman who spoke not a word of any known language. A tiny corner of the car was boarded over to serve as washplace and privy. At night rugs were draped from seat to seat and the oil lamps on the brackets were turned low; but sleep was elusive in such circumstances and passengers flitted to and fro along the swaying car during all the hours of darkness. With the livelong day to doze, what need to sleep at night.

In the afternoon of the third day out from New York they had reached the rolling grasslands and the view from the window, at first impressive, had become monotonous in the extreme. From the beginning the two girls had taken it in turn to sit on the inside where every passer-by jogged their arm or dropped cigar ash on them or even leaned against the arm of their seat to talk to the people over the way. In that seat it was not possible to sleep. Adela had the desirable window seat and was asleep with her mouth open and her hair coming down. Phemie had a book open on her lap but she was not reading: the swaying and jolting of the train over the hastily laid track made this almost impossible. Instead she was trying to recall in her head the material she had read while the train was halted at noon for almost an hour to let an east-bound train pass by.

"Ten minutes to eat breakfast," Adela had grumbled, "and then over an hour here, miles from anywhere."

The east-bound had come in at last, its cars half empty and the passengers looking at the other train with glassy-eye in-curiousness. The drivers exchanged incomprehensible items of news about 'hot-boxes' and reaches of 'sprung line' and then the two trains had clanked slowly apart. The delay had made them late at the township where they were due to have their dinner, a tiny place far out on the plains containing little more than a store, a saloon and a water-tower. The driver hissed to a halt in the siding and called out to the agent who stood by the track. The agent, a wizened ancient, replied with a barrage of picturesque bad language which described the ancestry, personal appearance and subhuman habits of a gentleman who had taken and wrecked a freight two miles south of Stratford. Phemie, who had climbed down with their plates and jug as soon as the train was still, listened fascinated to this exchange. The line had been cleared for the east-bound but now the wrecking car was bringing the engine and two salvaged freightcars back to the depot and the line would be blocked for an hour or more. An hour . . . time for a leisurely meal . . . time even for a walk. She collected the inevitable beans and salt pork and the harsh coffee which was drunk with objects which Phemie might have called scones had they been lighter and more digestible but which the purveyors called biscuits. Thus loaded she climbed back on to the train. Adela was awake, though still frowsy with sleep, and ready to take the food from her. They put it to keep warm on the stove and went to wash in the washroom while the rest of the passengers in the car were away gobbling their pork and beans in the saloon. Already three days had been enough to establish this as a routine.

They ate the unappetising food, eking it out with delicacies bestowed on them by Lady Lacombe, and then, washed, brushed and fed they set out for a walk. The township was too small to serve as an object. They could command its possibilities in two seconds from the steps of the train. Beyond and around stretched the plains, chequered into farms, the houses far away and tiny like toys. Only the railroad track provided a reference in that scene so they walked beside the train until they reached the immigrant cars next to the engine: bare comfortless versions of their own. Here the immigrants were washing, cooking, eating, singing, talking and laughing in a babel of languages. Already washing was draped from the car windows in the sun. Children played at Hide and Seek among the iron wheels and couplings. Adela averted her eyes from this intimate glimpse into other people's lives but Phemie watched entranced, noting as she always did the rickets here, the rheumatism there and the sore eyes elsewhere. There was a small group of children squatting down and watching two people play some game. Phemie went closer and looked over their heads. It was a game of cat's-cradle and had reached its most intricate point. It was a favourite with Joanna and after her stay with the Lacombes Phemie was well-acquainted with the finer points. The structure was carefully transferred from one pair of hands to another, the middle fingers dipped and the patterns unlimned smoothly into a single loop of string. The players looked up and laughed at their audience and Phemie found herself staring straight at Louisa.

5

IT WAS A SILENT TRIO which stood among the pile of baggage at the side of the tracks and watched the west-bound pull out without them. Adela looked worried and unhappy at being thus stranded in the middle of a foreign land, Louisa was tearful and mutinous and Phemie determined.

"Your mother was uncommonly good to me and I'll not be a party to distressing her," she had told Louisa. "I'm taking you straight back to New York . . ."

There had been an outburst of horrified protest of which she took not the slightest notice.

". . . and it's not the least use to argue."

Louisa was heard to say in a voice choked with emotion that All she had wanted to do was to Help.

"That's as may be," said Phemie dryly. "A grand help it's been, I must say, to have to turn back and the journey nearly half done."

"You said I'd have to have Experience before Miss Nightingale would let me train, and where can I get it if I don't come."

"You don't have to travel West to find sick folk . . . especially without telling your people where you'd gone."

"They'd be bound to guess."

"That's as may be, my dear," Adela intervened, "but they didn't *know*. They'll be worried out of their minds."

"You have behaved selfishly and unkindly," observed Phemie.

This severity from her idol finally dissolved Louisa into

speechless sobs. Adela stared and then offered up her last clean handkerchief. Words at last inserted themselves among the tears.

"I just . . . want to . . . learn . . ." hiccupped Louisa, ". . . and when Miss Forsyth . . . you *needed* someone . . ."

"Your Mama and your father both said you might not go. Did you think I wouldn't pack you off home as soon as I clapped eyes on you?" demanded Phemie.

"That was just because they don't want me to become a nurse. I don't care . . . I will . . . I will . . ."

"Haivers!" said Phemie. "They know you're not yet fit to be a nurse. You're undisciplined and emotional . . . and you'd be precious little use to us out there . . . and they know it. And this escapade proves them right, my lass, let me tell you!"

After such blunt speaking Louisa took refuge in ill-used silence from which Adela tried in vain to coax her. The last trace of smoke vanished from the western horizon and Phemie went to discover when they might expect the next train to the East. The agent in charge was lame, bad-tempered and didn't hold with wimmen-folk. He told Phemie with sour glee that the next east-bound was not due for some time owing to a bridge being washed out by the spring floods up the line. Phemie accepted this news philosophically and requested permission to camp in the wooden shed which served for waiting-room, parcels office and ticket office. He refused uncivilly and told them to be off to the saloon. Phemie looked him in his rheumy and malicious eye and told him that the party included a girl of sixteen and she for one would not take her within a hundred yards of such a place. The old man spat resoundingly at a bucket and observed that it warn't no concarn of his'n.

"Now," replied Phemie in an ominously quiet voice, "my friends and I have paid our fares and we are entitled to any or all of the facilities provided by the Railroad. We intend to sleep in that wee shed and you will supply us with water and firing or I'll report you to the directors for an ill-conditioned foul-mouthed, unco-operative old . . ."

Sustaining this attack with phlegm the old man spat again,

laughed creakily and said he'd dang his buttons if it warn't allus the littl'uns who'd the spunk and he'd fetch in some kindlin'.

He was even better than his word. He fetched in his own coffee pot and the Chinese cook from the saloon who smiled blindingly upon them and returned in half an hour with a loaded tray. The old man shared the pork, beans and biscuits and told them (through the commodities in question) that his monicker was Jedediah and they could call him Jed. They also gathered that he intended to sleep in the telegraph office next door with something he called a scatter-gun.

"An' ef any dangblasted nester tries it on he'll get a bellyful of lead!"

He clinched this reassurance by spitting explosively on to the red-hot stove and leaving them to their own resources.

Safe they may have been but they were far from comfortable. The furniture consisted of two narrow benches and two three-legged stools. The floor was of beaten earth and the privy (indicated by Jed earlier in a dislocatory jerk of the head) was a draughty hut surrounding a bucket. Phemie placed her companions on the benches and heaped them in blankets and cloaks. She then sat down on one of the stools to tend the stove until it should be time to rouse Adela and take her turn upon the bench. In the event she did not do this, but slept beside the stove on the earth floor. At dawn she woke shivering and went in search of wood and water. She was greeted as she emerged in the chilly grey light by a boy of about twelve who was loosely attached to a large mule breakfasting off the weeds which grew between the tracks.

"You one of them ladies got offa the west-bound yestiddy?"

Phemie agreed.

"Many on yer?"

"Just the three," said Phemie, amused by his directness.

"Three," ruminated her questioner and eyed her critically. "Any on 'em bigger ner you?"

"Oh, yes," Phemie said, puzzled by the trend of the conversation. The boy hauled up the mule's head and pointed it in the direction of the risen sun.

85

"Any on yer hitched?" he enquired.

"Hitched?"

"Marriet," explained the youngster scornfully.

"No," said Phemie.

"Giddap!" yelled her interrogator and hit the mule a resounding blow in the ribs which caused it to set off eastwards in a flurry of dust. Phemie watched them dwindle into the sunrise and wondered.

Breakfast was coffee and biscuits brought by the Chinese cook and alleviated by marmalade from their own store: Jed appreciated that. He produced a filthy frying-pan from his telegraph office and placed it on the stove. Into the elderly grease congealed inside he sliced chunks off a side of bacon.

"Side-meat," he explained above the hissing and spitting, "ain't no kinda breakfast without a bite of side-meat."

He gave each girl a fragrant and sizzling slice and then startled them by spreading a biscuit thickly with marmalade and putting his slice of side-meat on top.

While they were watching him demolish this delicacy a bell tinkled in the office and he rose grumbling blasphemously to answer it. Within a few minutes he was back.

"West-bound due in two hours," he announced. "It's to stop over more than a half an hour. Guess the east-bound jest might be a-comin' after all."

While they waited Adela and Louisa followed Phemie's example and washed at the pump as far as was possible in front of an audience. The boy on the mule was back.

The smoke of the west-bound had just smudged the horizon when the sound of hooves attracted their attention. A rig (they had recently learned to call it a buckboard) drove into the yard. It was drawn by two enormous plough-horses and driven by a large raw-boned farmer who looked not unlike one of his own horses. He had a long, bony weather-bitten face and his hair, once fair and now greying, made his skin seem even more sunburned than it was. His eyes, set in slits which had been put there by peering into the merciless sunlight of the plains, were vivid blue. Behind him sat a family of seven children ranging

86

from a twelve-year-old girl to the year-old baby she held in her arms. There were three boys in clean but crumpled checked shirts and levis and two girls in skimpy gingham dresses, all of them brushed and washed into a preternatural neatness. The driver raised his hand to greet the boy on the mule, hitched the horses to one leg of the water-tower, surveyed the children on the buckboard and nodded slowly.

"You stay quiet," he told them. "You see they do, Ulla."

He slapped some of the dust off his own levis with a broad-brimmed hat, smoothed back his hair and approached the group sitting outside the door of the shed. Jed who was waiting by the track and staring eastwards emitted a hoarse noise which might have been a laugh.

"Hi, Olaf," he greeted the newcomer.

" 'Day, Jed."

An almost imperceptible softening of the 'J' marked Olaf for a Scandinavian.

"Guess you come to look over my house guests," said Jed and gave his creaky chuckle again. "Don't let the grass grow under you none. Thisyer's Miss Louisa, she's headed for home again. Thisyer's Miss Witherspoon and Miss Wedmore. They're headin' West. Thisyer's Olaf Pedersen, gals. Farms a ha'f section herabout."

" 'Day," said Olaf Pedersen and nodded stiffly. He then surveyed the group in front of him and after a few seconds his eyes came to rest finally and solemnly on Adela, who blushed.

"Good day, Mr Pedersen," said Phemie. "Have you come to meet the train?"

"No," said Olaf, without taking his eyes off Adela, "to make a proposition I haf come."

He turned round and as if to gather strength looked at the children sitting obediently on the buckboard. The train howled mournfully in the distance.

"I haf eight children," he told them, "eight. Peder, he's the one on the burro, Ulla, Erik, Little Olaf, Bernt, Judi, Anna and Baby Jonni. Baby Jonni is not yet one year. Ulla not twelve."

He turned back to look at Adela.

87

"A big family, no?"

"A fine healthy family," Phemie responded.

"Ja," he agreed, "fine and healthy now. Next year . . . who can say . . . I do not know. Their Mama dead. Two weeks and three days."

Adela looked across at the silent children.

"The lambs!" she exclaimed, "the poor lambs."

The approaching train howled again, drowning Olaf Pedersen's next words.

"What did you say?" asked Phemie when the noise had stopped.

"I ask if this lady . . . ." He swept his hat in Adela's direction. ". . . will marry me and be their mother."

The three women stared at him, open-mouthed, and Jed apparently intent upon the coming train gave a snort.

"Marry you!" Phemie was the first to regain her voice. "But you never saw her in your life before!"

"Lady," returned Pedersen quietly, "in this town we haf only the wives of other men, little girls like Ulla there, or women of bad character like those in the saloon. Eight small children I haf and I must haf a wife. I cannot leave them to go find one. I must take my chance as it come. It come today when you come. I hear you are Nightingale nurses and of these even I haf heard. You are good and you care for people. I am fifty year old but healthy and strong yet and I haf one good farm. The house is of wood, not sod and there is a pump in the kitchen. Ulla is a good girl and will help."

There seemed to be no answer to this. Louisa stared round-eyed and Adela, her face scarlet, studied her hands as if she had never seen them before. Before anyone spoke the rails began to shake and the west-bound huffed importantly in.

"I go now to the store. I come back in one ha'f-hour and you tell me what you think. Come, children."

He strode off without a backward glance, the children scrambling about him. The three girls stared after him. Adela looked as if someone had knocked her on the head with a

88

hammer. She turned to the others like a ship in a sea-way and pressed her hands over her burning cheeks.

"Did he truly ask me to marry him?" she asked. "Me?"

"Yes," replied Louisa, her eyes as round as blue coins, "he did then, for I heard him. Eight children. Goodness me."

"The poor lambs," said Adela once more and her eyes filled.

"And that child Ulla to look after them all," said Phemie. "She'll be old before she's twenty. Worn out and old."

Jed stirred out of his trance and moved towards the train.

"He's a good man, Olaf," he announced and spat emphatically.

The passengers began to disembark and stream down the track into the saloon. Louisa gave a little squeal, pulled at Adela's arm and pointed at a car in the middle of the train. Climbing down from the entrance was Captain Wolfe. The person he turned to assist was bonneted and veiled to the point of disguise but Louisa had little difficulty in penetrating it.

"Miss Lambe!"

Their arrival was a satisfactory circumstance to most parties present. It appeared that the Captain and Miss Lambe had been despatched by Sir Hector as soon as the absence of his eldest daughter had been detected. They had had instructions to return with Louisa even if they had to travel as far as the railhead to meet with her. To find her before the third day of their journey was over was more than either of them had hoped. For Phemie it was an unspeakable relief not to have to return to New York and then endure the outward journey again. There was only a very short time before the east-bound drew in on the loop-line. It was spent by Miss Lambe in spattering Louisa with incoherent reproaches and by Captain Wolfe and Phemie in sorting out baggage and arranging its transfer to the other train. Adela, unusually for her, did nothing to help but stood and looked constantly at Captain Wolfe. Her attention was not distracted even by Louisa's dramatic and tearful protest at being handed over like a Parcel to the Mailman or a Prisoner to the Gaoler.

During that fraught ten mintues Captain Wolfe took no notice of Adela at all. He climbed upon the east-bound, hauled the sulky Louisa none too gently after him and handed her over to Miss Lambe. In a very few minutes he and his charges had dwindled into a speck under a plume of smoke. They left Phemie with a letter in her hand from Lady Lacombe and a sensation of infinite relief. Adela looked throughtful and also miserable as if she found the thinking process unaccustomed and painful.

"Phemie?" she said at length.

Phemie looked up from repacking her valise before stowing it in the waiting train. The passengers were already beginning to return from the saloon.

"Aren't you going to get ready?"

Adela frowned.

"How old is that Captain Wolfe?" she asked.

"How should I know? Maybe eight or nine and twenty."

"Then someone of six and twenty wouldn't be too old to . . ."

Adela didn't finish her sentence.

"That Miss Lambe evidently doesn't think so," said Phemie drily. "She's thirty past."

"I'm six and twenty," said Adela.

Phemie said nothing. There was really nothing to say. While they had been at the Lacombes Adela's pathetic passion for Captain Wolfe had been obvious to everyone except the gallant Captain himself. Adela transferred her gaze from the dwindling smudge on the eastern horizon to the group which had returned to the buckboard. Olaf was swinging the younger children up on to it into Ulla's charge. Peder sat on his burro, his legs dangling disconsolately nearly to the ground and his disreputable hat tipped over his face. Despite this Adela could see that he was watching her.

"Jed?" she asked suddenly. "Is there a school here?"

Jed spat.

"We got a schoolhouse. Thar she is. And the Rev'rend he teaches thar ever' so often when he's in town which ain't more'n three-four days a month."

He spat again. Jed had a vocabulary of spits. This one was

90

regretful, deprecatory . . . Adela looked across the yard to the buckboard.

"Phemie," she blurted out, "you think I'm stupid, don't you?"

Phemie looked up from her letter, startled and embarrassed.

"Not stupid . . . no," she said after a second's pause. "You don't care for book-work, that's all. Not everybody does."

"But I could teach . . . someone . . . children . . . to read and write and count, couldn't I?"

Phemie realised suddenly where this conversation was leading.

"Yes, of course," she agreed.

"And I can cook and clean?"

"None better."

Adela watched the children settling among the boxes and sacks.

"I like children," she said, "I always liked them. And . . . being plain like I am . . . I didn't expect . . . and no one ever . . ." She faltered and looked imploringly at Phemie.

"Adela Wedmore," said Phemie and moved so that they were face to face, "for nearly two years I have taken nearly every decision you have needed. What we should do, where we should go, what we should eat, what we should wear, whether we should come here . . . Are you trying to make me take this decision for you as well?"

Adela flushed. "No, no!"

"Because," continued Phemie, "I won't."

She looked hard at her friend but Adela would not meet her eyes.

"I never thought I could ever be married," she muttered.

"He's twice your age," stated Phemie.

"A young man would never look my way."

"His wife's only been dead a fortnight. What you'll be is an unpaid housekeeper."

"It'll be my house," said Adela.

"It'll be your prison," declared Phemie earnestly. "Look at this place . . . look at it!"

"It'll grow, I wouldn't wonder," said Adela, "and I never was one for company and that."

"Eight children."

"Maybe more," said Adela and promptly went scarlet.

"No doctor," observed Phemie grimly.

"I can help more folk than them, then."

Phemie shrugged despairingly.

"Adela, you've no more sense than Louisa. I'm sorry for Olaf, I'm even sorrier for Ulla, poor lassie, but we can't marry every widower in America with eight children, however sorry we are."

"I don't know the others. I've seen these."

"It'll be drudgery, I promise you. Endless grinding work."

"We're used to that."

"And there's another thing," said Phemie, driven to her last argument, "I'm going to need you."

But Adela shook her head, slowly and deliberately.

"No. You don't need people. People need you. And they . . ." She nodded her head in the direction of the family. ". . . they need me more."

Almost like a sleepwalker she moved over to the buckboard and spoke to Olaf. They were too far away for Phemie to hear what was said but Peder threw his hat in the air, let out a wild, shrilling war-whoop and set off on the burro raising a great dust-cloud. The noise brought Jed out of the ticket office.

"Dang my buttons ef she ain't took him!" he exclaimed and spat.

Phemie stared at the empty track running into the infinite west and considered the future.

"And then there was one," she murmured under her breath.

It was one of those days when the Rev'rend was in town. The loco-man agreed to delay the train by a matter of fifteen mintues in the cause of true love and at the sight of Jed's scatter-gun which he had taken with him to back up the argument. While Adela sorted out her possessions, Jed emitting the creaky noises which served him for a laugh went in search of the Rev'rend.

Phemie hastily looked out some items from her own bags to leave with Adela. The children clambered down once again, huddled around Ulla and eyed Adela uncertainly. Olaf stood mumchance twisting his hat in his hands until Adela picked up her heavy carpet bag. Then, as if that had been some kind of a signal the whole family descended upon her and strove for the privilege of taking it to the rig. Adela relinquished it, startled and stood aside while it and the rest of her belongings were stowed away. Olaf swung up the little hair trunk and the boys struggled with the bag. Ulla held aloof, baby Jonni clutching at her and peering at the strange face. Adela looked a little helpless and said nothing. Phemie restrapped her valise very slowly, hardly daring to breathe. Olaf turned round just in time to see his daughter hitch the heavy toddler higher on her hip and move over to Adela.

"You want you should hold Jonni?" she asked shyly and Adela dropped her reticule into the dust and held out her arms. Thus transferred Jonnie's face puckered with dismay for a tense few seconds until Ulla hastily produced a stick of candy which he grabbed and began to suck noisily oblivious of whose arms he was in. An expression of relief appeared on the face of every member of the Pedersen family with a simultaneity which struck Phemie as irresistibly comic. She gave a spirt of laughter and after a breathless second all the Pedersens joined in. She had a sense of an obstacle passed, a danger over.

They were still laughing in the inconsequent and passionate way of young children, rolling on the ground and hugging themselves for very glee when Jed returned with a long lugubrious figure who regarded the hilarious family without a smile. He wore an Abraham Lincoln 'plug' hat which made him look even taller and narrower than he was and although it was midday and the heat intense his dusty frayed frockcoat was buttoned up to his throat. Phemie surmised that this might well be to hide the absence of a shirt.

"You folks aimin' to git hitched?" he enquired of Olaf.

"Ja," said Olaf, nodding in Adela's direction and went scarlet.

"Got a ha'f an hour afore I ride out," said the Rev'rend hauling out a vast, silver, turnip watch. Phemie thought suddenly of Sir Aloysius, half a world away; her sharp eyes noticed that it declared the time to be seven fifteen. After a solemn glance at the dial the Rev'rend exchanged it for a battered Testament in a manner which smacked of sleight-of-hand.

"Dearlybelovedbretheren," he began without further ado, "wearegatheredhereinthesightofGodandthepresenceofthis congregation . . ."

The two central figures in this drama, finding that the play was beginning without them hastily took up their positions in front of him. Adela was still holding the by-now damp and sticky Jonni. Ulla ran up to take him back. None of this caused the Rev'rend to hesitate for a split second.

". . . foreverholdthypeace . . ."

He glared at the group behind the couple for as long as one might count to three but nobody moved.

"Whogivesthiswomantobemarriedtothisman?" he demanded accusingly. Before Phemie could collect her wits and step in Jed had responded to the challenge.

"Dang my buttons ef I don't!" he declared and scored a resounding bulls' eye on a kerosene can. He grabbed Adela's arm and handed it to Olaf as if it were a parcel just come by the railroad and stepped back to rejoin Phemie.

"The Rev'rend, he done the fastest marryin's in the whole state, I guess," he confided.

". . . lawfulweddedwifetohaveandtohold . . ."

Olaf's response was loud and heartfelt.

"I do that."

The Rev'rend drew a much-needed breath, turned to Adela and then hit a snag.

"Anddoyou . . . Say, ma'am, how d'they call yer?"

But it was only a momentary snag. In less time than seemed possible—or legal—Adela Wedmore had become Adela Pedersen.

"Kissthebride," concluded the Rev'rend and the Testament dropped in his pocket before the words were off his lips.

"Five dollars," he added and put out a long bony hand to Olaf who had the bill ready.

Less than six minutes after he had arrived the Rev'rend tucked the bill securely in his pants pocket, mounted his rosinantine horse and rode out. The loco-man back in his caboose blew the hooter summoning Phemie to leave her friend. Adela and the Pedersens stood and waved until she could no longer tell one from another. Phemie from now on would travel alone.

6

THE FORT AT MOUNTAIN VIEW which was the temporary railhead was so new that wood of the palisade smelt of raw timber like a carpenter's shop. Inside the troopers still slept in tents but two or three wooden huts had risen among the tents and it was to one of these that Phemie was directed by the Sergeant, summoned by a scandalised gate-guard unable to find any precedent for dealing with a small, solitary female who requested an interview with 'the gentleman in charge of this establishment' and refused to go away and write a letter. The Sergeant provided an escort who was told to take the lady to Captain Devayler and no shenanigans mind. Phemie glanced at the scarlet and tongue-tied boy by her side and decided that the Sergeant was a humorist. Her escort delivered her at the smallest of the huts, saluted clumsily and fled back to his post on the gate. Phemie tapped on the door and was told brusquely by a voice from the interior to "Wait!"

During the few minutes in which she obeyed this instruction she could hear someone inside being subjected to an interroga-tion. While the words were not audible the staccato rhythm of question and answer was. At first the answers were firm and clear, then as the questions became shorter and more frequent, the answers became hesitant and uncertain. The interview con-cluded on a quiet and remorseless note—an unmistakable 'carpeting'. There was a short silence, the clumping of boots on a wooden floor and a young officer emerged precipitately, very red about the face and neck.

"Cap'n says to go in . . . ." he mumbled as he adjusted his cap.

The fact that Phemie barely came up to the third button of his coat, was dressed in skirts and carrying a parasol and not a carbine did not appear to reach his consciousness until she had passed inside with a murmured word of thanks. His head turned, his jaw dropped and his eyes bulged.

". . . ma'am!" he added belatedly.

Phemie's first impression of the Captain was of swarthy good looks. Her second was of ill-temper and her third amply confirmed her second. He stared at her for an incredulous moment, the stare was changed to a glare and . . .

"What knothead let *you* in?" he demanded.

Phemie furled her parasol and put a firm hand on her own temper.

"I believe you are taking a reinforcement to the garrison at Fort Argentana."

"Correct," he snapped. "The day after tomorrow."

"I would be obliged if you would permit me to accompany you," she told him calmly. "There appears to be no other way to reach the town of Argentana."

He did not reply at once, simply glared at her unbelievingly then . . .

"Out of the question," he announced. "Good day to you."

He bent over the pile of papers on his desk as if Phemie had already gone.

"Why?" asked Phemie coolly.

"Isn't it obvious? You're female. This will be a military operation. There's no place for females on those."

"A gentleman would ask me to sit down," mentioned Phemie, "a feeble female, like me."

"A lady," he stressed the word as if it tasted unpleasant, "a lady would not have come here. And however feeble you may be, you will not be staying long enough to require a seat."

"Indeed," said Phemie. "Tell me, why would the presence of a female make your operation difficult?"

"I am not obliged to give you my reasons," he replied without looking up. "Good day."

"You might at least give me a proper hearing."

"Quite unnecessary when my answer must be 'no' in any case."

He went on writing.

"I have been in Mountain View for six weeks," said Phemie bitterly. "I was told that a stage for Argentana would leave from here. So far as I can discover it hasn't run for three months and no one can tell me when it is likely to run again."

"The last coach was attacked by the Comanche."

"I know."

"If you know, why come pestering to go to Argentana? You must know it is impossible."

"Because I have a post to take up in Argentana, a post of some importance . . ."

He looked at the tiny figure in front of him and his mouth twisted sourly.

". . . As I told you, I've waited for six weeks for the trail to be cleared. I can wait no longer."

"This has nothing to do with me."

"I beg your pardon," said Phemie, "but I think it has."

"I fail to see how."

"Your company or troop or whatever it is offers the only chance of a safe passage to my destination."

He flung down his pencil and rose to his considerable height. He towered over Phemie who stood her ground but knew a certain misgiving.

"I command a military unit not a freight company. It's no part of our duties to escort females to whatever dubious occupations they may have found for themselves."

Phemie flushed with anger.

"You are insulting, sir."

"And you, ma'am, lay yourself open to insult to make such brass-faced demands," he returned, "and by coming un-escorted into a military establishment."

"You appear to have no great opinion of the men you command," said Phemie with a calm which she did not feel. "I would be in no such predicament entering a British army establishment, I assure you."

This deliberate provocation resulted in a sulphurous silence for as long as it took for Captain Devayler to restrain himself.

"Have the goodness to leave, ma'am."

His voice was quiet but the suppressed rage made Phemie quail a little, though her voice did not betray this.

"Of course," she continued as if he had not spoken, "there can be no real comparison between the two forces. I understand, Captain, that your command was sent out here to control the Comanche. And no stage has been able to run for three months."

She shook her head sadly and unfurled her parasol. "That tells its own story, Captain. You have my fullest sympathy in your misfortune."

Without waiting to hear the reaction to this thrust, she smiled, bobbed a curtsey, went through the door and down the two wooden steps to the sunbaked earth. She then walked with dignity to the gate, pretending complete unconsciousness of the large figure which emerged from the doorway soon after she did and which was watching her progress with an intentness which she could almost feel.

For unmarried (and virtuous) women in Mountain View there was only one place to stay. That was Mrs McCorquodale's Boarding Establishment which was a white-painted frame house on the main street immediately opposite the Palomino Hotel which dignified name graced the three-storeyed façade of a rather squalid saloon. Mrs McCorquodale had left her native town of Philadelphia and come West, partly to make money, and partly as a missionary of civilisation to the barbarians. Her Boarding Establishment was unrivalled in all the Frontier for its lace-edged blinds, delicate china, snowy napery and monogrammed silver. Meals were served with oppressive ceremony though the highly polished dishcovers concealed only the beans, stews and side-meat of the Frontier cooked by Mr McCorquodale. He did not appear in the dining-room to enjoy the results of his labours preferring the amenities offered by the Palomino. Mrs McCorquodale, resplendent in black satin, ecru lace and a vast mourning brooch all plaited hair and urns, presided over the meals, though the dishes were actually handed by a parlour-maid in black bombazine and white muslin aprons from whose monumental caps floated streamers unrivalled even in Belgrave Square. Rumour hinted that those caps had been worn by Mrs McCorquodale herself in a similar capacity but no one had ever dared to enquire the truth of this. Mrs McCorquodale had been heard to remark that, of course, she would have preferred to employ a butler but they were rare on the Frontier and even her ambition wavered at the thought of Mickey, the Irish handyman, rigged out in a butler's panoply.

Her boarders ranged from one Mrs Kinloch who owned the town saloon (though the concession was contracted to another female of Spanish extraction called Florita) to the Reverend Hartmann who had eluded the determined pursuit of the townswomen for a number of years by dint of emerging from the Establishment only to officiate at weddings, funerals and the Sunday Services.

His parishioners were visited only when they were in extremis so that the sight of the Reverend emerging from a house was the signal for his fellow-boarder, Luke Machin, to look over his store of ready-use coffins.

For nearly six weeks Phemie had occupied a room under the shingles of this respectable institution. It was the cheapest room available, Esther, the parlour-maid, and her black bombazine having been evicted to the even tinier and stuffier box-room in order to make room for her . . . or so Mrs McCorquodale had decreed. In fact Phemie had investigated the box-room on her first day and prevailed on Esther to remove her folding bed back to its place so that they shared the room quite unknown to Mrs McCorquodale who rarely penetrated to the upper reaches. The result had been the establishment of a firm alliance. During the long hot nights Phemie had learned how Esther had come from Ireland to her brother in America only to discover that his cheerful letters home disguised the pathetic debt-ridden realities of a Boston slum. Esther had sold herself to help lift that burden, and Mrs McCorquodale had bought her for a three-year period.

After that—she had some six months to serve—the Good Lord knew what she would do, but one thing was for sure and she wasn't going back to Ireland with her tail between her legs.

She had followed Phemie's attempts to make the hundred-and-thirty miles journey to Argentana with interest and sympathy. The fruitless visit to Captain Devayler had been at her suggestion and she heard the story of Phemie's reception with a mixture of indignation and amusement.

"Ye never said that!" she exclaimed.

"I did," said Phemie gloomily. "I lost my temper again. Now I haven't a chance of getting there."

"Och, ye never really had a chance there. Everyone knows Lee Devayler hates women like poison."

Phemie stared.

"You never told me that."

"Och . . . what was the use. Ye'd have gone anyway."

Which was true enough.

After supper Phemie retreated upstairs to write letters: one to Mayor McDowall to explain her position (though when he would receive it was anybody's guess); another to the Lacombes asking for their help to get back East; and a third, the most difficult, to Miss Nightingale. Phemie had an uncomfortable feeling that whatever her explanation, in London, where Comanche was merely an outlandish name and not a hovering threat, it was going to look uncommonly like cold feet on her part. In fact it was an unattractive evening's programme. She had got no further than looking out her writing paper and dipping her pen in such muddy ink as Mountain View's general store afforded when Esther came in and flopped on the bed.

"It's dead on my feet I am," she announced and rolled over to face Phemie. "I was thinkin' while I was washin' the dishes with Mickey . . . why don't you up and make the beastly man take ye?"

"If I could, I would," Phemie said grimly. "But how?"

"I've an idea how it might be done . . . something Mickey was sayin' . . . Mind you now, it wouldn't be easy . . ."

"How many things are?"

"Dangerous too. Them Comanches is a rough crew, no lie. But Mickey says they keep in the hills. He says anyone would be safe as a baby in its mother's arms till they got near the hills. They don't come down only once in a while to steal cattle."

"What's your notion?"

Esther frowned.

"Now I've to put it in words it sounds demented. You see the soldiers must go the one way . . . that way."

She pulled a piece of paper towards her and took the pen.

"The trail runs this way . . . over the ford by Claydons, but nobody lives there now, the Comanche got them . . . and then between the bluffs all the way to Nine Tree Hill. They'll camp there."

"How can you be sure?"

Esther shrugged. "No cover near, Mike says, water . . . that kind of thing."

"What's your idea?"

"You get there first."

Phemie looked at her and frowned.

"They can't turn you back once they've got that far, d'ye see," Esther went on. "They've had a day's ride and the horses'll be tired. And they can't leave you all alone in the middle o' the murderin' Comanche either . . ."

Phemie thought of the dark face of Captain Devayler.

"I wish I could be certain of that."

"Och, but he couldn't just leave you—think the scandal there'd be."

"It might work," said Phemie. "It might just work."

"There's the two difficulties I can see."

Phemie raised her eyebrows.

"I'm glad it's only two."

"Och well," said Esther, "but these is serious. One's gettin' out of the town without some nosey busybody askin' what you're at. The other's a horse . . . you'll be needin' a horse. Have you enough left to buy one? It can't be no hunk of cat's meat neither . . . It's better than a hundred miles to Argentana."

Phemie pulled a heavy gold locket out of her dress and opened it. Twenty sovereigns tinkled on to her palm.

"That's my standby," she explained.

"Ye could buy the Captain's charger for that."

"There's another difficulty you haven't seen."

"And what may that be?"

"I can't ride."

Esther stared. "Lord be good to us, I never thought of that."

Phemie put away pens and paper, reached for her bonnet and stood up. "Come along," she said, "I'm going to need your help."

Esther sat upright. "Where are you off to?"

"The livery stable. We're going to buy a horse and I know nothing about horses."

She moved to the door. Esther scrambled for a shawl and squeezed her feet back into the shoes she had kicked off.

"But what the devil use will that be if you can't ride?" she wailed.

"You've twelve hours to teach me."

In fact it was Mickey who roused out his crony at the stable and chose the horse, an elderly, sedate but sound gelding with an air of melancholy.

"Murder!" Mickey exclaimed when he saw him, "if he isn't the dead spit of the Mister."

And the beast did have a look of Mr McCorquodale and so was named for him. Later Mickey said:

"And he's like his namesake—he'll never move out of a trot but he'll go on for ever."

It was Mickey too who taught her the rudiments of equitation first of all by lantern-light in the lane behind the Establishment and then by dawn-light up near the cemetery. Phemie applied herself in her accustomed style to the acquisition of a new skill and won the approval of Mickey. At breakfast time he helped her dismount.

"You'll do," he told her. "Think no shame to hold the pommel if you must. There's one thing—you ride a feather.

103

That beast'll never know you're on him. I'm thinkin' ye'd make a grand jockey in the Leopardstown Races.''

Captain Devayler and his troop were due to leave the fort at dawn. Phemie decided that with 'Mr McCorquodale's sober pace and her own very limited skill she had better give herself a good twelve hours' start. She was lucky in that there would be a moon nearly at the full. Accordingly, at about five o'clock that evening she set off along the trail to the mountains. No one took any heed, for there were a number of houses along the way and she might have been going to visit any of them. Esther, busy in the Establishment, heard the hoofbeats fade into the distance, fingered the crucifix under her dress and murmured a little prayer to St Christopher. As luck would have it no one looked out of the last house Phemie had to pass and she and 'Mr McCorquodale' clopped into the dusty defile which led down to the ford. By the time it got dark she had splashed through the shallow waters of the river and was well along the trail to the foothills. Stiff beyond belief and very weary she dismounted to eat and rest under a clump of cottonwoods until the moon rose. She hobbled 'Mr McCorquodale' as Mickey had shown her and the horse cropped rhythmically away at the coarse grass. When the sky lightened she was ready to go on. The plains at night were full of noises, near and far, which could be Comanche on the prowl.

It was while she was struggling to remount the tall horse that Esther sat up in bed clutching at her crucifix and said aloud:

"Dear God! I've killed her so I have! Mary forgive me for a fool's daughter. The Comanche'll have her by now, and her without a gun!"

Whereupon she got out of bed and prayed hard, first for Phemie's safety and then for the gift of discreet tongue. The first prayer was answered at least, for from moonrise to moonset Phemie and 'Mr McCorquodale' plodded safely along the trail, unmolested by man or beast. Soon after dawn she found a little stream (though she called it a burn) running down from the hills to the river and both she and the horse drank thirstily and shared what was left of Esther's sandwiches. In the distance about two hours' ride away, she thought, she could see the bare knoll with its scattered pines which could only be Nine Trees Hill.

It was not an isolated hill, in fact it was a spur of the foothills through which the trail now began to wind, and it was considerably more than two hours' ride away. By the time she reached it and dismounted she was so tired and sore that her head was swimming. She hobbled the horse and removed his bridle so that he could graze comfortably. The saddle was too heavy and the horse too tall to allow of her taking it off to ease the beast but she loosened the girths. 'Mr McCorquodale' seemed content enough, drank his fill at the spring and moved off in his hobbles. Phemie then opened the saddlebag she had unstrapped and with creditable determination o disguise her exhaustion and discomfort from those who were due to arrive she stripped to her petticoat and washed off the trail dust. For good measure she washed the dust out of her long, pale reddish hair. Next she brushed her dress clean of dust, mud and horse-hairs, found a clean white tucker and dressed herself again. Then and not till then did she sit down and begin to comb her hair, her back to a tree-trunk. Almost at once, her head nodded and she fell sound asleep, comb in hand and her hair about her shoulders.

When Captain Devayler led his weary troop up to the top of the hill about five in the evening the first thing to catch his eye was 'Mr McCorquodale' scratching his rump on a broken branch. The sight of the saddle set the Captain to look for the rider and it wasn't long before he spotted her. Neither the clatter of hooves or the bustle as the soldiers began to make camp had wakened her. He saw the gleam of her white tucker under the tree he had picked for his own sleeping place and went over to investigate. With her hair down and deeply asleep Phemie lost her competent, confident air which made up for her lack of height. Under that tree she looked like a clean and tidy child not the demanding female who had invaded his office . . .

''What in tarnation . . .'' he exclaimed and dismounted. Though not one of the soldiers ceased in their preparations for the night everyone in the command realised the situation and

105

were amused and curious to see how he might deal with it. He stood for a moment frowning, went down on one knee and pulled gently at her skirt.

"Ma'am! Ma'am!" he called. "Hey . . . wake up . . . this is no place to sleep!"

Phemie made a comical sound of protest as unconsciousness was inexorably wrested from her and Lee Devayler smiled. Phemie's eyes opened in time to get a momentary glimpse of this phenomenon: it was momentary because as soon as she was awake he recognised her. The smile vanished to be replaced by a look of angry dislike.

"You!" he snapped. "What in blazes are you doing out here?"

Phemie rubbed her eyes and collected her wits.

"I am on my way to Argentana," she informed him. "This seemed a good place to rest so I did. I must have fallen asleep."

"Let me tell you you could be a squaw in a lodge by this time, if any brave was fool enough . . ."

He eyed the mass of reddish-gold hair which she was now twisting into her customary and ugly chignon.

". . . or a hairless corpse. What in blazes possessed you?"

Phemie stuck in the last hairpin with a vigour which left no doubt where she would have preferred to stick it.

"The stage wouldn't take me. You wouldn't take me." She shrugged. "I decided to go by myself."

He stood for a second in exasperated silence glaring down at her.

"You, ma'am, are a pestilential childish nuisance . . . of all the self-willed, foolhardy . . . Don't you realise that it's still more than a hundred miles to Argentana and the most dangerous part of the trip still to come!"

"How fortunate I fell in with you."

His face darkened and he breathed audibly through his nose."

"Oh, no," he said softly. "Oh, no . . . you don't get your way as easily as you seem to think, my girl. First thing in the morning I am going to send you back to Mountain View with an escort. I categorically refuse to take you on."

"And I categorically refuse to turn back," said Phemie but without real conviction.

"You will do precisely what I say," returned the gallant Captain, "if I have to rope you into your saddle."

"Then I will start again as soon as the escort is out of sight."

"Not," he concluded grimly, "if I have you left in charge of the Marshal."

He turned on his heel and walked off. Phemie, her cheeks pink and her eyes bright with temper, watched him go. Under her breath she muttered a phrase heard in the wards which would have caused Mrs Wardroper to faint had she heard her.

"Stiff-necked bother!" muttered the demure Miss Witherspoon.

Next morning the escort was told off, a sergeant and two men and the humiliating instructions to consign her to the Marshal given in front of the rest of the men who stood pokerfaced and silent. 'Mr McCorquodale' was led up and Phemie after a night's immobility so sore that she could hardly stand or walk, but determined not to show her disability, prepared to mount. Her head barely came up to the saddle and she doubted her ability to pull herself up even with the proffered 'leg-up' from the Sergeant. Devayler, mistaking her hesitation for obstinacy, picked her without ceremony and dumped her, none too gently, in the saddle. Phemie winced and gave a little grunt of pain. Devayler raised his eyebrows.

"Sore, are you?" he enquired.

"Certainly not," lied Phemie.

"If it's any comfort you'll be sorer still by sundown," he observed callously and slapped 'Mr McCorquodale' on the rump so that he started off in a kind of sliding scramble nearly unseating his unskillful rider.

They had been on the trail just under an hour when it happened. Phemie who by this time did not care where she was going so long as she could arrive and dismount from that punishing saddle and whose whole attention was concentrated on maintaining a decent fortitude before her taciturn and

107

pardonably irritated escort was riding beside an enlisted man called Paterson while Sergeant Smith and Corporal Romanes rode some yards ahead. Suddenly she heard a curious coughing grunt from the man beside her. She turned her head and saw an arrow sunk almost to the flight of feathers in Paterson's back. The others reined in at her shout and galloped back, two arrows thumping into the ground near them, to find her holding Paterson in her arms while he vomited blood over the horse's withers.

"Can't stop here," said the Sergeant and hauled Paterson across his saddle.

"Bring the hoss!" he shouted at Romanes and himself grabbed 'Mr McCorquodale's bridle.

They clattered uphill off the trail to a cluster of big rocks where they could find cover. Two more arrows hissed past them and Paterson's horse squealed angrily as a third grazed its rump.

"Ain't more'n a couple or so, I guess," said the Sergeant, his slow calm voice contrasting with the speed of his movement as they dismounted among the rocks and took up positions which commanded the open ground between them and the wooded trail.

"If they'd been more they'd ha' jumped us. Here's hopin' they ain't got no guns."

He and Romanes slowly and methodically began to watch the area in front for signs of movement while Phemie did what she could for Paterson. This wasn't much. The arrow had virtually skewered him and he was dying fast, his breath coming in shallow sighs and blood welling from his mouth. Smith fired two shots at a movement behind a tree and the second ricocheted across and across the narrow defile. Romanes saw another movement down below, nearer the trail and loosed off two more when he was sure. An arrow lurched into the air wildly off course as if the archer had released it prematurely.

"Got him," said Romanes with satisfaction.

"I'm goin' to get me an Injun," said Smith and slid away uphill to find a more advantageous position.

Romanes shifted his position so that he could command more

of the ground, put a quid of tobacco in his mouth and prepared to wait on events. Phemie closed Paterson's eyes and wiped the blood from his face.

"He's gone," she said.

"Reckoned he might," said Romanes. "Guess there's consid'able movement in that tree. You use a gun, Mis' Witherspoon?"

An arrow whistled overhead and splintered against the rock, startling the horses.

"No."

"Time to learn, I guess. Get Paterson's."

Phemie rose from the dead man's side and pulled it from the saddle holster. Another arrow whistled over her head almost touching her hair and she ducked.

"There's more'n two or three of them varmints, I guess." said Romanes. "That came from over there. Smith'll get him. Lay there."

He jerked his head at the spot which the Sergeant had vacated.

"Thisyer weapon's a Winchester . . . great little gun. Fires itself, loads itself . . . you don' need to more than point it in the right direction."

Phemie examined the oil-smelling weapon. Romanes' eyes never ceased their watching of the ground in front.

"See yonder rock . . . thatyer with the grass on it like a scalp?"

"Yes."

"Try can you hit it."

Phemie raised the gun to her shoulder, copying him.

"Now . . . line up the bead with the horns."

Again she obeyed, getting the foresight between the horns of the backsight.

"Get that bead lined up on the foot of that rock."

The gun was heavy, and Phemie's arm ached. The barrel quavered into position.

"Now pull, very slow and easy."

Phemie obeyed, and through the shock of the quite unexpectedly violent recoil heard a whining ricochet.

109

"Waal, say . . ." Romanes' expressionless face was split in a smile. "If you didn't hit it! Now try again, an' this time you keep your eyes open."

"I did," said Phemie indignantly.

From above them came two shots in rapid succession.

"Reckon the Sarge done got the varmint."

Smith came slithering back as he said the words.

"Got them all, I guess," he observed. "Get them hosses."

"Paterson, he's dead," drawled Romanes.

"Put him acrost his hoss. We'll plant him later. We're goin' back to the company."

"Not to town?" queried Romanes.

"Nope."

"What about Mis' Witherspoon?"

"She'll just have to ride along with us. See here, ma'am . . ." Smith jerked his head for her to come and be thrown up on to her saddle. ". . . thisyer little commotion warn't no more than a scoutin' party. As I see it, an' I've fought Injuns sence you was in yo'r cradle ma'am, there's a war-band trailin' the company. It's my guess that they're between us an' the town now an' I'm not bumpin' no heads with them—not just the two of us and a woman, beggin' your pardon, ma'am. And Devayler . . . he oughter know 'bout the varmints for they're mighty li'ble to jump him. So, ma'am, we got to ride some."

When they did 'jump' them, nearly two days later, Phemie's dominant emotion was not fear but relief. It had taken a gruelling seven hours to catch the company and when he heard the news Devayler had pushed on relentlessly. His idea was draw the Comanche into a position where they could be caught between himself and a party from Fort Argentana. To this end two gallopers were sent ahead to warn Argentana. Of Phemie's continued presence he took no notice at all except to detail Romanes to look after her. For the rest of that first day they rode without stopping and paused only when it was too dark to ride safely. No fires were lit and no talking was permitted while they rested and as soon as it was moonlight they moved out again. By midday on the second day Phemie was riding in a haze of pain and weariness. She had knotted the reins on 'Mr McCorquodale's' neck and clung to the horn of the saddle because she was afraid that her numbed legs would relax their grip. She trusted that the horse would stay with the troop without any guidance from her. It seemed likely: it had become increasingly obvious that 'Mr McCorquodale' was a cast army mount. Romanes riding on her left glanced at her from time to time. Once when they halted briefly to breathe the horses he spoke to Devayler. The Captain looked across at her but Phemie who had seen what was happening straightened her back and gave him a smile of triumph, adding insult to injury by beginning to plait the mane of hair from which the last of the pins had long since fallen. Devayler had glared, said something brief and pungent to Romanes and turned away. Romanes returned looking grim and brought her a canteen of water.

"Get down while you can, why don't you?" he suggested.

Phemie shook her head.

"I'd never be able to get on again," she admitted, "and who'd want to spend the rest of the journey bundled across a saddle-bow . . . like him."

She nodded at the canvas-shrouded bundle which was Paterson's body.

After all too short a time her ordeal began again but before they had gone more than a mile or two the rear-guard came up at full gallop to report that a war-band of some four or five hundred was trailing them and they were less than three miles away. Devayler ordered the company to gallop and 'Mr McCorquodale' obediently followed suit, his rider clinging desperately to the saddle. The trail was uphill and the horses laboured panting up into an open space. Stumps and the charred remains of an old log hut told their own story. From beyond the clearing cliffs reared into the sky for more than a hundred feet and a stream tumbled down into a shallow pool at the foot. Devayler's hand went up and the troop halted. Phemie would have

111

blundered into the men in front but for Romanes' hand on her bridle.

"This is the place," said the Captain and nodded at the Lieutenant who began to shout orders. The horses were tethered along the base of the cliff behind a line of bushes and rocks, boulders and logs from the wreck of the cabin were dragged over to form a kind of low breastwork which was topped by saddles dragged from the sweating, steaming horses. Phemie dismounted, if such a term could be used to describe her scrambling descent from the hateful saddle . . . staggering with exhaustion when she reached the ground. Romanes found a moment to arrange a saddle and a blanket and give her another drink before he ran off to take his place in the ring of defenders.

The next hour dragged past. The men talked quietly and ate and drank but kept their weapons under their hand. The cook lit a fire and before long each man had had a mug of coffee. He brought one to Phemie who drank the hot bitter stuff gratefully and greedily and nibbled the hard-tack biscuit which came with it. Gradually, the men fell silent at the breastwork, fidgeting and chewing tobacco. The shadows lengthened and the birds stopped chirping. Back down the trail a coyote howled and was answered by another much nearer. The older men looked grim and nodded knowingly at one another.

But sunset gave place to night and no attack came. Devayler set watches and allowed half the company to roll up in blankets and sleep at their posts while the other half kept watch. Phemie, comforted by food and warmth, slept too and did not even stir when the watch was changed after midnight.

The attack came at dawn. There was a stir over on the right, a man came running across the enclosed space to where Devayler lay. He was up and across in a second and a man moved round the sleepers rousing each one. There was no sound but the occasional click of accoutrements. The messenger came to Phemie.

"Cap'n says you're to stop back with the horses an' not to move on no account," he told her and helped her to her feet.

She was not as stiff as she had been the day before but she ached and burned with saddle-sores and even that short walk was painful. She had barely reached the horse-lines when the firing began. It was soon apparent that however the scouting party might have been armed the main party had guns and plenty of them.

Before long she was joined by three or four wounded men who were carried over and left. She made them as comfortable as was possible. In one of her saddle-bags she had packed the barest essentials for nursing, not wanting to arrive in the town totally unequipped. Both bags were strapped to her saddle which lay out in the open. While she was struggling to unstrap them with hands which were still sore from yesterday's ride, Devayler bellowed at her to get under cover. She took no notice and went on struggling with the buckle. In a second she was picked up and forcibly removed back to the horse-lines. In spite of this she managed to keep a grip on the saddle and that came after them.

"Will you stay where you're told!" Devayler spat at her and went back to the firing line.

With a few blankets rigged over the bushes to provide shade, the contents of her saddle-bags and the primitive medical kit carried with the company she established a fair imitation of a medical post. She had four or five men lying under the awning and was busy probing for a bullet which was lodged agonisingly in a knee when a shadow fell over the writhing figure on the ground.

"Hold him for me!" she snapped and at once two large hands held down the leg. The bullet yielded to the probe almost at once, there was a groan from the wounded man and the misshapen object slithered sickeningly out. She applied a pad of lint to the wound. The shadow remained and a pistol dropped beside her.

"We're under pressure," said Captain Devayler. "In spite of your unflattering opinion of my command I think we can hold out until we are relieved by Argentana . . . always supposing my gallopers reached them and they know our predicament. If they do not come and the Comanche break in . . . use this.'' He nodded at the gun.

"Shoot them first . . .'' He nodded at the row of wounded under the blankets. ''. . . and then yourself.''

Phemie stood up, holding her bloodied hands clear of her skirt.

"I dare say you'd like to do the last part of the job yourself,'' she observed.

He looked at her without expression.

"I cannot depend upon being spared for that privilege,'' he returned and went back to the barricade. Phemie knelt again beside the man with the wounded knee and the first thing he heard as he came round was her laughter.

In the event Phemie had no need to use the gun on anyone. While the fighting was still at its height, a large detachment from Fort Argentana arrived and the Comanche, pinned between two strong forces, pulled out and melted into the trackless hills beyond the trail. Phemie intent upon a boy whose elbow had been shattered hardly realised that the shooting was over. The shadow fell across her patient again.

"We're moving out, ma'am. Get your horse.''

Phemie looked up and waved her hand at the row of wounded.

"What about these? None of them can ride.''

"Fort's sending spring-wagons for them.''

Phemie tied off her bandage and gave her patient a drink.

"Then I'll stay till they come.''

"No. There are still Comanche about. Get your horse.''

"No,'' said Phemie. "These men are my patients and they will remain so until the medical officer from the fort arrives. Your so-called medical orderly appears to have no notion of his duties beyond the carrying of wounded men into safety—dragging rather . . .''

"Do you want me to put you on that horse?''

"That is what you'll need to do.''

She moved off to examine the man with the bullet wound in his knee who was moving restlessly. After a second Devayler followed, ducking his head to get under the canopy of blankets. It is hard to lay down the law convincingly when a man is bent nearly double but he made an attempt.

"Will you please do as I . . ."

"Here's the Captain to see you, boys," announced Phemie and then proceeded to take him from one to the other as she might have taken a doctor through Elizabeth Ward in St Thomas's, an action which effectively spiked his guns. At the end of the 'round' he cleared his throat and glared at Phemie who glared back. He muttered something inaudible but plainly uncomplimentary and stalked away. Phemie permitted herself a smile and for a second or two forgot her poor maltreated backside . . . but only for a second or so.

The following afternoon a spring-wagon rumbled into the township of Argentana. Phemie had spent the night in the fort being spoiled by such wives as had ventured to join their husbands in such a posting. Ointment had been obtained from a grinning doctor and applied to her sores and balm to her feelings.

"He's well known for the way he's rude to all women," said Sergeant Smith's wife, "I can't tell you why. Nobody knows much about him except that he comes from the South but he fought with the Union during the war."

"What I think," mentioned the Corporal's bride, "is some woman must have treated him real bad."

"What *I* think," Phemie put in from her post by the chimneypiece (sitting had temporarily lost its charm for her) "is that the score's just about even by now and given half a chance I'll tell him so."

But not even half a chance had presented itself, only a wagon, a driver and a guard.

"Cap'n's orders, ma'am, an' we're to take you into town."

And with 'Mr McCorquodale' trotting behind that was just what they had done. Phemie climbed down, thanked them, shook their hands, untied her horse and watched them turn round and head back to camp without more than a wistful glance at the Silver Nugget Saloon. Phemie and 'Mr McCorquodale'

115

soon found themselves surrounded by the curious habitués of that establishment who had emerged at the sound of hooves and now demanded to know who she might be and how she done come in with the Injuns on the prod like they was. Phemie parried most of the questions and asked the way to the livery stable. At least twenty people volunteered to escort her and they set off towards the other end of the street. Argentana seemed like any other Frontier town that she had seen, wooden shacks, boardwalks, grandiloquent shop-signs and incipient squalor. Most of the street was lined with houses and businesses of various kinds but on the right they passed one vacant lot with a battered sign leaning over drunkenly and half obscured by the weeds which grew around it.

T E
LI CO N M MOR AL
HO P T L

it proclaimed faintly.

"Where is the hospital?" Phemie asked.

"There ain't none," said one of her escort.

"It jest natcherally never gotten built," volunteered another.

"It was some crazy notion of Mayor McDowall's, weren't it?" asked the man who was leading the horse.

"Ain't nothin' crazy 'bout a hospital," contributed a voice from the edge of the crowd.

"Only two kinds of sickness in the town," shouted the first man, "shootin's and birthin's. Don't need no ten-thousand-dollar hospital out of my taxes for them."

Phemie digested this information in silence.

"Mayor McDowall could've used a hospital," said the man at 'Mr McCorquodale's' head, "he died a spell back with a misery in his belly. Suthin' in his gut went bad on him, Doc said."

"Where does the Doctor live?" Phemie asked.

There was a silence in which she could detect both amusement and embarrassment.

"Find him in the Silver Nugget mostly," said the first speaker, "leastways ef anyone gets tromped or shot we fetch him outa there."

"Anyone gets shot in this town it's in the Nugget," commented a new voice, "an' Doc's right handy . . ."

At the stable Phemie arranged for the horse's keep and then enquired for respectable lodgings. Silence fell and heads were scratched.

"Not, alas, a commodity in great demand in our community," admitted a newcomer, a large prosperous-looking gentleman in a larger hat for whom the group of loungers made way. "However, you are more than welcome to stay with Mrs Barstowe and me until we can arrange something. Saul Barstowe at your service . . . I run the bank around here and I have the honour to be Mayor of this town."

He held out a damp white hand but before Phemie could respond to this offer a small man in well-washed levis pushed forward.

"My sister'll board you, miss. She's a widdy-woman an' dog-poor but you'll be comf'able . . ."

"The very thing, the very thing . . ." said Mayor Barstowe in haste. "I can vouch for Mrs Sellars, ma'am, a veritable pillar of our church and most respectable . . . you are fortunate indeed."

So Phemie was escorted once more up the street to a narrow little house near the saloon. Here she was welcomed in by a narrow little woman who cast a look of comprehensive scorn and dislike over Phemie's escort and told her brother to "tell that riff-raff to get offa my porch!" She cast another over Phemie and then showed her up a staircase so narrow that it had better be called a ladder to a stark little room under the shingles with no furniture but a bed and a wash-stand.

While her escort drifted back to the Nugget, still wondering who she might be and why she had come, Phemie explained her position to the widow who appeared to be mollified and said that it was just like that Mayor McDowall and there was sure to be work for her as a midwife for there were more babies borned than folk could feed, and supper would be on the table at five

117

sharp for it was early to bed and early to rise in this house if in no other in Argentana. With that she departed to the kitchen where Phemie heard her clattering the pans as if she hated them.

Phemie stood at her window looking out at the dreary street and considered her equally dreary prospect. But . . . but . . . however dreary it was a good deal better than requesting an escort back to the railhead from Captain Devayler . . . a gleam of pure glee lit her face as she pictured his reaction to such a request. No, there was no escape from this situation. She lay down on the lumpy mattress and began to consider ways and means . . .

7

THE YEAR WHICH FOLLOWED was an epic. Some of the facts are to be found in the series of letters which Phemie wrote to Miss Nightingale, and some in the columns of the town newspaper. Others became part of the history of the town of Argentana.

Phemie arrived late in May and reported on what she found in a letter to Miss Nightingale written on the following day.

P.W. to F.N. May 1867.

> . . . I find matters are not as we would wish [she wrote]. Our correspondent is dead, his hospital is not built and his successors show no great enthusiasm to build one. For many of the people of the town a hospital is but one step removed from a workhouse or a lunatic asylum and combines the worst of both. The Doctor is one Sophocles Stevenson, but he had better be called Papasilenos for he is perpetually drunk; though I have to admit that his condition makes little difference to his doctoring which is rough and ready but in the circumstances (also rough and ready) effective. He bleeds, purges, blisters and salivates with all the skill of the doctors of half a century ago. The town is virtually under siege by the Comanche and medical supplies are low.

> However, I have found some support for the idea of a town hospital among a very influential section of opinion. My landlady (who is what we in Scotland would call 'far

119

ben' in church society) is a power among those church
ladies and we are to call a meeting under their aegis of all
the leaders and some of the followers of Argentana Society. We have been very mysterious about the agenda and
thus depend upon female curiosity for a good turn-out . . .

Saul Barstowe the Mayor looked up from his copy of the
Argentana Argus (every Tuesday and Friday, price one bit) as
his wife came into the room taking the pins out of her second-
best hat.

"Well," he enquired, "what was the hen-party about?"

Agnes Barstowe sat down opposite him.

"I declare, Saul, just about ever'body was there . . . that old
Town Hall was chockful, clear to the doors. Mrs Sellars took the
chair—isn't she the dowdy one—and Sister Witherspoon spoke
so sweet. I do so like that darling Scotch twang, don't you?"

Her husband coughed.

"And most of the wives from the mining camp were there and
wearing their husbands' boots I declare . . . and did you ever
hear tell of a man McHarg?"

Barstowe nodded.

"Miner," he said. "Scotch, 'bout nine feet high. Don't tote a
gun. Don't need to."

"Mrs McHarg was there. She's a Scotchwoman too but with
very red hair and the most ungenteel voice, not in the least like
dear Sister Witherspoon . . ."

"Agnes," interrupted her husband, "what was the meeting
for?"

But his wife did not hear.

"Would you credit it, Saul, that painted creature from the
Silver Nugget was there, in a scarlet satin gown . . . imagine!
And a Chinese shawl which must have cost . . . I don't know
how much . . . Of course I avoided speaking with her but
imagine the nerve of her coming to a meeting where all the *good*
women of the town . . ."

Mayor Barstowe breathed a sigh of relief. To his shame, he
had good reason to know exactly how much the shawl had cost

and while he relied on Jane's shame he didn't care to hear she had been in the meeting. He picked up the newspaper.

"Stop cacklin' woman and lay the egg!"

"What egg?"

He drew a deep breath. "What," he asked carefully, "was the meeting to discuss?"

"Oh, that!" said his wife and went towards the kitchen. "Like a cup of coffee?"

"Nope!" said the Mayor. "Give!"

"It was about how we're going to raise money for—"

"Don't tell me—Missions to the Heathen . . ."

"No. We aim to build a hospital. We got the ground for it, all we need's the lumber and stuff."

Saul Barstowe got his voice back. "A hospital! Here, in Argentana! We need a hospital like we need a hole in the head."

His wife sniffed. "Folks get sick here like back East."

"Let them get sick at home," said her husband. "Taxes is high enough already."

"Don't make no never-minds what you think," announced Agnes, "the decision is took."

Mayor Barstowe flung down the paper and followed his wife into the kitchen.

"And who in tarnation gave a parcel o' wimmin the right to make decisions in this town?"

His wife dropped some wood in the stove which blazed up in an appropriate fashion.

"Sister Phemie said, we raise the money, we have the say and there ain't nothin' you menfolk can do about it."

"Did she now?" remarked Saul grimly.

"The motion was carried by a large majority," Agnes told him, "and we proceeded to elect a fund-raising committee. Say, Saul, where's that Katie at?"

"I told her she could visit the Dutton's bound girl, she'll be back . . . So you elected a committee, did you? I lay the fur flew . . ."

"There was some argifying," admitted his wife, "but we didn't take that long . . . and there's someone from all sections of Argentana Society just like Sister Phemie said . . . and guess what?''

''Don't need no guess . . . you're on this tomfool committee.''

''Yes . . . I'm to represent the 'very significant commercial section' . . . that's what they said and ever'body clapped. It was that exciting!''

''Who else?''

''Sister Witherspoon, Mrs Sellars, she's on for the Churchy folks, Mrs McHarg for the miners' wives, Laurie Meechan from the store for the shopkeepers, Mrs Dutton because she wouldn't be left off, and me . . .''

Barstowe snorted. ''Wouldn't care to drive that team in a buckboard . . .''

''And guess what?''

''I daren't.''

''We're givin' a basket supper in aid of the fund . . . an' I said you'd auction the baskets, so there.''

Her husband groaned.

Some extracts from the minutes of the meeting described above:

> Mr Lemuel Dutton, the undertaker, rose at the back of the Hall to say that he must disagree with his good friend the Reverend Baker. Argentana was a plain town and plain folk lived there. They could not afford luxuries like hospitals. Taxes was high enough. Argentana had got along very well without any hospital before and in his opinion this idea was plain tomfoolery. Sister Witherspoon rose to apologise to Mr Dutton for proposing a measure which must lead to a reduction in his potential custom. However, she hoped that in time the population of the town would be increased by it so that while his customers might be reduced proportionately they would most likely increase absolutely. Mr Dutton stood for some seconds in silence . . .
>
> . . . Mrs Dutton rose to protest very strongly against the

122

unchristian nature of the fund-raising activities so far proposed and for her part she would consider a weekly prayer-meeting with hymns and a collection for the fund to be adequate for the purpose without encouraging the young in lewd behaviour. Mrs McHarg said the young needed no encouragement . . . the debate became heated and general. Sister Witherspoon proposed that all the suggested activities should begin and end with a hymn and a prayer and this was adopted as a compromise . . .

The morning after the meeting Saul Barstowe left his bank in the charge of a clerk, put on his broadbrimmed white hat, lit a cigar and strolled along the street to the cramped offices of the *Argentana Argus.* Here he found the Editor, Eddie Thompson, scribbling busily. The Mayor sat heavily on the Editor's desk and jabbed the wet butt of his cigar at the manuscript.

"That a report of the tomfool meeting last night?"

Mr Thompson nodded.

"A most interesting and worthy project in my opinion," he pronounced, straightening his pince-nez which tended to slide awry during the throes of composition. "I intend to swing the support of the *Argus* solidly behind the Hospital Committee, in fact . . ."

"They won't get nowhere," said Saul.

"Oh, but surely . . ." protested the Editor, "I mean you cannot be against such a deserving cause . . . I mean . . . a hospital!"

"If," said Saul, "*if* it ever gets to be built, what will it be? Who will want to make use of a charity in this independent community of ours?"

"Why," said the Editor, "I can think of—"

"Nobody!" Barstowe went on ruthlessly. "Nobody hereabouts wants charity . . ."

"Nobody *wants* charity," agreed the Editor, "but surely . . ."

"I tell you, that hospital—*if* it ever gets built—will be used by every scallawag and saddletramp with the workshys and

123

what is more," announced Barstowe, warming to his theme, "as soon as they hear of this durnfool hospital this town is where they'll head right for. Folks will get mighty tired of givin' good cash-money for them and then where will the hospital look for money. I'll tell you . . . the taxpayers' pockets. The whole blasted scheme will come on us!"

The Editor looked unhappily at his copy. A phrase sprang up at him: '. . . a blessing to the poor and a comfort to the better endowed . . .'

" 'Sides," Saul dropped his election manner and reverted to his usual laconic conversational style, "I've got a better use for that lot, come the next election, than build a hospital on it."

"But Saul," exclaimed Eddie startled, "that there's town land and presented for the purpose of building a hospital. I've got Mayor McDowall's speech in the files . . ."

"Man," observed Saul and threw his cigar in the cuspidor where it smouldered unpleasantly, "I *am* this town. Ain't hardly a man in it I can't buy and sell . . . includin' you, Eddie, includin' you."

Eddie did not mistake his meaning. He picked up the copy on his desk, tore it across and dropped it into the wastebasket.

"What you want I should say?" he asked rather wearily. "I can't just lambaste the whole idea—it's a good idea, whatever you may say, Saul . . ."

"Just treat the whole thing as woman-talk," Saul ordered. "Well-meanin' but on no account to be taken serious. Advise the dear creatures to go back to their tattin' and leave runnin' the town to their betters. And you could use that Witherspoon creature as an example of the New Woman, pert and forward and ask if your readers want that their daughters should grow that way . . ."

"I can't do that!" protested Eddie. "Look, Saul, I'll give you all the space you want to knock the hospital but I'll not say a word against Sister Phemie . . . my wife'll kill me if I do!"

"Your wife wouldn't be too pleased neither, if you found yourself without no paper to edit," hinted Barstowe. "Guess I'll read Friday's issue pretty close."

He strolled back to the bank pleasantly conscious of a blow struck in that best of causes, public economy.

P.W. to F.N.

. . . I regret to have to tell you that there is a degree of resistance to our project. There is no co-operation from the council and the newspaper has adopted a singularly irritating attitude of condescension combined with a denigration of myself as an example of the New Woman . . . however, better a New Woman than an Old Wife, say I. Despite this, the Fund is growing. I am also making a living, being now in demand for 'birthings' and childish ailments and 'women's troubles'. Doctor Sophocles is a skilled man but unreliable. I am seldom paid in cash. Corn, side-meat, vegetables, honey, jam and pickles appear on Mrs Sellars' porch. I have absorbed much herb lore and superstition pursuing these avocations and find many of the more sensible receipts efficacious, which is as well in the dearth of drugs and other medical supplies. There are some practices I eschew—such as the treatment of putrid sore throat with a cow-dung poultice tied on with a stocking. The stocking for some reason must be inside out. Earache may be cured, so I am informed, by the insertion of a tight curled negro hair into the affected ear. This I have not tried as at the moment we have no negroes in town. To bring down a high fever it is customary to catch a grasshopper, put him in a bag with some crumbs and when he is hung round the neck of the sufferer the fever will fall when the wretched insect dies. Goitre (we suffer from this very much here) is to be cured by the touch of a dead person's hand. If he has been hanged so much the better. My patients remind me of my father's country patients in their dependence upon whisky for everything which ails them. If there is anything in this Doctor Sophocles should live for ever for he is properly pickled in the stuff . . . his patients pay him in bottles. I often wonder if they are full bottles,

125

for the belief here is that to pay the doctor's bill in full is to invite further illness.

Yesterday, Maggie McHarg dragooned some hobbledehoys into clearing and digging over the site of the hospital. I strongly suspect that their absence from the schoolhouse was connived at by Miss Elvira, our teacher. They were nearly as big as Maggie herself and more than a match for Miss Elvira. Together we pegged out the area of the buildings (I enclose a rough plan) and marked where the cellar is to be dug. This leaves a considerable area unused so I intend to plant a 'physic garden'. This would, no doubt, please Mrs Wardroper. It will provide me with standby remedies in circumstances such as the present. Maggie McHarg has sent round to the notable herbwife of the district to ask for recommendations and cuttings . . .

Argentana Argus: Society Column. July 10th.

A basket supper was held at the charming home of our worthy Mayor and his wife on Tuesday night. It was held in aid of that latest of feminine fads in the town, the Hospital Fund. The youth and beauty of the town attended in force and much rivalry was shewn in bidding for the baskets prepared by the fair hands of our budding beauties, none of whom could overshadow their charming hostess, Mrs Barstowe who presided graciously in puce satin with yellow velvet trimmings. Mayor Barstowe auctioned the baskets with his accustomed wit and humour and himself bought the chairwoman's (Mrs Sellars) basket for a handsome sum. A gay and sociable evening was enjoyed by all present. Mrs Dutton, wife of Lemuel Dutton, our undertaker, asked a blessing on the assembly and the hymn, 'With weary feet and saddened heart . . .' was sung before the merrymakers departed.

The day on which this report appeared was the day appointed for the monthly meeting of the Town Council. It was held, as was usual, in the back room of the bank and Saul, also as usual, supplied refreshments and entertainment in the form of an unopened bottle of redeye and a new deck of cards. The first of the city fathers to arrive bore a copy of the *Argus*.

"Here, Saul! I reckoned as how you didn't cotton to this doggone hospital notion! What's this piece here?"

The same sentiments were echoed by all the members as they arrived. Saul poured each of them a glass and bided his time.

"Gents . . . gents . . . I wish to reassure you. Argentana will not if I can prevent it be burdened with a hospital on the taxes."

"Then why all this basket-supper foolishness?"

"Because gents, we must take in account the contrariness of folks. If we give our support to this dadblamed scheme taxes get bigger and our votes get fewer. *But* if'n we come right out and say it's a lot of foolishness there's some not so far off would declare we uns was a lot of scallawags to let folks die like dogs for the lack o' lovin' care."

He shook his head. "That wouldn't get us no votes neither. However," he added comfortingly, "t'won't never come to nothin'. Why fight shadows? Thisaway we keep our dollars in our pockets and smile approving . . . Whichever way things turn out it ain't our blame."

After the passage of the seconds necessary to allow those present to work out this machiavellian pronouncement a murmur of appreciation was heard. Saul smiled, shifted his cigar to the other side of his face, put his tooled-leather boots on the table the better to admire them and threw the deck at Undertaker Dutton.

"Your deal, Lem," he announced.

Maggie McHarg rose to her full five foot eleven and glared down at Elmer Lowenfeld and his wife.

"Are ye baith daft as brushes?" she demanded. "Tell me wha mak's the siller in this warld? Men or women?"

"Men," admitted Mrs Lowenfeld regretfully.

"An' how many men's in this toon?"

"Near enough two hundred I reckon," answered Elmer.

"An' how many's Temperance?"

"Just Elmer here, and my brother Samuel," said Mrs Lowenfeld regretfully.

"An' ye'r wantin' the Hospital Fund Commytee tae come on a Temperance March to demand the closing o' the Nugget when a' the one hunner an' ninety-eight drink there . . . forbye the subscription from Mr Jenkins *and* the collecting box on the bar. There was mair nor twenty dollars in it last time!"

"You're never accepting money made in that evil trade?" asked Mrs Lowenfeld and Maggie snorted.

"It buys the same lumber as the stuff oot the Kirk baggies," she told her, "an' the hauf o' the patients'll be drunks. Let them pey as weel's the sober."

Argentana Argus: August. Social Calendar.

> The concert held in aid of the Hospital Fund was voted a complete success. The participants displayed both a variety of talent and a skill in execution which all present must agree was a privilege to witness.
>
> Congratulations to our worthy Mayor and his spouse for their spirited rendering of *The Country Maid*, a duet to which Mayor Barstowe brought a powerful and tuneful baritone and his partner an unsuspected talent for the portrayal of a flirtatious minx: a most affecting piece. Mrs McHarg delighted us with a selection of Scotch Songs and if the words were a mite hard to understand we could certainly hear all of them. The greatest applause was reserved for a pathetic rendering of *The Ballad of Mary's Ghost* by Thomas Hood the English comic bard. Doc Stevenson froze our very blood by his ghoulish tale of the fate of poor Mary's Corpse at the hands of the denizens of the dread dissecting room. Our worthy barber obliged the company with a selection of tunes on his violin which set our feet tapping.
>
> Thanks were returned to all the participants at the close of the entertainment and a special vote of thanks was made to Mrs Dutton for her services at the pianoforte so kindly

lent for the occasion by Mr Jenkins of the Silver Nugget. The Editor would like to take this opportunity of apologising to Mrs Dutton for the misfortune with the egg during his juggling act. He would like to add that he was quite unaware of the regrettable condition of the contents.

Mrs Sellars the chairwoman then declared her pleasure in announcing that the Fund now approached the astonishing total of five hundred dollars and building could now commence. The Committee announced that they wished to submit a petition to the Town Council and invited those present to append their names to the document now circulating in the Hall. The proceedings closed with a prayer offered by Mrs Dutton and the assembled company singing the hymn,

'When Thy summons we obey,
On that Dreadful Judgment Day!'

". . . and arisin' out of that, Mr Mayor, what are you meanin' to do about thisyer petition?"

Saul Barstowe blew out his customary plume of smoke and admired his boots.

"I propose to do nothing, gents," he replied, "absolutely nothing at all."

"Thar's sure a lot of names, Saul."

"Lotta wimmin-talk . . . passel o' nonsense," growled another city father and tossed in his hand, "I seen it in the paper."

Saul smiled to himself, blew another cloud of smoke and considered the card he had just drawn.

"Raise you a dollar," he said around the cigar and two more hands were tossed in.

"I still think," persisted the first speaker, "if them wimmin has raised all that cash-money we oughter . . ."

"Nope," said the Mayor and laid down a full house with queens high, "I don't see no need for a hospital in this community at the present time. We manage very well as we are . . ."

129

"When he's sober . . ."

". . . and moreover, gents, I don't see no percentage in it. The menfolk don't want to pay extry taxes for no hospital and the ladies, bless 'em, don't have no votes."

Which was conceded to clinch the matter. Saul scooped the pool.

P.W. to F.N. September.

> . . . no co-operation from the Mayor, but this was not unexpected. Nothing overt, you must understand . . . all co-operation short of actual help. The main difficulty is that as Barstowe has most of the businessmen in the town in his pocket we are having some difficulty in finding people to do the building. It seems that he could foreclose on most of the population. However, I am mobilising my forces . . .

"Blast, woman! Give me one good reason why I should spend my off-duty buildin' a hospital!"

"Mrs Smith says Sergeant Smith's there all the times he can spare. And Corporal Wills, and Corporal Romanes. And wasn't *you* lookin' for your stripes, hmn?"

Captain Devayler to Sister Witherspoon. September.

> Ma'am,
>
> I appreciate that what my men do in their off-duty is no concern of mine. It is, however, a matter of some importance in these uncertain times that so many men should be out of the camp at one time. Moreover, the Surgeon informs me that he has had to treat a number of minor injuries due to their present off-duty activity, mainly cuts, bruises and blisters. Two men, however, have been incapacitated for duty, one with a crushed foot and the other with a strained back. This is a serious matter in a small

garrison already much overextended. I would be obliged therefore if you could look elsewhere for your building labour.

Lee Devayler, Captain, U.S. Cavalry.

P.W. to L.D.

. . . I am happy to report that the building is almost complete. What remains to be done, I can do.
P.W.

Phemie, Maggie McHarg and some conscripted truants were putting the finishing touches to the building one afternoon in late September. Two boys were putting up a neat name-board which declared the building to be THE LINCOLN MEMORIAL HOSPITAL. Maggie was trying to make sure that it was not installed upside down, a distinct possibility as after some years of systematic truancy neither of the boys was able to read. Phemie, her brown skirts pulled modestly about her ankles was perched on a ladder nailing the last row of shingles onto the porch roof. A third boy, his head rigidly averted held the foot of the ladder and a fourth sulkily weeded the 'physic garden'. This industrious scene was interrupted by the sound of a horse being ridden into town at a dead run. The boy on its back was brandishing a huge old-fashioned Walker Colt. He reined in to a sliding halt and fired three times in rapid succession.

"Injuns!" he yelled. "Injuns raidin' at Painter Creek!"

At the noise the townsfolk poured into the street.

"Big party, son?" asked Saul Barstowe from the steps of the bank.

"Better'n fifty, I guess," the boy shouted and as the bell above the church began to ring the alarm, 'Clang, Clang, Clang!' he swung down from the horse which stayed where he had halted it, head hanging, flanks heaving and the cart harness

131

still hanging about it. The boy sprinted across the street and ran up the steps of the hospital porch.

"You Sister Phemie?" he asked Maggie anxiously.

"No. I'm up here. Wait. I'm coming."

Phemie came neatly down the ladder and round on to the porch.

"What is it?"

"Maw's poorly. Babby started comin' so soon's she heard the shootin'! It's Peary's up by the Creek."

Phemie jerked her head at the boy holding the foot of the ladder.

"Saddle the Mister," she told him.

By the time she was ready to leave the messenger was back astride his weary beast and bugles were sounding at the fort. The church bell still rang urgently in threes and men, horses and guns were milling round the steps of the bank waiting for the Mayor to organise them into a posse. Phemie nodded to young Peary and they set off as fast as the Mister could be persuaded to move.

"Phemie!" yelled Maggie. "Wait on the sojers! Ye cannae tak' on the hale Comanche nation! Phemie!"

Unable to make Phemie listen she turned on the confused mob of men outside the bank.

"Ye bluidy sheep!" she bawled. "Will ye let Sister be murdered by yon heathen savages! Get efter her, ye muckle sumphs! Or gie me a gun an' a horse an' I'll gang masel'!"

Her abuse was drowned by the thunder of hooves as Captain Devayler's troop came down the street in a cloud of dust. The menfolk tired of waiting for Saul to appear swung in behind the troop and rode after them.

"That's mair liker the thing," approved Maggie and grabbed an escaping conscript by his outstanding ear. "Never heed, son, ye'll can fecht the Injuns when ye're growed. Back tae the kail."

At Peary's matters were beginning to come to a crisis. The raiding party were busy at the cabin half a mile away and the yells and shots could be heard very easily. Mrs Peary hunched in

132

her rocking chair was fending off the inexpert help of half a dozen of the earlier arrivals while Paw and two of the earliest stood guard at the window and the door with Winchesters. A half-breed girl was weeping in a corner. Phemie looked about her and took charge.

"Got a root-cellar?" she demanded.

Paw Peary did not move his gaze from the plume of smoke rising above the pines which hid the next cabin.

"Trap's under the rag-rug."

A rickety ladder led down into the earth-smelling cellar and Phemie bundled the six youngest down among the potatoes and carrots with two cherished rag-dolls, a stump of tallow candle and strict instructions not to make a sound or try to lift the trap whatever appeared to be happening above them. As she closed the trap and replaced the rug she reflected that even if the cabin were set on fire it would be better for them to be smothered by the smoke than to fall into the hands of the raiders. Mrs Peary was assisted into the imposing brass bed by Phemie and the half-breed girl, a tall, raw-boned girl with Indian features and hair and incongruously blue eyes. She answered to 'Mattie' and knew enough English to fetch and carry while Phemie delivered the tenth young Peary. It was an easy delivery and the boy though small was sturdy and healthy. Mattie wrapped him in the well-worn baby flannels and after she had made the mother comfortable Phemie put the bawling scrap on the pillow beside his mother. Maw Peary shivered.

"Don't seem hardly worth all the trouble," she croaked. "Looks like he'll be a corpse beside the rest of us, come mornin' time."

This remark drew Phemie's attention to the fact that the yelling and firing was now much closer than it had been. It seemed that the raiders were coming their way. Paw suddenly fired and reloaded.

"Here they come," he remarked calmly, "murderin' varmints."

Almost as he spoke a fusillade rang out from the other side of the house where his sons were stationed.

133

"Best you wimmin get down on the floor," he advised sighting carefully, "they'll likely fire through the windows."

Phemie settled her two patients on the floor in a nest of patchwork quilt and told Mattie to stay near them, but went herself to join Paw at the door."

"I can shoot," she told him. "Is there another gun?"

He didn't answer at once but drew his Winchester inside the door and removed the remaining cartridges.

"Ain't no call to waste ammunition," he said at last. "The army's out there an' I guess they'll do the job without'n our help. But thankin' you kindly, ma'am."

"You've got a fine son, Mr Peary," said Phemie now there was time for such trivialities.

"He'll make the seventh," said Paw.

"I'd ha' liked a girl," said Maw wistfully.

Half an hour later it was all over. Phemie and Mattie fed everybody on the soup which had bubbled peacefully on the fire during the whole affair, tidied the cabin and repacked Phemie's bag. Paw put the guns above the chimneypiece and went back to the barn with the grown sons while the boy who had fetched Phemie went to bring 'Mr McCorquodale' round to the door. He had just assisted her into the saddle and was handing up the midwifery bag when Sergeant Smith cantered up. He was dirty, dusty and dishevelled and he looked worried.

"Sister Phemie! I was afraid you'd have gone back to the town. Can you come?"

"What's up?"

"It's the Captain," said Sergeant Smith and looked uncomfortable. "He stopped an arrow."

Phemie hauled on 'Mr McCorquodale's head, he was hardmouthed to a degree, and followed the sweating trooper.

"Is it a serious injury?" she enquired.

"Well, I guess not . . ." said the Sergeant, "but it sure is uncomfortable. And Surgeon Masters he's dead . . . he got an axe in his skull trying to help Devlin. They're both dead."

Lee Devayler was standing by his horse looking at once

134

drawn and sheepish. At the sight of Phemie he flushed angrily and glared at the Sergeant.

"Why did you fetch her?" he demanded as if she was nowhere near at all. "I won't have a woman . . . I . . . Oh, blast it! Where's Surgeon Masters?"

"Dead," said the Sergeant succinctly, "stone dead."

Devayler started at the news and then winced. "Dead! How many wounded?"

"Countin' you, sir, three. Other two's a ha'f ways to the fort, I guess. Four dead countin' the doc, Surgeon Masters, sir."

"Better get Stevenson."

"Drunk," said Phemie, echoing the Sergeant, "dead drunk."

"Then he'll have to be sobered," said Devayler. "Get him, Sergeant and you may escort Sister Phemie back to town at the same time. The raiders have gone but there may be one or two lying up waiting for stragglers."

Phemie slid out of her saddle. "What's wrong?" she asked.

Devayler refused to answer.

"Captain's bleedin' some," volunteered Smith.

"Will you go get Stevenson!" said Devayler between his teeth.

The Sergeant saluted and left hurriedly before he was again ordered to take Phemie with him. He was not a man to overestimate his own abilities. Phemie tied 'Mr McCorquodale' to a tree and came over to the Captain. When she was close his injury was obvious enough. The leg of his breeches was soaked in blood and his boot as well. From high on his thigh protruded the flight of an arrow.

"One thing's sure," Phemie told him, her face as serious as a judge's, "I can't ask you to sit down."

She considered the wound and saw the blood was still flowing.

"I must get that stitched at once," she said, "you can't wait for the doctor."

"No," said Devayler grimly, "I'll wait."

Phemie removed a knife from her bag.

135

"Do you want to spend a fortnight on your front?" she asked. "Or even to bleed to death? If Doc's drunk as he usually is it'll be two hours and more before he's fit to bandage a cut finger."

They glared at one another.

"Hadn't you better be sensible. I won't hurt you more than Doc would, in fact he'd probably have less regard for your sensibilities . . . He might even consider he had the makings of a good story."

There was a charged silence.

"If you were to kneel down and bend over that boulder," she suggested, "it won't take more than ten minutes."

What followed was gory and painful to a degree for a barbed arrow in the thigh is no joke to the recipient. By the time Phemie had extracted it Devayler was grey and sick. She cleaned and stitched the wound and dressed it with spaghnum. Bandaging presented something of a problem but she solved it by ripping some eighteen inches off the hem of her petticoat and winding it tightly round the dressing and what was left of Devayler's breeches.

"Lawks-a-mussy-on-us," she observed, breaking the silence, "this is none of I . . ."

"Do you often have to cut your Petticoat All Round About?" asked her patient rather faintly as she tied it off.

"No . . . not often . . . Now, I don't know which'll be more uncomfortable, riding or walking."

He rose slowly and stiffly and Phemie watched him closely wondering if he might not keel over after all. She had been disturbed by the amount of blood he seemed to have lost. He walked a pace or two and winced.

"Riding'll be over sooner."

He yanked his army cloak off the saddle and slung it round his shoulders.

"Mustn't upset the town riding through with such a bloody wound."

He heaved himself painfully into the saddle from the offside and Phemie, using the blood-stained boulder as a mounting block, followed suit as Sergeant Smith rode up.

"Doc Stevensen is sober, sir," he reported, "Jenkins doused him in the horse-trough. But he's busy. Couple of the townsfolk got hurted. Sister Phemie fix you up, sir?"

"Expertly," said Devayler sourly and rode on.

Phemie and Smith rode together, their eyes on the tall cloaked figure in front.

"Wouldn't hardly know there was a hole in him, would you?"

"He'll bear watching for all that," replied Phemie, "he's lost more blood than is healthy."

"Take more'n an arrow in the leg to faze him, I guess. Served during our war, did the Captain. He weren't more'n a kid Lieutenant. Wounded twice. Once at Antietam and again at Appomatox."

"Were his company manners another casualty of war?" asked Phemie sweetly.

Smith looked a little unhappy. "He ain't no beau, that's for sure," he agreed, "but I guess it ain't all his blame. Way I heard it, his fiancée upped and married his brother."

"A woman of discernment evidently," observed Phemie. "Why?"

"Brother got the family plantation. Captain, he took and fought for the Union and old Father, he was a dyed-in-the-wool Johnny Reb, he cut him out in favour of the brother. So the girl upped and married the brother."

"She had a narrow escape, didn't she?"

"Captain, he got the worst of it all ways. No girl, no plantation and no promotion."

Phemie looked at him. It had not occurred to her that Devayler was old to be a Captain.

"Army don't have much time for Southerners now," explained the Sergeant.

P.W. to F.N. October.

> . . . I have had a well dug which will save much carrying of water. A squad of soldiers arrived at dawn yesterday . . .

L.D. to P.W.

     . . . I hope these excavations in your backyard constitute recompense for a similar operation performed by you.

P.W. to F.N.

     . . . but the money is finished. We need beds, blankets, pots, cutlery, kitchen equipment, plates, cups . . . I have asked the Town Council if they will advance a little sum towards this but they (or rather Mayor Barstowe) refused. They are polite and complimentary but unhelpful. The townsfolk have shot their bolt for the time being. I manage to buy and beg a few items each week . . . a blanket for delivering a baby, for example, or a cup and plate for a house visit, but it is slow work, for such items are scarce . . . The most faithful members of the committee are knitting squares for blankets or piecing quilts. My heart misgives me when I think of all we still need. However, it is something to have achieved the hospital within a sixmonth and no doubt we will contrive . . .

Argentana Argus: November. News Item.
SERIOUS ACCIDENT AT THE LUCKY SEVEN MINE!

     Mr Lester Sims and Mr James Lennon just preparing to leave the scene of their daily labour and make their way out of the Lucky Seven when part of the roof caved in trapping them in the current working.

     Mr James Lennon, (Big Len to his friends) was unhappily caught under the fall by one leg and severely injured. It was a fortunate circumstance that the fall was not enough to completely block the level. A small aperture remained and through this Les was able to raise the alarm.

     At great peril to themselves the rescuers worked their way towards the working, propping the roof as they went. At 7 a.m. Les was heard to call out that something had better be done for Big Len because the pain of the injury was so severe as to cause loss of consciousness.

However, the way over the fall was too small to admit Doc Stevenson who weighs better than 240 lbs.

At this point Sister Witherspoon from the new hospital volunteered to make the attempt. Nurse Witherspoon is what our French friends would call petite and Americans vest-pocket-size. She retired and changed into male attire whereat some of the ladies present raised a great outcry. This was suppressed by Mrs McHarg whose husband Alexander was directing the rescue operations.

Sister Witherspoon worked her way over the fall into the cavern at great risk to herself, for all are agreed that the roof was rotten as cheese. She examined Big Len and declared that his leg must be taken off immediately if his life was to be saved. At this point Mrs Lennon who is in expectation of a Happy Event broke down and was taken home by neighbours.

Chloroform and instruments were sent in and room was made for Doc Stevenson at the other end of the aperture.

The operation was then performed by the Sister under the instructions of the Doctor: an action deserving of the highest admiration. Sister Witherspoon and her patient were brought out soon after midday and taken at once by Mayor Barstowe's buggy to the hospital. We are happy to report that Big Len is making a rapid recovery and is now sitting up in bed whittling himself a wooden leg.

P.W. to F.N. November.

. . . because of a fortunate accident the hospital has gained the wholehearted support of the mining community. We now have a considerable sum for equipment and what is more we have the promise of a regular donation from one of the larger mining Corporations. I am having a pump installed, as carrying water from a well absorbs too much time and energy. Our problem now is when we can have the equipment brought in. The stage runs only seldom and then under heavy escort and there are no freight runs at all. Meanwhile we make shift with what is available.

A crowd, well-wrapped against the chill December wind, was gathered outside the new hospital waiting to see the Lincoln Memorial Hospital declared open. The snow had been scraped and shovelled away and a few gay flags snapped in the wind. Inside Mrs Dutton presided over a table laden with food and drink by the fund-raising committee in order to regale the party who were to witness the official opening.

It was, perhaps, unfortunate that the Reverend Baker, the obvious candidate to perform the ceremony was sick and Mrs Baker who had played an anonymous but Trojan part in the campaign was attending him. A hasty meeting of the committee had rejected Mr Dutton (proposed by Mrs Dutton) as being likely to inhibit custom; proposed Phemie and been refused ("you need someone impressive, not a pennyworth of well-water") and then heard Mrs Barstowe propose with a somewhat petulant note in her voice that surely the Mayor would be the ideal person to perform such a ceremony and that she would personally guarantee that he would be very happy to be asked. This statement was received in a somewhat sceptical silence by Phemie and Maggie McHarg who had excellent reasons to suppose that Mrs Barstowe took rather too much for granted.

"Well!" boomed Maggie after this loaded silence. "*I* think we should spier at the auld doctor."

As an alternative to Mayor Barstowe her suggestion was welcome but certain difficulties presented themselves . . .

"Never heed," said Maggie, "I'll keep him aff the bottle for one forenoon."

It was a vain promise. Five minutes before the time when the official party was due to arrive Sergeant Smith, who was to represent the army on the occasion, trotted up looking somewhat heated and handed a note to Phemie. Mayor Barstowe taking in this (not unexpected) development pulled down his

140

vest prior to taking his rightful and accustomed place in the centre of the picture. The note read:

> . . . the auld docks as drunk as Davys sow. Hed a botle hid in the privy. Speer at the Sargent will he cut the string he biggit the place when alls sed.
>
> Maggie

Phemie, aware of preparatory mayoral throat-clearing behind her, smiled sweetly at Sergeant Smith.

"Sergeant," she said, loudly enough to be heard by the assembly, "the Committee and I would be much obliged if you would overlook the short notice and take the place of Doctor Stevenson so suddenly and so unhappily indisposed, and open the hospital. We are extremely conscious that without the help of you and your comrades it would never have been built at all."

The Sergeant slid from his horse, thrust the bridle into the hand of the nearest man (who happened to be Saul Barstowe) saluted and said in a suspiciously studied manner:

"On behalf of my fellow-workers, Sister Phemie, ma'am, ladies and gentlemen, I am proud to accept your invite."

The ceremony proceeded. Mrs Dutton offered up a prayer and then called for the hymn of her choice.

> "Safe home, safe home in port,
> Rent cordage, shattered deck,
> Torn sails, provision short,
> And only not a wreck . . ."

After this the Sergeant attempted without further ado to cut the tape with Mrs Dutton's scissors; these being small and blunt and the tape thick he did not at once succeed. He worried the near edge for a few moments and then pulled out a businesslike clasp knife. The tapes fell to the ground, the hospital was declared open for business in ringing parade-square tones and the crowd cheered. At the window of the Male Ward Big Len waved his all but completed peg-leg in acknowledgement of having become an official inmate.

The feeling of triumph and achievement was dispersed by

Maggie. She came running across from the Silver Nugget, her skirts held high and her red hair hanging in loops about her face.

"Sister Phemie! Sister Phemie! Ye'd best mak' up anither bed! The Doc's awfu' no weel. He's fair vex'd me that I cannae see the wee green thingies sclimmin' doon the lum tae cut aff their heids. Jim Drinkwater's sittin' on him till I get help . . ."

P.W. to F.N. December.
> . . . so the hospital could be said to be inaugurated by the doctor, though possibly not as either of us could wish . . .

8

Argentana Argua: December 1867.

DEATHS:
Stevenson, Doctor Sophocles. Died in the Lincoln Memorial Hospital following a long illness.

'After life's fitful fever, he sleeps well . . .'

[a number of irreverent ex-cronies of the good doctor were heard to suggest that this effecting quotation might have been amended to . . . 'he sleeps it off . . .']

BIRTHS:
Lennon: To Mr and Mrs James Lennon on December first, a son, James Witherspoon.
Smith: To Sergeant and Mrs Smith at Fort Argentana, a son, Witherspoon Albert.
OBITUARY: It is with the deepest regret that we record the death of Doctor Sophocles Stevenson. 'Doc' as he was affectionately termed by most of the town had served its citizens long and faithfully. His little weaknesses were understood and rarely interfered with his ability to attend to those who needed him. His passing unhappily leaves the towns without medical aid unless one excepts the activities of the indefatigable Sister Witherspoon . . .

For once there was no call for the afternoon. Phemie shared some soup with her two patients, a miner with a badly damaged hand and a boy from a farm who had put a pitchfork through his foot. Both were nearly ready to go home. Maggie was clattering happily in the kitchen, singing 'Ye Banks and Braes o' Bonnie Doon' powerfully out of tune. Phemie went into the tiny cubicle at the back of the building which was her office and (since the episode of the 'male attire' made her unwelcome under the Paulian roof of Mistress Sellars) her bedroom. She sat down and began a letter to Miss Nightingale.

> . . . there was a time when I believed that we were hardworked by Matron Wardroper but life in St Thomas's was a cushion of ease compared with my present existence. It has been a long, cold and sickly winter and much of it passed without the benefit of either doctor or drugs . . .

144

Her pen dried and as she dipped it Maggie's voice echoed across the yard from the kitchen.

"In the name o' the wee man! Wha's daen *that* tae ye, ma wee doo?"

Phemie peered through the tiny window and saw Maggie, sleeves rolled up and her head bare towing a familiar figure behind her through the yard. It was Mattie, the half-breed girl who worked for the Peary family. Phemie dropped her pen and ran out to meet them and was shocked to see that the girl's face was a mass of bruises and her clothes were torn almost off her back.

"Cold water, Maggie . . . and some swabs from the box. Sit down, Mattie."

She had taken Mattie into the empty Female Ward to examine her injuries. It was clear that the half-breed girl had had the father and mother of a beating. Maggie came in with the water and the swabs.

"My, but she's had a richt larrupping! The puir lassie!"

"This one will need a poultice," observed Phemie.

'This one' was a contusion on Mattie's left shoulder so severe that Phemie took care to make certain that there were no bones broken.

"Churn-paddle did it," said the victim.

"Cider-vinegar and ginseng-leaves," said Phemie. "I'll fetch them from the still-room. Did you keep the brains from that jack-rabbit we ate?"

"I did. I'll bring them."

When Mattie was bathed and poulticed and tucked for the first time in her life into a bed and sheets, Phemie cleared the debris, washed her hands in the bowl which stood on the stove and took a stool to sit beside the bed.

"And now, lass," enquired Phemie kindly, "who did this? And why?"

Mattie stared sullenly at the unpainted wooden wall. "I stole," she said.

"Stole what?"

"Food."

145

"Did the Pearys not feed you?"

Phemie was well aware that the shortages of the winter might make the presence of an extra mouth in the cabin a burden. A 'mere Injun' might well be kept short. Mattie shook her head.

"They feed me."

"Then why steal?" insisted Phemie.

"For my people," the half-breed burst out, "for my mother. They are hungry in the lodges. Many die. Children die every day."

"Your people?"

"My people the Comanche . . . my mother Comanche. My father . . ."

She spat and Phemie frowned with distaste.

"You mean that the Comanche round here are starving?" she asked and wiped the spit off the floor with a rag.

Mattie nodded. "The white man has driven away the buffalo," she explained. "They could dry no winter meat. The raids brought few cattle and the deer are scarce. They could not trade meat for corn. So, they starve. I stole because my mother is near to death and my sisters are dead. Peary beat me. So I came here."

Phemie looked down at her new patient and pulled the gaily coloured blanket over the girl's chest.

"And we'll see to you . . . never fear. Go to sleep."

Back in her room, Phemie sat in thought for some time. After a while she seemed to make up her mind and pulling a thick shawl about her shoulders she set off towards the newspaper office. Eddie Thompson, his eye-glasses wildly askew, was correcting the next day's issue in form. He looked up, tweezers in hand as Phemie came in on the heels of a bitterly cold March wind. Before he could speak she began:

"You haven't started printing yet? Good. Can you put this in?"

She handed him a dollar note and a scrap of paper which he accepted reluctantly and then made for the door again.

"Must see about the Hall," she explained. "Sorry to put you about but it's important. Thank you."

146

The door slammed behind her and the gust of wind rattled the dusty piles of old papers. Thompson sighing heavily looked at the paper in his hand and stuffed the dollar into his pants pocket.

"THE INDIAN PROBLEM!" it read. "There will be a meeting TONIGHT in the TOWN HALL to discuss the best solution. Everybody welcome!"

Eddie Thompason scratched his thinning hair and considered. There wasn't time to consult Barstowe about this development. He considered the advertisement again. Barstowe would be bound to hear about the project and if he wanted he could quash it for himself. Meanwhile there was a dollar in Eddie's pocket and the notice would fit comfortably into a space below the Editorial if the next item were cut . . . He sighed. The *Argus* would be late for bed tonight and so would he.

The meeting was well attended. This was less because the Argentanians considered that a solution of the Indian problem was possible—or even likely—than because the winter had lacked variety and such a meeting promised a few knock-down drag-out arguments. When the hall was nearly full, Phemie, her heart beating hard but her face expressionless began to clamber up on to the tiny platform which was dignified with the name of stage. Sandy McHarg who was acting as steward picked her up like a doll, placed her firmly on the centre and bellowed for silence in a voice which even his wife might have envied. The meeting quietened down and looked expectantly at the platform. After ten months they had learned that where Sister Phemie was life could be strenuous but it was rarely dull. Saul Barstowe, curious and suspicious, had come and was standing near the door with Kellow Pike, his clerk . . . a very confidential clerk indeed, some said: Eli Jenkins the owner of the Silver Nugget had been heard to say that they could each put the other in jail if they were so minded. Jenkins was there too, looking more like a college professor than a tavern-keeper, and so were nine out of ten of the town worthies. Two of these standing near Barstowe were muttering hoarsely together.

"Ef'n it's Sister Phemie ramroddin' I guess them Injuns might just get soluted at that," observed one and the other

147

signified his agreement by nodding sagely and tipping back his hat with his thumb the better to see the small figure on the platform. Barstowe frowned and chewed on the butt of his cigar as if he were trying to solve a problem of his own.

A final fusillade of bangs on the platform from Sandy's fist reduced the last conversations to resentful silence and Phemie was able to begin.

"Ladies and gentlemen, this meeting was called because yesterday I learned that the Comanche were starving."

This statement was received enthusiastically with cheers, hats thrown in the air and much stamping of booted feet. Phemie waited, stonyfaced, until the racket died down.

"Their women and children are dying," she went on quietly. "Some of you have seen your children going hungry. Did you enjoy the spectacle?"

The silence in the hall could almost be felt. It was broken by a woman holding a baby who shouted from the benches at the side.

"My man was killed by them murderin' heathen. That's why my childer's goin' hungry. I don't care ef'n they all starve. Good riddance, say I!"

There was a rumble of agreement.

"That's one solution to the Indian problem," replied Phemie, "let them all die slowly of starvation. It's a pretty heathen one, I must say."

The crowd emitted an indignant murmur.

"*And*," she went on, "it's not a specially good one, because some of them are sure to survive and in a year or two they will be at your throats again, raiding your cattle, lifting your scalps, stealing your corn, stopping the stage-run . . . making this town like a desert island. Do you really want this to go on?"

There were cries of "No!"

"Wouldn't it be better to find a more permanent solution?"

Cries of "Yes!" and "Kill 'em all!" were heard and Mayor Barstowe pushed his way forward through the crush to confront Phemie from the floor.

"We ought to find a way to *live with* them!" shouted Phemie

148

above the din. "And I think we've got a chance to find that way today!"

"Little lady!" interrupted Barstowe unctuously, "I'm sure you mean well. What you say's right. An' we all 'preciate how an English gal—"

"Scots!" came from Maggie at the side of the hall and the meeting laughed.

"All righty," agreed Saul grinning around his cigar, "we all 'preciate how a Scots gal raised like you was must feel to hear 'bout such matters. But I guess you jest don't understand how we uns feel 'bout Injuns. There ain't no one in this Hall, I guess, who ain't lost by them varmints—a loved one scalped, a cabin burned, property stole. We don't see them like other folk, lady. We know them, we know they jest ain't human. The only end to the Injun problem, Miss Phemie as anyone in thisyer Hall will tell you, is a dead end."

On this somewhat grim note he turned about to receive the plaudits of his voters but before the plaudits could begin Phemie began to reply.

"What you say, Mr Mayor, is obvious and easy . . ."

From the back of the Hall came a grumbling comment, "Like always!" which might have originated with Eli Jenkins, though there were some who attributed it to Eddie Thompson on duty with a notebook.

"We all know those wretched Indians can't hold out for ever against the odds. You've only got to sit back and admire your boots, Mr Mayor . . ."

The meeting expressed its appreciation of this observation and Barstowe scowled.

". . . it's the army who have to do the work and run the risks, not you . . ."

A woman's voice from the body of the hall demanded to know, "Where were you at Painter's Crick, Mister?"

"At their present rate of progress," Phemie continued, "it will only take them twenty years or so to wipe out the whole tribe. But while you sit and wait for them to do it how many of the townsfolk are going to be killed in raids, or die of neglect

149

because no doctor would want to practise in such a place? How do you expect the town to grow and prosper? Tell me that. I am beginning to wonder if you want it to grow and prosper . . . and so are other people.''

There was a murmur of agreement and Barstowe scowled more than ever.

''You ought to be ashamed!'' he shouted. ''Any decent woman would be ashamed screeching up there about things you don't know anything about! You go back where you belong—leave us run our town our way. You don't belong here. This town don't want no forward hussies telling them how to run things!''

''I might just take your advice,'' retorted Phemie. ''*If* I could find a stage to take me and *if* when I did I could be sure of arriving at Mountain View with my hair!''

''I'd back you 'gainst any Injun, Sister Phemie!'' yelled Matthew Johnston the barber from the back of the Hall. The crowd laughed its agreement but Phemie concentrated on Barstowe.

''I don't relish being up here any more than any other woman,'' she told him. ''I've work to do. But I need time and peace to do it in. We won't get it if you're allowed to idle this chance away.''

''What chance?'' came from a dozen voices up and down the Hall.

''A chance to live in peace with the Comanche!''

A confused response to this gave a general impression that such an object even if it were attainable was not in the least desirable, and that the only trustworthy Injun was a dead Injun.

Phemie's face flushed with anger.

''You call yourselves a Christian community!'' she raged at them. ''You've taken their lands, killed their buffalo, driven them into the barren hills to starve and you grudge them even the right to exist. Is that Christianity? It isn't a brand that Christ would acknowledge, I'm sure of that!''

From the corner down near the stage where Mrs Sellars had herded her Church ladies there came a shocked hissing murmur of "Blasphemy! Sheer blasphemy! She should be struck down!"

"I'll tell you what a real Christian would do," Phemie went on. "He'd forget about the raids, and the thieving and the deaths, he'd raise every scrap of food and rag of clothing that he could and take it to Lodge Pole Crossing. He'd give the children food and then talk about peace. That's what a real Christian would do!"

"Are you proposin', Sister Witherspoon," asked Barstowe, "that this township which has suffered more from them varmints than any other that I heard tell—are you proposin' we send food to them thriftless, painted, naked, murderin', heathen thieves?"

Phemie, who by now was well under way, turned on him.

"Why not?" she demanded. "And I'd expect a handsome contribution from you, Mr Mayor. You've plenty of stores—and you haven't wasted them by giving to the people in the town during this hard winter, I notice. I look to you to set an example! And . . . to pay back a little, a very little, of what you stole!"

The silence which greeted this could be felt. Barstowe's face went cheese-colour and for once he was lost for words.

"I know how you made the money to buy this town, Mr Mayor," said Phemie striking while the iron was hot.

"Every dime on it was made honest!" shrilled Pike, who might have had an interest in the matter.

"It was made contracting to feed the railroad workers," said Phemie. "On buffalo-meat mostly. And the skins fetched fancy prices in the East. You must have slaughtered twenty years' food-supply for those wretched Comanche and wrecked their supply for the next forty . . . if not for ever. It's you and your like the people of this town have to blame for the Indian war. And you grudge them a month's starvation diet!"

She turned back to the meeting.

"This is your chance. Feed them and then talk peace. You've nothing to lose but a sack or so of corn and you may get a treaty which will let you and your children live in peace, let the settlers

151

on Stone Creek live without fear of getting their scalps lifted. It might let you run a stage-line, visit your folks back East if you want to. Let the town start growing instead of stagnating. If you don't at least try it you're more foolish than I think you are.''

The people in the Hall stared in silence at the tiny figure in front of them. For a few seconds nobody said a word and then Luke McShane who helped at the livery stable shouted:

''Doggone it! Why not give it a try! Can't make nothing any worse than it is, and like she says it's worth tryin'. I got a keg of salt-horse you can have, Sis!''

His words tilted the feeling of the meeting over to Phemie and within a few moments offers were rolling in from every side: corn, salt meat, potatoes, flour, biscuit . . . Eli Jenkins offered his buckboard to take it in, and Barker of the livery stables two mules to pull it.

''Mules is best over rough trail and the Lodge Pole trail's real rough.''

Meechan at the store offered flour, salt pork and blankets and half the women in the hall volunteered to bring some contribution, however small, to swell the load.

''Just a minute!'' Barstowe's voice cut through the din. ''Will some kind-disposed person tell what durn fool's goin' to take this load to Lodge Pole? *I* ain't volunteerin'. *I* ain't tired o' life.''

At first glance this seemed to constitute a fairly strong objection to the scheme. Wives dared husbands to volunteer and the young unmarried men studiously avoided one another's eyes.

''There y'are,'' said the Mayor scornfully. ''What'll you do with yer Christian charity now you got it? Give the Injuns an invite to come eat it in the town? I'll eat every one that comes!''

This offer was received with acclaim and Phemie had to wait for the noise to die down.

''No need for you to meet them or eat them,'' she said calmly, ''I know they wouldn't let a man within a mile of the lodges. So, I am going to drive the wagon and the Pearys' Mattie is coming with me to interpret and explain who has given the stuff.''

At this point there were a scatter of protesting voices.

152

"Has anyone got a better idea?" enquired Phemie and without waiting for an answer she continued, "If you would bring your contributions to the Silver Nugget before dawn on Thursday, I'll be leaving at that time. Now, ladies and gentlemen, I must thank you for giving me a hearing and for your offers of food and clothing. And I think that concludes the business for which this meeting was called. Good night."

She jumped down from the platform, disappeared into the body of the meeting and left.

Considering the uproar which greeted her announcement and the protests which flew about the Hall after she had left at the prospect of allowing a slip of a girl to go into what could not but be described as acute danger it was surprising that there were no candidates for the role of driver: either the representations of their friends and relations, or the cold water poured on the scheme by the Mayor, or, more likely, a nagging suspicion that Sister Witherspoon did not regard the male sex with quite the respect they reckoned their due served to restrain their ardour.

As soon as he had seen Phemie slip out of the door Mayor Barstowe clambered awkwardly on to the stage. He threw out his chest and began to address the meeting before it could escape.

"Friends!" he opened in the nasal tone of the practised political orator, "if some female is prepared to butt heads with the Comanche because she has a bee buzzing in her pretty little bonnet I guess there ain't no call to stop her . . . the Comanche will do that soon enough. She won't get far and if she gets her come-uppance, ain't no one to blame but her fool self. If she gets any place I promise I will personally donate the money for the Children's Ward in her hospital . . ."

He paused and took a puff from his cigar.

"Don't worry, gents . . . I know my money's safe. And so do you. You know, my friends, the curse of the present age is the New Woman. I decry her desire to interfere with things which is the proper sphere for men. I decry her wish to abandon home and hearth to attempt tasks properly and naturally reserved for men. I decry her willingness to neglect her family and interfere

153

in things far too complicated for her puny understanding. I decry—"

At this point in his peroration he was struck on the ear by a large potato: which of the indignant ladies at the back of the Hall had so far forgotten her dignity and decorum as to perpetrate this expression of political frustration was not clear; but it was well known that Mrs Devlin of Wardellers' Cabins was able to hit a chosen offspring in this manner at thirty paces nine times out of ten and the Mayor presented a much easier target than her quicksilver brood. She and eight of her eleven children were certainly in the Hall and those eight were certainly not cheering the Mayor. Barstowe glared at the crowd, but was unable to go on for the laughter.

Phemie and Mattie left the Silver Nugget at dawn on Thursday with a full load of mixed provisions and a multitude of tearful good wishes. Maggie McHarg, left in charge of the hospital, dragooned the patients mercilessly to ease her feelings and in every household in the town relations between the menfolk and the women were somehow strained. Even Miss Elvira felt the current of emotion: when two vast habitual truants shambled into their unaccustomed seats in class that morning her gentle face assumed an expression of awful scorn.

"I expected that you'd be here today," she observed and positively sneered. "Men! Huh!"

The girls murmured agreement. Miss Elvira then turned to the board where the day's lessons were written up.

"Today," she told them with relish, "we will read our portion of scripture from the Book of Esther . . ."

Meanwhile Phemie drove her team into the hills, quite unaware of the devil's brew of emotions which she had left behind. Her decision had been taken because she considered that a man would almost certainly be killed at sight. She had been allowed to go because the men agreed with her and no one found themselves able to stop her. This circumstance did not stop them from feeling somewhat ashamed of themselves and consequently angry with Phemie for making them feel so . . . a feeling

154

which was in more than one instance taken out on their wives.

Phemie coaxed the mules along the steep and stony trail to Lodge Pole Crossing and beguiled the tedium of the journey by learning some essential Comanche words from Mattie. Apart from some anxiety as to whether the rig would stand up to the bucketing it was getting on the trail the journey was uneventful. Dusk was just beginning to fall when Mattie sniffed.

"I smell the fires. Stay. I will go and tell Grey-Wolf-Who-Comes-in-The-Night that we come."

She slipped down from the seat and vanished into the brush. Phemie tied the reins to the whip-socket, applied the brake and pulling a battered copy of *Annals of the Parish* out of her pocket prepared to make good use of what daylight remained. She looked up smiling from Balwhidder's account of the operation performed upon the Muscovy duck to find herself the centre of a circle of Comanche, staring at her with bright sunken eyes. Phemie closed her book and stared back, noting automatically the symptoms of prolonged underfeeding evident in all of them.

"Good evening to you," she said and waited, her heart thumping like a drum and her armpits clammy with sweat but her face calm as cream in a pan.

The oldest of the men there grunted and then came to peep under the tarpaulin which covered the sacks and barrels. He jerked out a phrase which appeared to please the onlookers, replaced the cover and nodded peremptorily at one of the younger men who came and stood by the rig.

"My father says, your gift is welcome. The Stranger's Child has told us why you come. You are to come to our fire. It gets cold."

"Will your father accept our gift?" enquired Phemie.

The young man looked at her with a sardonic eye. "How can he refuse?"

In the village the women were standing silently waiting: even in the firelight they appeared like wraiths and the children clinging to their deerskin skirts were little better. Mattie came forward to meet the cart and the women crowded behind her.

"Mattie!" called Phemie urgently as eager hands hauled the

tarpaulin off the rig, "tell them not to eat too much too fast, they could do themselves harm . . ."

"The Healer need have no fear," Grey-Wolf's son reassured her, "our people are too well-acquainted with hunger to be so foolish."

She watched while the cartload was divided among the lodges and her heart sank at the smallness of the share each family received. The gift represented food for a few days only.

"Oh, I do wish it were more!" she exclaimed suddenly to no one in particular. Grey-Wolf's son put his hand on the side of the empty buckboard.

"A gift is a gift," he said, "and we are grateful."

"Winter is a bad time," said Phemie.

"When my father was young it was not so. We dried buffalo-meat and traded with our cousins in the south for corn. There were buffalo robes to keep us warm and game in the forest to hunt even in the worst of winter. Today . . . the white man's cattle graze and the buffalo comes no more. White men plough our hunting grounds and cut down the forest. We cannot trade for corn because we have nothing to trade. When we try to steal food to feed our families the white man kills us. So, we kill him."

His voice expressed neither anger nor bitterness. Phemie could think of nothing whatever to say.

The two young women spent an uncomfortable and wakeful night in a crowded lodge. In the morning Phemie sought out Mane-of-the-Swift Horse, Grey-Wolf's son, and asked him bluntly if there could be peace. The Comanche looked at her and made a resigned gesture with his hand.

"That is for my father," he said. "But he lives still in the days when he was young. He cannot accept what is now."

"You accept it?" asked Phemie.

He did not answer at once.

"The white men are as many as birds in autumn flying south," he remarked at last. "They are many beyond counting. I have seen them. My father has not."

They were interrupted by a Comanche woman who came and spoke urgently to Mane-of-the-Swift-Horse.

"My sister," he explained. "She had three sons. Two are dead and the last lies very sick with a wounded arm. She had heard you are a Healer and asks if you will see him."

"I will see him," said Phemie and added cautiously, "but I cannot promise that I will be able to help him."

The boy lay in a lodge upon a heap of skins and he was very ill indeed: he was delirious and babbled gibberish. The heat of his body when she tested it on the inside of her wrist made Phemie open her eyes very widely indeed. She could not remember having met so high a fever. His neck-glands were hard and swollen and his skin harsh and dry. The source of the fever was plain to see. The boy's right arm was swollen to three times its usual size and was ominously red and streaked. A concoction of leaves was tied over a hideous suppurating wound the smell of which permeated the air in the lodge. The child was horribly thin and his belly swollen from famine. Phemie looked at the poor creature and his mother kneeling beside him and knew a kind of white fury at a world which could let this happen.

"I can make him more comfortable," she said at last, "but he may be too close to death for me to pull him away. And he is starved. Tell your sister what I say and ask if I may open her boy's arm to let out the poison."

A brief exchange followed in which the mother listened stone-faced to her brother's translation and then nodded. Phemie did not wait for Mane-of-the-Swift Horse to tell her what she had said but sent Mattie scurrying for her bag and a bowl of hot water.

Accustomed as she was to dress wounds and attend disease Phemie was still forced to exercise all her self-control when she lanced the throbbing arm. It was somehow the more unpleasant for the mother's rigid determination to show no emotion at all. After a few minutes which Phemie did not afterwards care to recall, much of the matter had escaped and been cleaned away and a pad of wet lint tied over the wound. In the meantime

157

Mattie had been preparing a brew of sage and dried elderflowers and the mother persuaded the child to drink a bowlful of the decoction. Afterwards he seemed less restless but Phemie feared that this was less because he was more comfortable than because the lancing had left him very weak. Through Mattie she gave instructions that he should be given some strong broth when he woke and then remembered with a sinking heart how difficult such an instruction would be to carry out. The mother made no protest but nodded and sinking to her knees stayed motionless beside her son.

"Bury those rags," Phemie told Mattie, "and empty that bowl well down stream. Next thing you know they will have sickness from drinking infected water as well as famine."

They emerged into the chilly morning and were confronted by a wrinkled and toothless ancient who screamed abuse at them and waved a much decorated hatchet. He was not a lot bigger than Phemie herself but Mattie lost colour and shrank behind Phemie, insofar as she could . . .

"It is Eye-of-the-Day, the Wise Man," Mattie explained. "He is angry because you have been to the child."

This was something of an understatement. Eye-of-the-Day advanced upon them yelling threats and with a crowd of noisy supporters behind him.

"He says if the boy dies he will let the women cut you into little tiny pieces . . . and me with you!" quavered Mattie.

Eye-of-the-Day reached what appeared to be the climax of his commination and spat on to the hem of Phemie's already bedraggled dress. Phemie had spent a sleepless night and her nerves had been stretched by the scene in the lodge, the drive to the village had been a nerve-wracking affair and she was tired and on edge. Her temper snapped.

"You filthy little toad!" she rapped out and spat back.

Silence fell. Eye-of-the-Day stepped back and glared at her with a concentrated malevolence.

"Oh, Sister . . . Sister . . . you should not do that!" wailed Mattie and cowered away from the angry old man who flung back his head and let fly a high warbling yell. At once Phemie was seized by two of his supporters and taken at a humiliating pace to the fire where she was pushed roughly on to her face in front of Grey Wolf-Who-Comes-in the-Night. He appeared not to notice this interruption to his morning meditation. Phemie looked around for Mane-of-the-Swift-Horse but to her dismay there was no sign of him. Eye-of-the-Day made a long high-pitched complaint to his chief and punctuated it by kicking Phemie in the ribs. When she tried to get to her feet he pushed her down and made two of his followers hold her there. Grey-Wolf made no sign. Slowly Phemie's indignation and fury turned to cold fear. Behind her she could hear Mattie whimpering.

The tirade was suddenly interrupted. From the edge of the forest clearing where the village stood there came a rifle shot. A familiar voice shouted a phrase in halting Comanche. The kicks in her ribs ceased and so did the tirade. The voice repeated the phrase. The grip on her arms relaxed, and the feet were taken off her shoulders. Phemie found herself able to lift her head.

The first thing she saw was a ring of cavalry around the group at the fire, their carbines at the ready. Lee Devayler dismounted and pushed his way through to confront Grey-Wolf who raised his head and stared past the Captain and into the distance. Devayler evidently demanded an explanation of the scene he had interrupted but the chief gave no sign of having heard him. Devayler hauled Phemie roughly to her feet and shook her.

"What do you mean by it?" he demanded. "Can't you ever mind your own business? What in the name of Providence are you doing here? Of all places in the territory and of all times, this one!"

Phemie jerked herself out of his grasp and glared.

"And what business is it of yours what I'm doing?" she snapped.

"Plenty! You've wrecked . . . do you realise what I've got over there?" he demanded and waved his arm in the direction of the trees. "I came up here with a load of biscuit and half a dozen beeves which I've perjured my immortal soul to wring out of Uncle Sam."

159

She stared at him and then to his increase fury she laughed.

"And why did I imperil my soul? You don't bother to ask do you, oh, no! Because I hoped their belts might be tight enough to get us a treaty—a treaty of peace, you feather-witted imbecile . . . And now you've wrecked the whole idea . . ."

"Oh, have I? Oh, have I, indeed! And do you suppose that such notions are the monopoly of beef-witted soldiers?"

She glared up at him with her hands on her hips and her hair escaping from its pins.

"Do you imagine that because for once in your career you've had a rush of blood to the brain that you are the only person in the world ever to have had an idea?" she said angrily. "What in the name of all that's holy do you think *I'm* doing here?"

This speech was not calculated to appease.

"I don't pretend to understand the vagaries of the female," he ground out, "and what is more I don't want to . . . All I know is that instead of coming in here with the food as benefactors we've had to move in as usual with guns and all to prevent some unwashed son-of-a-gun from doing what I'd like to do myself—beat you!"

By way of answer Phemie pointed at the buckboard which was standing empty while the mules, tethered to its wheels tried with concentration to find a bite to eat where there was neither grass nor bush.

"Last night that was full of food and clothes," she told him. "Mattie and I came up with a gift from the town. There wasn't more than a few days' supply but they did collect something."

"Last night! You've been here since last night! Why did nobody tell me?"

"I have a notion," said Phemie drily, "that the worthy Mayor hoped that the Comanche would do him a favour by removing a thorn in his flesh and he was unwilling to give you a chance to prevent them. You've made an enemy arriving at the last minute like this."

"How in the name did you manage to screw a load of goods out of that tight fisted, ornery bunch of Injun haters?. . ."

160

By this time the conversation—if that was the term appropriate—had attracted the attention of the whole assembly, both Comanche and troopers who were regarding them with interest and a degree of amusement. Devayler flushed and lowered his voice.

"May I enquire, if you brought them in a load of food last night and presumably spent the night with them in safety, what you were doing down there?"

He pointed at the spot where she had been lying.

Phemie brushed the dust and grass off her skirt and looked him in the eye.

"It was nothing of any consequence," she said, "a slight professional misunderstanding . . ."

"Indeed?"

"This gentleman and I . . ."

She looked round for Eye-of-the-Day, which gentleman was somewhat uncomfortably situated having the muzzle of Sergeant Smith's gun stuck firmly in his left ear. Phemie smiled sweetly at the Sergeant and removed it gingerly. She assisted the old man to his feet.

"I collect, Captain, that you have some knowledge of the Comanche language. I would be infinitely obliged if you would convey to this gentleman my sincere apologies for inadvertently attending on a patient of his . . ."

Devayler stared and then gave a crack of laughter.

"You overestimate my grasp of the tongue a trifle," he admitted, "but I'll do what I can."

His halting explanation did not seem to appease Eye-of-the-Day who spat into the fire in a manner which reminded Phemie forcibly of Jedediah at the railroad station and muttered something which was patently uncomplimentary.

"Roughly translated," Devayler told her, "that meant 'plaguey women!' "

"Not the first time I've had that said to me by a long shot," she said and laughed. "Would you ask him if he will tell me about his methods. Explain that I am a healer among our people, in a very small way of course."

161

"You mean that I should butter him well and deliver him to you to finish off?"

"Something of the kind . . . it works with doctors in England, why not with him. Could you ask if I may go with him to examine the boy and discuss what he is going to do for him . . . that should get us out of the way and perhaps you might get a chance to introduce the subject of bread and beef and put away the guns."

While Devayler was doing his best to put this to Eye-of-the-Day Phemie beckoned Mattie over to act as interpreter. The old Wise Man got rather unwillingly to his feet again and toddled down towards the lodge still muttering imprecations under his breath. Quietly Devayler ordered his men to sling their carbines and told Sergeant Smith to bring on the ambulance wagon of supplies and the beeves. The Comanche stared at one another with a wild bewilderment, not having expected to survive an encounter in which they had been taken at such a disadvantage. The last Phemie saw of the scene was the arrival of Mane-of-the-Swift Horse who came out of another lodge and squatted down between his father and Devayler.

Inside the lodge the mother rose to greet them and spoke excitedly, pointing at the little figure on the heap of skins.

"She says the evil spirit has left her son," said Mattie, "and that he has spoken in his own voice and knew her for his mother and her heart is glad and grateful."

Phemie looked at her patient.

"He is very weak still . . . warn her."

"She says she is familiar with the look of death upon a child and that he has not that look."

Eye-of-the-Day grunted a few words.

"The Wise Man says, the boy will live."

"Ask Eye-of-the-Day how he will make him strong."

The old man felt the boy's chest and listened to his heart. Then he felt his stomach and last he smelt him very thoroughly.

"He says," Mattie translated, "he says that the small one must have strong broth three times a day prepared with herbs

162

which Eye-of-the-Day has gathered and that while it is preparing he will say words of power in the steam."

"Ask if it is permitted that I should see these herbs and hear the words of power," asked Phemie and opened her case which was still lying where she had left it after lancing the boy's arm. "Say that it may be that my herbs are the same as his."

Somewhat to her surprise he nodded at the request made rather timidly by Mattie and then told the mother to be gone. When she had hurried out he beckoned to Phemie and squatting down on the floor of the lodge he pulled out of the welter of furs about his waist a greasy bag from which he drew an assortment of desiccated herbage tied in bundles as well as other objects such as dried lizards and smoked bird and animal claws. There were also insects and other portions of deceased creatures some of which were recognisable and others, perhaps mercifully, were not. He waved his hand at Phemie and made a request.

"He has shown you his herbs . . . now he would hear your words of power before he tells you his."

Phemie had to think very quickly. Any prayer she might make, however sincere, would not have the necessary ritual flavour. She wished she had attended the Episcopal Church instead of the sternly unritualistic United Free Church of her father's choice: but there was no time to regret this parental shortcoming. She rose to her feet, clasped her hands before her, put her head back and as she had done in the schoolroom not so very long ago recited fervently:

"Waly, waly up the bank
And waly, waly doun the brae,
And waly, waly yon burnside
Where I an my love were wont tae gae."

Eye-of-the-Day nodded in evident approval and Phemie who had forgotten the rest of the stanza launched herself upon

"Contented wi' little and cantie wi' mair,
Whene'er I forgaither wi' sorrow an' care,
I gie them a skelp as they're creepin' alang
Wi' a cog o' sweet swats and an auld Scottish sang."

163

Eye-of-the-Day appeared as pleased with Robert Burns as with Lady Grisell and repaid the favour with a shrill ululation which woke the patient with a start of terror. The chant which followed, however, was monotonous enough to lull him to sleep again. After this Phemie was encouraged to oblige with 'Oh, merrie hae I been teethin' a heckle', to which Eye-of-the-Day replied with a thrumming invocation which sounded like a train in the distance rocking over a sprung line. When he had finished he made a request.

"He wishes to learn some of the white healer's words of power," said Mattie.

Again Phemie had to think very fast while she nodded and smiled acquiesence.

"Tell him," she said, "that it is to be said over the food to strengthen the eater."

Mattie translated and Eye-of-the-Day nodded and grunted.

"Put your hands so," Phemie instructed, placing them palms together under her chin in the manner of a mediaeval angel. The old Comanche obeyed, though his aspect was less than angelic.

"Some hae meat," said Phemie, her repertoire by now nearly exhausted. Poetry had never been an interest of hers.

"Some hy met," repeated Eye-of-the-Day. "Som hy met."

"And cannae eat," said Phemie.

This time he was more successful.

"And some," continued Phemie conscious of the bony face and sticklike arms of her ancient pupil, "hae nane that want it."

It took him three attempts to master that.

"But we hae meat, and we can eat . . ."

It occurred to her forcibly that this was a revoltingly complacent statement, but Eye-of-the-Day unconscious of its overtones wrestled with the pronunciation and overcame.

"And sae the Lord be thankit," she concluded.

This was comparatively easy. Then with the retentive memory of the illiterate he had it by heart and repeated it five times in a row. Phemie nodded and smiled approval.

There had to be, of course, a reciprocal lesson and Phemie

164

was acquiring the appropriate stamp-and-go for the first chant when Sergeant Smith appeared at the door.

"Cap'n Devayler's compliments, ma'am," he began and stopped in bewilderment at the scene before him.

"Liar," said Phemie.

". . . and will you come at once," he continued.

"That's more the accustomed style."

". . . because we're all set to go."

"As soon as my lesson is over," said Phemie. "I will be delighted to accompany you."

And she resumed the 'wa-wa-*aha*!' which accompanied the dance while Eye-of-the-Day watched over her progress with a critical eye. Sergeant Smith's jaw dropped and he retired in confusion.

When Eye-of-the-Day and Phemie returned to the fire, by now the most excellent of colleagues, there was a meal prepared; Devayler rose as she approached and made room between himself and Mane-of-the-Swift Horse.

"Did you get your treaty?" asked Phemie urgently under her breath.

Devayler jerked his head in the direction of the young Comanche.

"He is coming to Fort Durgan to discuss terms. He is no fool. I think we might get one."

Before Phemie could express her feelings at this development Eye-of-the-Day rose, turned to Phemie, put his hands palms inward beneath his chin and began on 'Som hy met'.

To do them justice neither Lee Devayler nor the Sergeant moved a muscle at this curious Comanche custom.

"It's a compliment," Phemie whispered. "White words of power to make food strengthen the eater."

"And how do we return it?" enquired Devayler in exasperation, "with a few stanzas of 'When lilacs last in the doorway bloomed'? "

When they were all ready to leave Grey Wolf came to bid them goodbye.

"My father says, he wants peace very much," said Mane-of-the-Swift-Horse.

"We also want peace," agreed Devayler.

"But hunger begets anger, so says my father."

"True," said Devayler, "I will remember this."

Grey-Wolf's wrinkled and weatherbitten face cracked into a smile and he made a short speech in Comanche which his son smiled as he translated.

"My father says it was his great good luck when you came in search of your woman and brought us food and peace on the muzzles of your guns . . ."

Devayler flushed to the roots of his hair.

"She is no woman of mine," he stated categorically.

The Comanche looked puzzled.

"You speak to her like she your woman . . ." said Mane-of-the-Swift-Horse.

Phemie coaxing her mules into line behind the empty ambulance wagon heard this exchange and laughed until the mules laid back their ears uneasily and Mattie stared.

9

Argentana Argus: September.

THE COLORADO TERRITORY STAGE AND FREIGHT LINE take
great pleasure in announcing that they will be recommenc-
ing regular runs between the Mountain View Railhead and
Argentana as from August 24th in consequence of the
Treaty recently concluded with the Comanche Nation.
Fares and Freight Charges and Stage Times to be had on
application to our agent, Seth Barker at Argentana Livery
Stables.

THE STAGE WAS DUE in town around midday and the townsfolk had
prepared a great welcome for it. The shops were closed, banners
fluttered above the dusty street and the porch of the Silver
Nugget was lined with spectators long before there was any
possibility of the stage being sighted. Only in the Lincoln
Memorial Hospital was business more or less as usual. The
hospital was full almost to capacity. Three of the four beds in the
Male Ward were occupied; one by a farmer who had been
kicked by his cow and had three ribs stove in, a condition not
improved by his having locked up his cabin, led the cow and his
horse to a neighbour and then walked the seven miles into town
to the hospital. He was now immobilised in bed, Phemie having
made up for her inability to pull the bandages as tight as was
necessary by borrowing a corset from Maggie. The farmer
propped on his chaff-filled pillows was a bachelor and Phemie
was in no hurry to explain what he was wearing. The other two
patients were less unusual; one being a miner whose jaw had

167

been broken during a drunken brawl outside the Nugget—or rather while the brawl was in the process of being evicted from the Nugget. Jenkins preferred his clients to maul one another and leave his furnishings untouched. The third was another young miner but he was unlikely to get much older. Billy Quinn had brought his death with him from Ireland and was in the last stage of phthisis. Phemie looked in shortly before midday, attended to their needs, tidied their beds and noted their condition on her charts.

In the Female Ward it was less peaceful. Granny Bulmer was quiet enough lying in her corner, eyes staring into her long past youth and her mouth turned down clownishly at one corner. Young Millie Lennon was weeping with the pain of her arm which had been burned to the bone with lye. The remaining two beds were supposed to be occupied by two children, one of them Millie's (his lack of a father prevented Millie's respectable neighbours from caring for him) and the other recovering (fast) from a fall off a woodshed roof. These two were playing bears in caves under the beds and growling furiously. Phemie quelled the riot, put it back to bed and threatened dire pains and penalties. She gave Millie a dose of laudanum and water and changed her dressing, noting with concealed distress that the injury was showing signs of mortification: not an unexpected development but one which could lead to amputation. Despite the survival of Big Len, Phemie did not regard such a prospect with complacence. Her next task was the changing of Granny's sheets.

She carried the soiled linen round to the back of the building and put it in the steep-tub. Maggie had washed the previous day's accumulation and hung them along under the porch. They were dry, so Phemie began to take them down and she had just taken down the last pillow-case when she heard the sound of hooves, the rattle of wheels and the traditional whoop with which the driver of the stage-line announced his arrival. Without waiting to put the linen down she hurried round to see the great event.

The stage had halted outside the Nugget and two of the

168

waiting patrons had gone to the horses' heads. The rest of them were exchanging livid personalities with the driver and the guard who were relieving the coach of its roofload of luggage by the simple process of hurling it to the ground. The door of the coach swung open violently and the first passenger emerged. Phemie watched, hoping against hope for some professional-looking gentleman who might be a doctor. She was to be disappointed in the first one. He was a blackavised customer who wore a curious costume consisting of a rusty black frock-coat and ancient faded levis. Both garments were decorated with snake skins stitched on wherever there was space. Round the crown of his battered hat were threaded the rattles of more than twenty sidewinders. He leaped, rattling furiously, to the ground and began bellowing abuse at the guard in a deep hoarse voice. The guard did not miss a single champ on his bacca-chaw but hurled the wooden box he was holding straight at its indignant owner who received it on his chest and sat down hard on the rutted street making noises like an infuriated bullmoose.

The racket he made and the appreciation it roused in the spectators distracted attention from the next passenger to alight. He was elegantly dressed in pale grey wearing a flat-crowned grey hat with a broad brim. He carried a cow-hide cloak bag at least fifty years old and a silver-knobbed cane. He surveyed his new surroundings with interest, appearing to note the nameboard of the hospital with particular satisfaction and then turned away to help a third passenger. Meanwhile the first passenger having deposited his box with tender care was preparing to climb on to the stage and (according to his expressed intention) disembowel the guard. In this he was being frustrated by a barrage of hand-luggage and parcels which bounced off him from all points. Jeff Drinkwater the barkeep at the Nugget finding himself without customers strolled out to watch the comedy and called over to Phemie.

"Guess you got your new Doc, ma'am!"

Phemie's expression changed from apprehensive amusement to sheer horror.

"Not him!" she exclaimed, pointing at the gesticulating

figure who had reached the top of the rear wheel despite the assorted missiles ricocheting from his person.

"Yeah . . . that there's Doc Biedermeyer," said Drinkwater.

A blast of picturesque blasphemy drowned the laughter.

"Sure is," added the barkeep, pokerfaced, and returned to the bar.

Phemie, staring appalled at this prospective colleague, failed to notice the other two passengers approach the porch where she was standing. Indeed the first she knew of them was to hear a familiar, deep, brown velvet voice say:

"May I take that linen, Miss Phemie, ma'am?"

"Scipio Africanus Beauregard!" gasped Phemie.

Scipio removed his hat, bowed and, taking the linen, smiled happily at Phemie's surprise.

"The same, ma'am. Where may I find the kitchen?"

"But Scipio . . . what are you doing here?"

"I come to work with you, ma'am," he informed her kindly.

"But what about Lady Lacombe? Surely you haven't . . ."

"No, no, ma'am," he reassured her. "The Lacombes have returned to Europe. I did not wish to accompany them so I came here. Is that the kitchen?"

He moved off towards the cluster of outbuildings at the back.

"But Scipio," protested Phemie, trotting after him, "I can't . . . there isn't . . . Scipio, listen . . . there's no money. I can't pay you a red cent."

"You get paid, ma'am?" he enquired.

"Well, no . . ." she admitted, "not to say *paid* exactly . . ."

"I work for nothing most of my life," said Scipio. "Till Mr Lincoln said I was free. Then I could choose what to do. I chose to leave the Beauregard place and work for Lady Lacombe. Now, I choose to work here. You can feed me?"

"If you can eat side-meat and beans."

Scipio laughed. "I was raised on corn pone. You got a place where I can sleep?"

"Yes," said Phemie, "and there's plenty of blankets . . ."

"In that case," concluded Scipio majestically, "you have

now a hospital cook and handyman. And I know sick folk. I was about the hospitals in the war, Miss Phemie, ma'am.''

At this point they reached the kitchen. Maggie who was in there pounding jerky to make beef tea glared upon Scipio rolling pin at the ready.

"Is my lugs aye richt?" demanded Maggie. "Did I hear you say you were tae be working here?"

Scipio, despite his armful of linen succeeded in doffing his hat politely, bowing gracefully and dodging cautiously out of range of the pin.

"Maggie . . . Mistress McHarg," Phemie intervened, "may I introduce Mr Beauregard who has kindly volunteered to join our staff. He is . . ."

Maggie's glare turned to a stare and the rolling pin dropped to her side. Scipio dropped the linen into the appropriate basket and kissed Maggie's work hardened hand with Southern grace, taking the chance deftly to disarm her of the pin as he did so.

"Hey," exclaimed Maggie, unaccustomed to such manifestations, "ma haun' reeks wi' ingins . . ."

Scipio began to remove his coat and roll up the sleeves of his beautiful white linen shirt.

"I hope," he announced, "to relieve you of your more arduous duties here, ma'am, in order that you may more readily pursue the art of healing."

He considered the amenities of his new domain.

"In the name o' the wee man!" exclaimed Maggie, as quiet as any sucking dove.

Hastily Phemie hauled her out of the kitchen and into the herb-patch, hoping to be able to explain while the lull lasted. No sooner was the door shut than Maggie erupted.

"Phemie Witherspoon, are ye gaen clean gyte? Are ye putting yon muckle black callant in ma kitchen . . . is this a' the thanks I get after a' I've dune . . . he'll puishon us a' in wer beds, so he will! Let me tell ye, gin yon chiel comes next or nigh me I'll be aff oota here like a rabbit wi' a futret efter it . . ."

"Excuse me, please," came a soft Irish voice from behind them, "if you could just spare a moment . . ."

171

For the second time in quarter of an hour Phemie was left speechless. Maggie spun round and stood agape staring at the third passenger from the stage who put back the thick veil on her bonnet and smiled upon them both.

"My six months at the Boarding House is up . . ." said Esther happily, "and Mrs McCorquodale gave me twenty dollars for my own. I'd a notion to train for a nurse, Phemie—if so be ye'll have me."

The following morning Esther was being instructed in the St Thomas's (the definitive) method of giving a blanketbath to the accompaniment of heartrending groans from Granny Bulmer to whom regular baths were a new and unwelcome experience. In the Male Ward splutters of indignation quelled by Maggie's injunctions to haud their wheesht—

"Man! Man! It was a wumman that bore ye the puir mis-guided sowl . . . birl ower till I dae yer bum'—indicated that Maggie was doing the same for the men, while Scipio prepared a midday meal. The busy scene was interrupted by a thunderous noise which rattled the windows in their frames accompanied by an ear-splitting falsetto chant. The newly augmented staff of the Lincoln Memorial Hospital hastily dried the current area of operations and dashed to the windows which overlooked the street.

At the gate of the hospital there had appeared a stall. It was decorated with posters in strong primary colours which proclaimed in terms verging on the hysterical the virtues of Doc Biedermeyer's Fundamental Snake Oil Panacea. This specific, a pinkish green liquid was displayed on the stall in ranks of bottles the labels on which echoed the posters in smudged and minuscule print. Doc Biedermeyer himself had added to his odd apparel a loud-patterned Indian blanket, beaded moccasins and a faceful of war-paint. In this array he was dancing and chanting and beating on a war-drum. A crowd, mostly drawn from the customers in the Nugget, was gathering and while they watched he stopped his antics and began to extol his wares in a voice which might have been heard in his native Germany.

172

"You don' need no hospital!" he bawled. "You don' need no doctors! You got me! Friends! you got *me*. Just for you I have penetrated the age-old secrets of the Kiowa and at peril of my life stole the receipt for my life-saving elixir . . ."

He paused for breath and beat upon the drum. Phemie looking behind her saw that Millie had awakened out of her uneasy dose.

"Make Granny comfortable again," she told Esther and went forth to do battle.

However, Doc Biedermeyer was an experienced campaigner. He ignored Phemie's requests, appeals and latterly abuse as if she did not exist. His audience, maliciously amused to see Phemie for once at a loss backed their latest fancy and cheered him on. Phemie realised that a frontal assault would not serve. She left the quack in the midst of a graphic and wholly fictitious description of the twenty years he had spent undetected among the Kiowa and crossed the road to the bank. Here she sought official support from the Mayor in his office. Saul received her politely but with an air of amusement which suggested that he might have witnessed the preceding scene from the windows of the bank. He was smilingly unable to help her in any way. The street was free to all, he explained, as long as the traffic was not obstructed. He had no power to prevent any trader from carrying on his business on public ground. Miss Witherspoon might not be able to understand the great American tradition of Freedom for the Individual coming as she did from an effete and corrupt monarchy but he, Saul, was here to assure her that these United States were the land of the free . . .

At this point Phemie rose, shook out her grey skirts and remarked that she understood considerably more than Mr Barstowe gave her credit for. She then thanked him sweetly for awakening her to a full understanding of her own rights and privileges in this matter. Begging him not to trouble to remove his boots from his desk to see her to the door she took her leave. Saul felt slightly uneasy but found himself able to comply with her last request easily enough.

Her next call was at Big Len's cabin where she made certain enquiries and a request which Big Len was delighted to carry out. Having done this Phemie returned to the hospital and resumed her duties. Biedermeyer's bawling continued. Big Len borrowed a buckboard from his neighbour and was seen to drive off towards the mine.

About an hour after noon Big Len returned with a friend of his who had escaped from a premature explosion of dynamite with his life but little else save a lively sense of humour. He was employed as tally man in the company's mine. In the buggy was the wheeled chair he habitually used. Scipio unloaded this and placed it carefully under the hospital porch and Esther came running out with a stool to place beside it. Louie One-Eye was then helped down from the buggy and dragged his mutilated figure to the chair where he and Big Len, who possessed about a leg and a half between them, disposed themselves under a poster hastily daubed in lamp-black by Mrs Len and pinned up by Scipio. Louie One-Eye turned his scarred and disfigured face towards the crowd around Biedermeyer's stall and smiled with ghastly effect. Above him the poster read:

I TUK SNAKE-ILE ALL MY DAYS
JEST LOOK AT ME!

It was a crude gambit but appreciated by the crowd whose comments drove Doc Biedermeyer to remove himself and his stock in trade back to his room in the Nugget. Meanwhile, Phemie had arranged to purchase a bottle: it turned out to be a curious mixture of cheap whisky and castor oil.

It had become the custom since the death of Doc Stevenson for Phemie to hold a kind of outpatients' clinic in the closed-in part of the hospital porch. About ten in the morning three times a week a queue would begin to form and shortly afterwards Phemie appeared with the battered leather case she had taken over from the Doc and begin to work her way through the sore eyes, bad backs, poisoned fingers, boils, bruises and cuts. Sometimes Maggie was there to bring hot water and make bread poultices but more often Phemie would work alone and the queue would wait patiently on the rough bench and gossip. Two days after the stage arrived the queue was longer than ever and at least two members had brought the *Argus* to while away the time; various items from the paper were haltingly read aloud and fluently discussed. Phemie had just lanced a felon on Mary Ann Halfdansdottir's thumb and was bandaging on a wet dressing when Luke who helped out at the livery stable snorted like one of his charges.

"Citizens of Argentana!" he read. "A meeting will be held in the Town Hall on Tuesday next for the purpose of making nominations for the office of Mayor of this Town. A full attendance is confidently expected."

His neighbour, an old miner, spat over the porch rail into the dust of the street; Phemie reflected not for the first time that spitting appeared to be the all-American national pastime, and, remembering the prowess of Eye-of-the-Day wondered if they had acquired it, like maize and tobacco, from the Indians.

"Nominations my—eye!" commented the marksman. "Guess Saul Barstowe'll be Mayor around here for a long spell yet."

"Burg did ought to be called Barstoweville," agreed Luke and turned the paper over. "Seems like he's set on running ever'body in it."

"Why does he have to be Mayor?" enquired Phemie and popped a liquorice candy into Mary Ann's mouth. "Next, please."

Luke folded the paper into a square the size of an army biscuit and stuffed it into his pants pocket before he rose and limped to the chair vacated by the little girl.

"Because he done buy this town and ever'body in it just about," he grumbled and bent down to remove his right boot which was not the neighbour of the left boot, being larger in the foot, wider and shorter in the leg and brown instead of black. "Mule done it. Danged ornery critter stood on me. My foot's swole."

Phemie peeled off the ragged sock and prodded the discoloured member to see if there were any broken bones. The old miner watched and grunted in sympathy.

175

"Plumb ugly foot you got there."

Maggie brought a bowl of warm water and Phemie persuaded Luke to put his foot into this unaccustomed element to discover how much of the discoloration was bruising and how much could be removed with soap and water.

"Do you want to have Barstowe for a Mayor?" she asked suddenly.

The two men regarded her with pity for her limited understanding.

"Saul Barstowe he don't do nothin' but sit in a chair all day. He ain't no proper Mayor," said the miner and spat again for emphasis. "Might's well have Luke's ol' mule in that office."

"Then why don't you find another candidate?" she asked as she patted the mule's handiwork dry. "I mean, you don't have to vote him in."

Luke sighed. "Trouble with females," he complained, "is they jest don't hev no understandin' o' politics. Ef'n any other cuss tuk and stood for Mayor Saul 'ud squeeze him plumb outer the Territory. Saul he got the bank an' ever'body owin' the bank. Ever'body—the store, the stables, the undertaker, the newspaper."

"Ain't nobody in this whole town Saul can't twist round his little finger," agreed the miner.

"What about the Nugget?" enquired Phemie, spreading arnica on a linen rag.

The two men looked at one another.

"Eli Jenkins, he don't owe nothing to nobody," admitted Luke, "he don't even keep his cash money in the bank."

"Got a safe the size of a house. I seen him open it oncet. Got to twiddle at it," added the miner.

"Barstowe couldn't do much to Mr Jenkins, then."

Phemie began to wind a bandage round Luke's foot. The two men began to laugh.

"Miss Phemie, ma'am, you ain't suggestin' Eli Jenkins for Mayor, are you?" asked the miner.

"Why not?"

"A saloon keeper!" exclaimed Luke. "Tain't respectable!"

"Why not?" asked Phemie easing the bandaged foot back into the boot. "I'd rather have an honest saloon keeper for Mayor than Saul Barstowe."

Both men shook their heads in profound agreement.

"Church folk 'ud never stand for it," said Luke.

"Nor the wimmin folk," added his friend.

"I hadn't thought," observed Phemie sadly, "that the women had all that much influence on the politics of this town. And the church folk aren't all that many . . . and females for the most part. There. That should be a lot more comfortable in a day or two."

She nodded to the miner to take Luke's place beside the table. Luke shuffled aside but did not go away. He looked thoughtful.

"Come to mention it," he muttered, "that there brother of Louella Sellars . . . he was sayin' the same. An' she's church folk."

"Got a misery in my ear," said the old miner, "cain't hear nothing."

Phemie parted the matted hair and peered into the organ indicated.

"Blocked with wax and stone-dust," she told him. This was a common complaint among the miners working with the ore-crushers. "Clear it for you in two shakes of a lamb's tail."

She began to fill a large syringe with warm water under the apprehensive eye of the patient.

"Supposin'," remarked Luke thoughtfully, "jest supposin' folks did cotton to the idee . . . Saul couldn't squeeze out the hull town just for votin' him out."

"That's so," agreed Phemie advancing upon his friend with her syringe.

"D'ye reckon that Jenkins 'ud stand?"

"He'd need to be asked," replied Phemie.

"Guess he would at that," said Luke and wandered off in the direction of the Nugget.

Phemie smiled and pushed the plunger home. Under her hand the old man jumped like a hooked salmon.

Argentana Argus: September. Political News.

At the meeting of Tuesday last two candidates were nominated for the office of Mayor. Mr Kellow Pike proposed the retention in office of the present incumbent, Mayor Barstowe. This proposal was seconded by Mr Meechan of the stores. Mayor Barstowe rose to return thanks for this expression of confidence in his leadership but his speech was interrupted by Alexander McHarg who requested the indulgence of the meeting to propose another candidate, Mr Eli Jenkins, proprietor of the Silver Nugget Saloon. Mr Jenkins who was present signified his willingness to stand and the proposal was seconded eloquently by Mr Lucas McShane. This development was received by the assembly with evident surprise as Mayor Barstowe had previously been returned unopposed.

Editorial: same issue as above.

No doubt the sober citizens of Argentana can safely be trusted to repel this assault by the liquor interest upon the citadel of public affairs. We have confidence that our citizens know very well where their best interests lie; in *sober* judgment and respectable representation. We are sure that they will display their good sense this November by re-electing their present tried, trusty, true choice, Saul Barstowe.

The day after the meeting Saul Barstowe and Kellow Pike were closeted in the back office of the bank ordering the affairs of the town.

''Here's a letter from some doctor or other. Wants to set up in practice here.''

Pike thrust a letter under Saul's nose. The Mayor blew a smoke wreath at it.

''Write and tell him this town is the best prospect for a young doctor since the first Thanksgiving. Say we need a doctor so bad I'm prepared to loan money for him to set up. Get that off. Where is he at?''

Pike consulted a letter. "Abilene, I guess."

Barstowe's eyebrows rose. "Is he now? Right. Offer him anything he needs within reason. That's to put that upperty woman at the hospital in her place."

"Tell him 'bout the hospital . . . sounds good."

Barstowe blew another smoke ring. "No," he said. "I got plans."

Pike produced the *Argus* and pointed at the report of the meeting. "What are you doin' 'bout this?" he enquired.

There was a certain nuance in the flat New York voice which informed Barstowe that his clerk was not unamused by the situation.

"What you suggest?" he drawled.

"Ain't nothin' much you can do."

Barstowe stubbed out his cigar. "Suthin' you can do, friend. Listen here."

For about five minutes he explained what Pike was to do.

"Lookit," he concluded, "I ain't worried. Jenkins ain't got a snowball's chance in July. I got this town just about buttoned up. This is jest insurance and what I like is that it's right thrifty. Deals with two pesky things at the one time."

Pike nodded agreement.

"Ef'n you're right, Saul."

"I'm right," Saul assured him. "Where at did he get the money to start up the *Argus*? Weren't from me. Them flatbed presses cost a heap . . . not to mention paper an' that. *And* so far's I know—and I know a heap—he didn't have a red cent outside of his mine. Bar one thing."

He gave Pike a piece of paper.

"You try each one of those. I'll bet he borrowed from one of them. *And* I know on which collateral. You redeem it. Here's the money." He counted out a roll of bills into Pike's hand. "See you come back," he said.

"Don't worry. I'll be back," said Pike and tucked the list into the band of his hat. "And before the election."

Some days after Pike had left on the stage a hunter came out of the hills before dawn and hammered on the hospital door. Into Esther's indignant face he grunted out a story which sent her running for Phemie.

"Och, Phemie, come will ye! There's a man here says a bear's clawed a boy at Pinner's Level and he'll die if somebody don't sew him up."

In ten minutes Scipio had brought round a sleepy 'Mr McCorquodale' and strapped on the old doctor's bag. Phemie emerged in the frieze cloak which had come with her all the way from Scotland. Her small face was pale and set.

"I'll be back as soon as I can," she said as Scipio threw her up into the saddle. "But I don't like the look of Millie one wee bit. If you hear word that the new surgeon's arrived at the camp, send to Devayler and ask can he come."

"Where's the hunter gone?" asked Scipio.

"Mountain View for rifle-shells. He's expecting an early winter he says. Don't fash yourself, Scipio, I know the way . . . I know the boy too."

She hit 'Mr McCorquodale' on the rump and set off along the trail into the hills. Scipio went back up the porch steps glancing anxiously up at the fast moving clouds which hid the mountain tops.

During that day the thought of her stayed with everyone in the hospital. Maggie came and dressed Millie's arm disguising her alarm at the state of the injury with a blast of cheerful encouragement. As it drew on to evening it began to rain, gently at first and then more and more heavily. The wind began to rise making the little wooden building creak and groan and penetrating the smallest chinks between the boards with ankle-chilling draughts. Maggie refuelled the stoves with energy, said a cheerful good night to her patients and went over to the kitchen before she went home to make a meal for Sandy (now immersed in pre-election activity).

"Hey, Scip!" she said, her prejudice against the 'muckle black callant' not having outlasted the first day—and the first dinner. "I dinnae like it. Pinner's Level's ower the creek."

Scipio glanced involuntarily at the window where the rain beat viciously.

"The creek will surely be high after all this," he agreed. "Miss Phemie should wait till it goes down. She may be a day away. She will sleep at Pinner's for certain."

"Yon Phemie hasnae the sense she was born wi'," returned Maggie, "and she's sair vex't for Millie. Mark my words, she'll be on her weys hame, rain or no rain."

With these words in mind Scipio waited up until he fell asleep with his head on the kitchen table. Shortly after ten o'clock a furious gust of wind roused him and he looked in the shed for 'Mr McCorquodale'. It was empty. He stayed staring in for a few moments, lantern raised high; a voice called softly from the tiny room which Phemie now shared with Esther.

"Scipio! Scipio . . . Sister's not back yet. I can't be easy. She'd not stay away . . . not with Millie the way she is."

Scipio came to stand under her window.

"Think I'll go get me a horse, Miss Esther."

Esther did not answer at once and when she did it was rather doubtfully.

"Maggie's been talkin' to me . . . Scipio, I'm thinkin' the best thing you could do is rouse them up at the camp. You don't know the way she'll be comin' and no more do I. And from what I was hearin' they might be wantin' to hear was there anything the matter."

It must have been just about the time when Scipio was explaining his errand to a sympathetic sentry on the main gate of the fort (he had made one of the building party) that Phemie reached the bank of the creek. Behind the scudding cloud there was a moon and by the faint light she could see the water running smoothly and powerfully, streaked with yeasty foam and more than three times as wide as the stream she had crossed so easily in the morning. The wind blew the rain in her face and she clutched her heavy cloak miserably round her. There was seven miles of rough going behind her to Pinner's Level and there seven people and a dead child shared a cabin fourteen feet by eleven. Once across the creek it would be less than a mile to the old Finnegan place where she and the horse could at least shelter from the wind. They might even be able to sleep . . . the thought made her yearn to close her eyes. The ford was clearly marked with larch poles on each bank. She considered the position and decided to wait for a while. The rain was easing and it was possible that the creek would go down as fast as it had risen. Finding a sheltered spot among a tumble of boulders she slid off the weary horse and eased his girth.

As it happened the creek did not go down. High in the mountain which fed the creek the rain was as heavy as ever. After an hour Phemie realised that it was actually rising, not falling, and if she was going to cross at all it would have to be at once. The alternative was to try to find a crossing elsewhere. Upstream, as far as she knew, was a trackless forest and bear country. Phemie's vivid memory of the tragically mutilated child whose death she had been unable to prevent made her reluctant to attempt a journey through it in the dark. Downstream the nearest crossing was the cattletrail, more than twenty miles away and there the river spread over treacherous flats with quicksands and unexpected deep gullies.

It was the thought of Millie's arm which decided her. To die of blood-poisoning was a cruel death. She pulled off the voluminous cloak and rolled it into a bundle which could be fastened across the saddle-bow and might protect the instruments in the bag. The rock under which she had been sitting made a convenient mounting block. The Mister moved obediently to the larch poles but was understandably reluctant to enter the torrent. Phemie was too small to use her boot heels effectively and she never wore spurs, because they tore her dresses. Hitting the beast only hurt her hand and she had neither crop nor switch. She tried everything she knew to make him go in including a blast of language which would have made Mrs Wardroper faint. She was just going to back him away from the water in order to wrench off a withy from the bushes to use as a persuader when something—Phemie was never to be quite certain that it was a bear—decided 'Mr McCorquodale' to cross in a hurry. He plunged wildly and blindly into the water, jerking his rider off her balance. Almost at once he found himself out of his depth and swimming frantically: at the same instant Phemie discovered she had made a serious error. The saddle girth was still loose. The saddle slipped round under the Mister's belly and all but took its occupant with it. Phemie kicked her boot clear of the iron just in time but lost the rein in her panic and was swept downstream away from the horse, choking and spluttering in the savage water and wondering in some calm remote corner of her mind whether this wild wet darkness was the last she would know of living and where her sodden corpse would be washed up at last.

Captain Devayler, roused cursing from his bed, reckoned (correctly) that the woman he knew would try to cross the river. "She's fool enough," was how he phrased it to the detail waiting for him outside headquarters and they regarded him with totally expressionless faces; but he overestimated her knowledge of the area and did not take the bears into consideration. He selected Sergeant Romanes and five of the strongest men in the camp, and gave them a length of thick rope. Thinking that Phemie would have made for the crossing upstream he ordered the detail to make their way up the bank of the creek (as far as this was possible) looking out for Phemie and her horse on the way. He himself kept one of the lanterns and stayed by the main ford in case Phemie had not yet arrived, in which case he intended to give her a piece of his mind. He had a coil of rope on his saddle. After one glance at the angry water in the faint lanternlight it did not occur to him to search downstream.

The detail had vanished into the darkness and Devayler had been waiting by the ford and getting colder and angrier for about half an hour when he heard hooves plodding through the bushes not far from the trail on the downstream side. He turned his trooper abruptly and cantered towards the sound, lantern held high. What he saw was not reassuring. The Mister was riderless, his head was drooping with exhaustion and he was trailing a broken rein. The saddle hung under his belly and a broken branch was snagged in one of the irons. Blood trickled down over a white stocking from a nasty gash. Devayler stared at this sight, his face grim. He dismounted, caught the weary beast and cut the sodden girths to rid him of the saddle. The Mister then began to plod his way along the trail to the town. Devayler examined the saddle to see if he could find any clue to Phemie's fate. He found the cloak and the instrument bag still securely fastened to the horn and he swore viciously. It was fairly plain that on a night like that no one in their senses would remove a warm cloak unless they intended . . . He stood up and remounted. Slowly he began to ride down the bank of the creek, waving the lantern and shouting from time to time.

10

THE INSIDE OF THE stage was both cold and stuffy. Kellow Pike by
dint of sleeping in his clothes had managed to get a corner seat
and was asleep, his mouth lolling open to display broken and
discoloured teeth. The seat opposite was crammed with mail-
bags leaving room for only two more passengers. The woman in
the other corner was dressed in deepest mourning, sombre but
noticeably becoming to a well-made woman with large brown
eyes and biscuit coloured hair. She leaned her cheek upon an
expensively gloved hand and gazed forgivingly upon the un-
civilised landscape. The third passenger sat bolt upright between his more fortunate companions, his arms folded across
his chest and nothing to look at but the bulging mail-bags. The
stage rattled, creaked and bumped over the trail. Occasionally
the driver could be heard to address his team in terms of
affectionate and blasphemous opprobrium and the figure in
black would wince slightly. Pike snored in succulent fashion.

The sun was well clear of the horizon when the stage clattered
down the bank to the ford and splashed through the swollen
creek, the muddy water coming nearly to the floor-boards. At
the far side the driver vented a blast of exhortation at the team
which scrambled desperately up the treacherous bank; the stage
tilted violently backwards deluging the passengers with mail-
bags. By the time these had been restacked on the forward seat
the early morning silence had been broken. Kellow Pike introduced himself as a 'business man from our flourishing town
ship'. The elegant bereaved admitted to Virginian origins

(which declared themselves without admission) but shook her head mysteriously when Pike enquired her errand to Argentana. The third passenger asked if it were true that there was a hospital in the town and Pike gave him a knowing look.

"Doc Parsons?" he suggested.

Evan agreed, slightly startled by this apparent omniscience.

"Got a letter in your pocket from Mayor Barstowe, I guess."

"Yes."

"I writ that," announced Pike and held out a grimy hand. Evan shook it and again enquired about the hospital. Pike shrugged.

"Sure, there's a shack they calls a hospital. Dunno that it'll be much use to you."

"Who runs it?" asked Evan, rather consciously, adding, "I was under the impression that there was no other medical man."

"Ain't nobody barrin' Doc Biedermeyer an' his Snake Ile. Hospital's run by a passel o' no'count wimmen an' a negro."

He left his uninteresting subject and launched into a eulogy of Argentana in which it appeared as a kind of Promised Land for budding doctors. The stage rattled monotonously along and Evan wondered how Phemie took to being a no'count woman. He felt uneasy about her.

He was not alone. At the Lincoln Memorial Hospital Maggie and Esther conferred with Scipio about Millie.

"If it's no taen aff she'll dee," declared Maggie. "I cannae dae it an' nae mair can Esther."

"Nor I," admitted Scipio, "and the surgeon for the camp has not yet come."

Esther turned round from her post at the window where she was watching the road. "Where can she have got to?"

"She kent fine that this was likely tae happen," said Maggie sombrely. "She'd be here if she could . . . I doubt she's . . . I doubt she cannae . . ."

Esther burst into tears. Maggie rose and sighed.

"Best dae whit we can, lassie. Phemie'll mebbe come yet. Born tae be hangit, yon lassie."

186

However, hope waned when the detail returned soon after ten and delivered a weary 'Mr McCorquodale' to his stable. They had overtaken the beast plodding home, they explained and dumped a sodden lump of leather on the porch. Sergeant Romanes explained how they had come on the saddle when he and the detail had reached the ford. They had looked for traces of Phemie and the Captain for more than three miles below the ford but come on nothing. They did not say in so many words that they believed they must have been drowned but it was clear that they thought so.

"Got to get back and report," said Romanes heavily. "Let you have any news we get . . ."

They rode along the street towards the fort and passed the stage squelching through the morass which had resulted from the rain. By now the arrival of the stage was a familiar event and few people took much notice of it. Pike dismounted first and picked his way through the dirt to the boardwalk like an alley-cat, leaving Evan to cope with the problem posed by the sea of mud and their black clad companion who looked at it horrified from the doorway of the stage. She consented graciously to be carried to the door of the Nugget and once there silently expected Evan in his low shoes to do the same by her numerous bags and bandboxes. Pike, bored by this, moved away.

"Barstowe wants to see you, Doc. Come to the bank when ye're done doin' the little gent."

Among a kind of ponderous and reluctant chivalry which the widow appeared to be able to evoke from most males at a glance she became the star guest at the Nugget. With studied Southern courtesy she turned to thank Evan for his services but was a little put out to discover he had gone. His shoes filled past the uppers with mud he had gone back to the stage to get his own baggage and noticed the hospital name board. He splashed his way across to the porch, wondered briefly about the battered saddle lying there and knocked on the door. It was opened almost at once by Scipio who looked worried and distracted.

"Sister Witherspoon?" asked Evan. "Is she here?"

Scipio swallowed hard and shook his head and as he did he saw the unmistakable doctor's bag in Evan's hand. He looked at the visitor eagerly.

"Sir, are you by any happy chance a medical man?"

"My name's Parsons, Doctor Parsons . . ."

"Come in, sir . . . come in . . ." He drew Evan into the narrow vestibule.

"We have a case urgently needing your attention."

He opened the door of the Female Ward. "Ladies," he announced, and his voice had the ring of one who bore news, "*Doctor* Parsons."

Later Evan was to reflect that this was the most eventful day in his life. Before he had time to draw breath (or even change his muddy shoes) he was laying out his instruments for an overdue amputation and curbing Maggie's generosity with the ether which she was pouring rather than dripping into the funnel over Millie's face. The face and voice of the Professor at St Thomas's returned to him; ". . . it is to be hoped, Doctor Parsons that experience will be able to teach you more than I seem to have done . . ."

Not until the operation was over did he hear of their fears for Phemie and he had not quite taken in the news when a horse was ridden up to the porch steps at a dead run and someone hammered on the door yelling for Sister Phemie. It turned out that three somewhat battered miners were following on in a buckboard to be patched up after a damaging encounter with some carelessly handled dynamite. By mid-afternoon he was still bandaging and stitching and Scipio suggested that he should go across to the Nugget and book a room.

Over there the big negro found the whole place in an uproar. Evan's fellow-passenger was having a fit of hysterics on the bottom step of the staircase. The staff of the Nugget, being wholly male, was standing unhappily around at a respectful distance making helpful suggestions such as, "Fetch a glass of water", or "Don't you take on so, ma'am!" or "Why don't someone cut her staylace . . ." which last was ill received by all present. Jenkins who could cope decisively with commonplaces such as knifings and gun fights and gougings was standing behind the desk looking thoroughly put out and undecided. The huge blue rosette on his lapel which proclaimed him to be JENKINS THE MAN WHO WILL *ACT* seemed a trifle inappropriate.

Scipio dumped Evan's bag in the lobby and regarded the scene with some amusement.

"Doctor Parsons would like to engage a room for the next week or two," he announced in tones which pierced the hubbub.

Jenkins's air of gloom lightened.

"He would be very welcome, indeed he would!" said he. "In fact I wish he would come just as soon as he can!"

Evan, his confidence reinforced by the events of the day took hysterics in his stride. A firm voice, sal volatile and a promise of cold water externally applied and his patient's high pitched cries and sobs gradually diminished. She blinked at him miserably, dabbing her eyes with a rose-scented handkerchief.

"You see . . . I am quite alone now . . ." she told him and made a convulsive little sound which he suspected of being a hiccough. "I have not a soul left in the world . . . not a soul. Oh, Doctor . . . it is a lowering situation for a woman to find herself quite, quite alone . . ."

"Doctor!" Eli was beckoning to him from the desk.

"I am so sorry to cause all this commotion," she confided apologetically, "but it was such a shock . . . to hear such distressing news shouted out in the public saloon . . ."

The tears welled up again. Evan passed the smelling bottle under her nose and supported her to a chair.

"If you would excuse me for one moment, ma'am . . ."

At the desk Jenkins gave him a key.

"Room Eight," he said. "Doc Stevenson's old room. Guess if you look real hard you'll find a bottle or two hid there yet."

Back at the hospital there was time to draw breath. Millie was very weak but seemed to be drowsy and comfortable. The miners were bedded down on palliasses on the floor in the Male

Ward. The patients were all fed and tidied and Scipio summoned the staff of the hospital to a meal in the kitchen. There was time then to explain something of the situation to the newcomer.

"This chap who seems to have gone after Phemie . . . did you say his name was Devayler?"

Maggie nodded.

"That's the name above mine on the register across the road. Mrs Violette Devayler."

Maggie grunted. "Wonder how Phemie'd hae heard that news . . . puir lassie. It's in my mind she'd a notion o' the man."

Esther burst into tears again and Evan, who in England had obstinately measured his mother's selection of sonsy Hampshire maidens against his recollections of Phemie and found them wanting, found that this suggestion moved him less than the sight of Esther's distress. Such fickleness appalled him but did not prevent his putting out a large hand to pat Esther's shoulder comfortingly.

"Och . . . ." sighed Maggie, rising to go home, "she'll be a sair miss richt eneuch, will Phemie . . . But we'll no let her doon ower the heid o' this place, so we'll no . . . Whit for dae we no cry the hospital the Euphemia Witherspoon Memorial . . . I've nae notion o' politicians . . . fushionless bodies . . ."

However, this motion, appropriate as it might have been, was never to be discussed. Just as darkness began to fall an excited hubbub could be heard at the far end of the street. At first no one in the hospital took much notice for, with the election drawing near, meetings official and unofficial had become a regular occurrence. This meeting, however, appeared to be mobile for it came nearer and nearer. Processions in the town were not yet a commonplace and folk moved to their windows to watch. It was not an organised procession, just a crowd of excited, shouting people crowded round a single lame and weary horse, waving their hats for joy and firing questions at the man who was leading it. On its back wrapped in a cavalry cloak, her usually well-disciplined hair hanging in elf-locks about her face, but as upright as ever, sat Phemie. From every side people ran out to

190

squelch through the mud and shout their pleasure and relief that both were safe.

At the door of the hospital Devayler lifted Phemie down and handed her over to Esther and Scipio. They received her with huge delight and Scipio raised his arms high. With the accents of his childhood breaking irresistibly through subsequent sophistication he declared:

"De Lawd be thanked fo' all He mercies!"

Whereat the crowd responded with a heartfelt "Amen!"

Devayler refused to come inside, explaining that he must discover what had become of his detail. He accepted his cloak back from Phemie who by removing it revealed that she was wearing an army shirt many times too large for her in place of her usual trimly fitted bodice. He moved off towards the camp leading his horse and still attended by a few curious spirits. The rest of the crowd began to return home exclaiming over the ways of Providence. As Devayler passed in front of the Nugget he paused to refuse the pressing invitation of some people to have a drink to warm him up. As he paused a shrill outcry echoed from the window of the best bedroom.

"He is safe! He is safe! Thank God!"

Startled, he peered up at the window but it was empty. The doors of the saloon swung open and an elegant blackclad figure stood there, arms outstretched, haloed by the light from Eli's new kerosene lamps.

"Louis!" she cried. "Louis, my darling! Thank God you're alive!"

After which and with her hand pressed hard to her silken bosom she collapsed in a heap just inside the door (the boardwalk was really very muddy).

"Violette!" exclaimed Devayler and he sounded more exasperated than gratified at such a reception. He thrust the bridle into someone's hand and strode up the steps.

Phemie, who had been besieged by congratulations and questions on the hospital porch and prevented from going inside at once, saw this touching scene with astonishment . . . and another emotion which she was at a loss to recognise.

191

"His wife, seemingly," explained Esther and turned her round to face the door, "and here's an old friend of yours—all the way from England, so he tells me."

Evan blushed.

"You might recall . . ." he mumbled, ". . . on the *Indiana*. I did suggest that I might come out. I hope you don't object to my arriving without warning."

Phemie considered the enormous and self-conscious figure in front of her and gave a curious strangled little laugh. For the first time she realised what he had been saying when she ship's siren blew. Holding out her hand she said:

"Evan Parsons, my *good* friend. *How* pleased they must have been when you arrived. Tell me, how is Millie?"

Esther following them inside hardly knew whether to be relieved or disappointed at such a greeting.

Later that night Phemie gave them a brief account of what had happend.

"The Mister must have scrambled out somehow but I got swept away . . ."

She paused.

"Can ye swim at all?" asked Esther faintly.

"Not a stroke. My skirts were full of air and that held me up for a bit. There was a log jammed across the creek and I hit that. I hung on and hauled myself along to the bank. But I couldn't get up—it was too steep."

"What did you do?"

"Prayed that the log would hold till morning. But it soon began to grind and shift. The water was rising all the time."

"How long were you there before you heard Devayler?" asked Evan.

"I don't know . . . it felt like a lifetime. I could hardly hold on, it was so cold . . ."

She spread out her hands and examined the tips which were scraped and raw.

"I heard him shouting," she said at last, "I yelled back."

She giggled suddenly. "I've never heard anyone sound so surprised."

The last thing Lee Devayler had expected to hear was an answering shout. At the sight of the Mister he had given Phemie up for dead and his search was no more than a despairing gesture. After he located her he moved fast. The rope on his saddle already had a standing bowline tied in one end and he tied the other to a tree. Then he took the bowline in his hand and crawled to the edge to drop it down . . .

"The bank had been dropping clods and pebbles on me for a time," said Phemie, "so I had guessed it was rotten and undercut. I yelled for him to get back. He told me to hold my tongue and get my arms through the loop. I managed that. Then he shouted that he was going to haul me up and a great lump of the bank came down and landed beside me in the water . . . I thought it was him . . ."

She sipped at the coffee in the mug.

"It wasn't . . . he'd got back in time and he shouted for me to hang on and he'd have me out of there in no time. Just then the log gave way . . ."

Her listeners stirred uncomfortably.

". . . it lifted, rolled half over, lurched and away it went and me with it . . ."

Esther gave a little squeak of dismay.

"My dress was caught on the stump of a branch . . ."

Phemie put her hand on her left side to show where the snag had caught her and Evan put out his hand to calm Esther. Phemie didn't miss the gesture.

"It was a good strong rope," she observed, "and it was a heavy log. Something had to go and it was my dress. My bodice just ripped away. All that was left was one sleeve and a bit of the back."

"What happened then?" asked Scipio.

"Devayler hauled me in like a salmon. The slide had made the bank easier to climb so I could scramble out. After that . . ."

She frowned.

"It's not very clear . . . I was so cold and tired and heavy . . . with the water, you know. I remember sitting in front of a fire in the old Finnegan place and then waking up this morning . . ."

"How did you miss the detail?"

"They must have passed the cabin while we were still asleep and the fire would be low so there was no smoke. And I don't suppose they really expected to see anyone. Then when we did start home, Lee's . . . Devayler's horse went lame. That was a little difficult because I'd lost my shoes in the creek but he said I didn't weight as much as the saddle and made me ride. And that's about all. The worst of it was wondering what had become of Millie. Thank heaven you arrived in time, Evan."

"Oh, yes!" agreed Esther fervently, "I made sure she was going to die . . ."

"She's not out of the wood yet," said Evan.

"True," admitted Phemie, "but at least she's a chance now."

If she was aware that her account had left a number of questions in her listeners' minds she gave no sign of it, and even if they had asked those questions she was not prepared to answer them all. She undressed wearily, unbuttoning the coarse woollen shirt and wondering as she examined her many scratches and bruises just how she had come to be wearing it. Her memories of the previous night were vague and patchy after she had arrived shivering and exhausted at the top of the bank. Lee . . . Captain Devayler had wrapped her in his cloak and put her on the horse in front of him. She remembered gratefully how his warmth had penetrated to her back.

In the old Finnegan place she remembered nothing but the warmth and the light and an overpowering need to sleep. Sleep she had, waking in the grey light of morning to a consciousness of buttons pressing into her back and a heavy arm lying across her waist. Devayler, lacking any blanket but his own cloak had kept her warm in the only possible way. The fire was smouldering among a cloud of white ash and round it on the rope which had pulled her out of the creek were suspended every garment she had been wearing when she set out for Pinner's Level: her skirt, torn and mud-stained, two petticoats, one flannel and one cotton (lacking a flounce once used as a bandage), her linen pantalettes, her knitted woollen stockings and the rag which had

194

been a chemise . . . every last one. A startled exploration revealed that she was wearing one voluminous and scratchy garment which could be nothing but an army shirt. Resolutely she had closed her mind to precisely how she had come to be wearing it, but a certain consciousness had quelled conversation during that wearisome trail home.

Phemie pulled up the blankets and relaxed, waiting for Esther to bring her a promised hot drink. She reflected that she ought to be feeling glad to be alive; glad and grateful. Instead she felt unhappy and depressed. Firmly she told herself that things were sure to feel differently in the morning, but however firm she was she knew without the slightest doubt that her depression was not due to her exhaustion and shock. It was due to three things. Lee Devayler's decision to leave the army was the first: he had told her this over the biscuit they had shared at noon. It had been at that point she had summoned up the courage to thank him for coming to the rescue again.

". . . it is coming to be a habit with you," she had said.

"You'll have to be more careful in future," he replied, "I'll be away from the army in two months' time."

It was as if the earth shifted underneath her and it took all her self-control to say casually, "You'll be returning East, I presume."

"May do," he said. "Depends."

The second thing was to see Lee . . . Captain Devayler vanish into the Nugget. She remembered Sergeant Smith's gossiping tale and realised that the widow was probably Lee's sister-in-law. If the brother were dead that would be reason enough for Lee to leave the army . . . though possibly not for his widow to come West. She felt uneasy and that was perfectly ridiculous. She turned over and thumped her chaff pillow. As for the third thing, in the circumstances (and she did not quite define these 'circumstances') it was perfectly infantile to feel bereft because Evan had patted Esther's hand. While she was busily trying to avoid thinking about any of these things sleep surprised her, so that when Esther came in with a cup of beef tea on a wicker-work tray and a pile of letters from Europe she found Phemie asleep, frowning ferociously and with one clenched fist flung outside the bedclothes.

In the morning things did seem different. For one thing as she resumed the hospital routine her own vague unhappiness appeared very trivial beside Millie's bravely concealed concern about a one-armed future and Billy Quinn's lack of any future at all. By midday her adventure had begun to seem unreal like a nightmare. Evan rode off to attend to the calls that afternoon and Phemie took time off to read and reply to her letters. This she did in the warm bread smelling kitchen. There was a letter from Adela Pedersen: three pages in her laboriously elaborate handwriting much of which was devoted to questions about Phemie's welfare. Only at the end did she give news of herself:

> . . . we have school every morning, and Olaf makes the boys mind me and learn their letters. Ulla has become my friend and helps me very much. I love her dearly because she makes me think of you; she has the same quick im patient way with her . . .

Phemie knew a pang of guilt and remorse as she turned the page remembering the many times she had been made impatient by poor Adela.

> . . . in the New Year we are to have a new baby and if she is a girl Olaf and I are agreed she must be Phemie and we hope that you will stand godmother. I am so well and happy, Phemie, and Olaf is kind and good. I have never regretted leaving the train . . . only that I had to leave you . . .

Phemie scribbled a letter of congratulations, sent a kind message to Ulla and turned to the letter from Frank Dinwoodie, her brother-in law. He reported on the welfare of her sister and her two nephews; mentioned that Neil Linklater had married Miss Deuchars 'at last' (an obstinate man, Neil, reflected his ex-fiancée) and the wedding had been sumptuous. She skipped through the list of Glasgow worthies who had attended and came to the meat of the matter. Frank reported with a kind of reluctant enthusiasm on the progress of the Blackburn Colliery in which Phemie was now a substantial shareholder. He described the sums which were accumulating in the bank for her tocher and how he and his fellow trustee were investing them. Phemie laughed aloud—it must be dust and ashes in the mouth of Neil Linklater to be engaged in such an enterprise. The last paragraph was a plea to Phemie to come home like a sensible girl and buy herself a nice husband:

> . . . let me assure you, my dear sister, that you are become a most eligible parti . . . quite a 'catch' upon my word . . .

Phemie grunted: he made her feel like a pig or a fowl being fattened for the market.

> . . . if only you would abandon this eccentric nursing work and come home I am sure that you would be settled in a very short time . . .

'I believe you,' thought Phemie.

> . . . believe me, my dear, your most affectionate brother Frank.
> Post scriptum: we are in daily expectation of a new addition to our little family. We are quite decided, Jean and I, that if she should prove to be a girl she shall be Euphemia.

At this coincidence Phemie laughed aloud and reflected that her lamentable name was in a fair way to being perpetuated.

Miss Nightingale replied at affectionate and helpful length to a letter written some months earlier when Phemie had been all but single handed. It concluded with a warning about the dangers of overworking, citing her own invalidish habit as an example. Phemie laid the letter before her and sharpened her pen ready to answer. She considered that Miss Nightingale got through more work as an invalid than any six ordinary healthy people. She dipped her pen and began with the usual salutations and thanks:

> . . . matters have improved considerably. I have a new recruit to the nursing side and Scipio Beauregard of whom I have written before and who is a whole domestic staff in himself. Mattie the half-breed is studying to learn to read and will come to me when she can. Not only that but yesterday Doctor Parsons (perhaps you recall that he trained at St Thomas's) arrived, hoping to set up practice in the town. It could be said that he achieved this within twenty mintues of his arrival.
>
> In the circumstances I feel justified in making plans for . . .

She had reached this point when Scipio at his most superior ushered in the shabby figure of Kellow Pike.

"This person wishes to see you, Miss Phemie, ma'am. He says his business is important."

Phemie choked down a laugh and looked at 'this person'. Scipio considered him with evident distaste and returned to the door.

"I will be within call, Miss Phemie, ma'am," he informed her.

He closed the door with all the aplomb of a superior upper servant.

"That big black needs teachin' a lesson," said Pike indignantly. "You let them blacks get above theirselves and you got trouble. Easy seen you don't know blacks."

Phemie felt the back of her neck prickle and took a firm grip on her temper.

"Please sit down, Mr er . . . er . . ."

It didn't soothe her feelings to see that he had anticipated her permission.

"Name's Pike—Kellow Pike."

Phemie remained standing.

"How may I help you, Mr Pike?"

"Boot's on t'other foot, gal . . . I aim to help you."

"Indeed?" said Phemie sweetly. "You surprise me."

"Yeah . . . I aim to take this place right offa your pretty little hands."

Those same hands clenched on the back of a chair.

"I beg your pardon."

"Granted. You heard me, gal . . . I'm a-goin' to take over."

Phemie regarded him incredulously.

"I take it you are drunk, Mr Pike?"

"Guess not."

He produced a cigar in the manner of his patron, bit off the end and spat it into the linen basket.

"You got nine hunder' dollars?" he enquired.

"You must be well aware I have not."

"Then I take over. Simple."

He leaned over to light his cigar at the candle. Phemie considered him as if he were a very poor specimen.

"Please explain yourself."

By way of an answer he flung a sheet of paper across the table.

"McDowall he raised nine hunder' dollars in Abilene for to start the *Argus* and he used this lot you built on for collateral. I paid the folks in Abilene their money. Less'n you pay me nine hunder' dollars this lot's mine. You ain't got it, you get out, see?"

Phemie read the paper carefully and as far as she could tell it seemed to be in order. She folded it and looked at her visitor who had tilted the chair back on its back legs and was watching her arrogantly through wreaths of smoke.

"And what do you plan to do with a hospital?"

"This shack! Tear it down. I aim to build me a saloon. Got the plans right here." He tapped his chest. "Pillars in front and a balcony—real classy. Chandleers and red plush curtains . . ."

199

"Restrain yourself, Mr Pike, and don't count your pillars before the hospital is demolished, because I promise you you'll do that only over my dead body."

She glared at him.

"Price is nine hunder' dollars," repeated Pike. "Less'n you pay inside of a week the sheriff'll put you an' your trash out on the street. Dead body or no dead body."

He blew a smoke wreath right into her angry face. Phemie's grip on her temper slipped.

"Put that out!" she ordered unceremoniously.

"Guess I won't . . . leavin' in a spell."

Without a word she dragged the stinking weed out of his mouth and dropped it into the pig bucket.

"Out!" she said. "Get out. This is a hospital not a house of ill repute—not yet . . ."

Pike stared at her much aggrieved.

"I thought you was a lady."

"Did you now," Phemie bit out. "Well, I would never have taken you for a gentleman. Out! Come for your money in a week but don't come your footlength inside our gates before that time or you'll spend longer in here than you like. Now take your unwashed, unshaved, unpleasant person out of here before I call Mr Beauregard to throw you out."

"Mr Beauregard," sneered Pike.

All the same he condescended to get slowly to his feet. Phemie finally lost her temper and with a quick swipe she knocked off his greasy hat and kicked it over to the door. This gesture seemed to enrage Pike for he turned on Phemie snarling and raised his hand.

"Why you . . ."

The kitchen door swung open with a crash and Scipio stood there filling the frame as full as a box with a doll in it.

"You want me, Miss Phemie, ma'am?"

"Please see this person off the premises. See him right off and fast."

Scipio picked up the maltreated hat and placed it on its owner's head. He appeared to expect that there might be a chance of its falling off again because he pulled it right down over Pike's eyes. He then took a handful of the cheap jacket and left the room with the unwelcome visitor dangling from his fingers and protesting blasphemously and obscenely.

When her heart stopped thumping Phemie began to think. She caught sight of a phrase in her interrupted letter to Miss Nightingale, '. . . matters have improved considerably . . .' Improved! And she had exactly a week to find nine hundred dollars. She sat down and put her head on the table. For a few seconds she was sorely tempted to give up, to forget the whole project, leave on the next stage . . . she was tired to the very bones. Scipio came back and she sat up and looked at him. He did not even pretend he had not been listening.

"Where will you get it, Miss Phemie?"

"I don't know," she replied. "I don't know. But somehow we must."

"You could borrow it?"

"On what security? How could we ever pay it back? And there'd be the interest. Besides . . . who would I ask? Barstowe? He's behind this man Pike."

"Could you raise it in the town like the money for the building?"

She shook her head.

"They've shot their bolt for a while. There just isn't the money in the town."

"The mines?"

"They might let me have it, I suppose, but . . ." She shrugged. ". . . by the time they've sent the request to head office and it's gone all round the directors either the answer will be 'no' or it'll be too late."

They sat in silence for a moment and then Phemie sighed and got up.

"I can't settle to writing somehow. I'll go over and help Maggie with the dressings. Meanwhile, if you think of anything . . . anything legal that is . . ."

She stopped suddenly reminded of Frank Dinwoodie and the letter she had had from him.

201

"Scipio! I believe I *have* thought of something. Look at this!"

She thrust the lawyer's letter at him.

"I'm a wealthy woman, Scipio . . . once I'm married. And if I was married I could borrow on the strength of this letter, couldn't I? I could borrow even if I were just engaged."

Scipio stared at her.

"Now . . ." said Phemie. "Who'd be game to marry me?"

Two hours later a council of war was being held around that same table. Outside Mayor Barstowe's supporters were conducting a noisy torchlight procession. Inside Esther was protesting angrily at Phemie's decision.

"Marriage is important," she declared, "you can't go and marry yourself for the sake of a pile of lumber—it wouldn't be right . . ."

"It isn't just a pile of lumber," Phemie told her, "and you know that perfectly well. It's a place for Millie to recover . . . and she'd be dead in that unspeakable hovel of hers if it wasn't for the hospital. Granny's warm and comfortable here and she'd be a disregarded nuisance in Bob Bulmer's. And if they turn us out next week where will Billy Quinn go to die? The bank? For the love of heaven," she added scornfully, "people die for things, live for things, beggar themselves for things, why can't I marry for something?"

"It's not the same," persisted Esther. "For one thing it's two people . . . if you see what I'm at . . ."

"I wouldn't force anyone to marry me."

"Wi' a tocher the like o' that you'll not need tae," Maggie put in.

"And marriage goes on and on . . . it isn't just a single thing like dying . . ."

"This marriage would be on my terms," declared Phemie, "or it won't be any use to us."

Maggie intervened again. "This is a' haivers," she said impatiently. "Phemie ye're no wyce. Ye cannae marry on any Tom, Dick or Harry in this toon because the hauf o' them's here tae get awa' frae their wives. And Eli Jenkins kens that fine . . .

202

he'd no lend ye a penny if ye tak' ane o' thae scallawags."

"But there are decent men in the town . . . I don't have to marry a scallawag."

"But they're needin' *wives*. They'll no hae you on yon terms. Wha'd wish tae be merriet and get naethin' but a poochfu' o' siller an' a cauld hearth."

At this point Evan swallowed hard and carefully avoiding Esther's gaze rumbled out that he had offered for Phemie before and would be happy to offer again on any terms she cared to name. Before Phemie could reply to this Maggie turned on him.

"Ye tumphie! Phemie mebbe hasnae the sense she wis born wi' crossin' burns in spate, but she's nae fule, an' even a naitrel could see ye makin' yer sheep's eyes at Esther. Haud yer wheesht."

Evan blushed to the roots of his hair and relapsed into silence: Esther gabbled out an incoherent excuse about having to read to Millie and fled from the room.

"Ah, well . . ." said Phemie. "Are you married, Scipio?"

"No, ma'am. And I would be happy to oblige you in this matter were it not for two objections. The first is that someday I hope to meet the mother of my five children and marry her."

His listeners gasped.

"She was sold into Carolina just before the war," he explained, "and the three youngest went with her. I enquired about her and she was said to have come West."

"And the second?" asked Evan to break the silence which this glimpse into slavery had evoked. The answer gave them an even grimmer view.

"Argentana is full of Southerners . . . if I married you I'd be dangling at the end of a rope in no time at all."

"That's the truth," agreed Maggie.

"I am aware, ma'am," Scipio continued solemnly, "that to be a wealthy widow would suit you excellently. And I am anxious to oblige you in most things but I must draw the line somewhere and at hanging, ma'am, I draw it."

"In fact," said Phemie, "what you are both trying to tell me is that only a fool or a saint would marry me. Evan isn't a fool and you won't let him make one of himself and the only saint in the territory doesn't wish to be a martyr. Where do we go from here?''

Just then Esther came back into the room.

"Captain Devayler wants a word with you, Phemie.''

Devayler looked uncharacteristically flustered. He thrust his hat on to the dresser and sketched a bow.

"Phemie . . . Miss Witherspoon . . . may I have a word with you in private.''

"If you wish,'' Phemie told him, a little bewildered, and turned to the others who had already got up. "Would you mind? I am sure the Captain won't be long.''

Devayler closed the door behind them and turned to Phemie. He cleared his throat and then moved restlessly about the kitchen fingering the pots and pans.

"I expect you've heard,'' he remarked at last, "my sister-in-law has arrived in the town. My brother is dead. The estate is left to me. There are no children, you see.''

He hesitated and rasped his thumb down his jaw, a trick he had when he was embarrassed.

"She . . . she wants to marry me,'' he blurted out at last.

"She has made that moderately obvious,'' said Phemie carefully. "Am I to offer my congratulations?''

Devayler gave her a look compounded of scorn and irritation.

"I don't want to marry her. I don't want anything to do with her. I never want to see her again.''

"You had best tell *her* that.''

"It is not easy to convince her,'' he groaned, "you see, there was a time when I . . .''

"I know . . .'' said Phemie, "she was engaged to you once.''

He stared. "How in tarnation did you get to hear that?''

Phemie raised her eyebrows. "I cannot recall.''

He moved restlessly away. "I can't imagine how I could . . . I can't bear the sight of her now . . .''

Phemie sat down and folded her hands in her lap. "Captain, I sympathise with you in what must be a most embarrassing predicament but I fail to see what it has to do with me.''

204

He swallowed hard and rasped at his jaw again. "Because, ma'am, I informed her tonight that as you and I had passed a night together quite unchaperoned, your reputation would be bound to suffer and that I was in honour bound to marry you."

He looked imploringly at her. "I would be much obliged . . . most deeply obliged, Phemie, if you would support this story by becoming betrothed to me."

Her hands gripped together in her lap and she stared at him as if she had never seen him before. Then she began to laugh and he grinned reluctantly.

"Fair's fair," he pointed out, "I've come to your aid before this."

"I'll strike a bargain with you," Phemie told him breathlessly, "I'll be betrothed to *you* . . . if you will be so good as to marry *me*. It's a fairly usual arrangement I understand."

11

Argentana Argus: December.

. . . Our little community will be pleased if not surprised to read that two of our number have decided to enter the ranks of Hymen: Sister Witherspoon and her Gallant Rescuer Captain Louis Devayler of the U.S. Cavalry announce their betrothal in this issue. We are sure that we speak for all when we wish the happy couple every felicity. While we will miss the indefatigable Sister Witherspoon and her work among us, Doctor Parsons has demonstrated that he can more than supply her place . . . as for the hospital, so-called, most of the sensible citizens will admit that it was a premature venture and we will do well to wait until the growth of the community (and grow it will under the proper leadership) warrants such a luxury . . .

PHEMIE FOLDED THE PAPER and went back into the wards. As she followed the morning routine she thought about that loaded little paragraph.

"Evidently Barstowe thinks that this is my way of saving my face," she commented to Maggie later.

"If that's whit he thinks he's in for a real surprise the morn's morn. Let's see where it says you an' him's tae be wed. Ken this, I never kent his name wis Louis."

Devayler had agreed to the scheme reluctantly. At first his reactions had been unpromising to say the least, for he did not think Phemie could be serious . . .

"This is *not* a subject for joking," he had snapped. "I realise that it is an . . . an . . . out-of-the-way request to make but . . ."

"Oh, do come off your high horse, Captain," Phemie had begged penitently, "and let me explain. You see I'm in a pickle of bother as well . . . real trouble this time."

He had regarded her grimly and sat down on the rocking. chair.

"The last two or three times being nothing but a trifle, I take it?"

"Well, compared to this it seems that way . . . and *not* my own fault this time. Listen . . ."

She had explained the predicament and shown him Frank's letter.

"I know it's a lot to ask but it's easier to be divorced in America," she ended. "I mean, I wouldn't make any difficulty. And your going away makes it easy. We can announce the engagement with all the noise we can make but keep the wedding a dark secret."

He frowned at that. "Why?"

"Because once you have gone and I stay behind people won't think it strange if we eventually decide that we don't suit. It does happen."

"True," he agreed.

"Meanwhile, as soon as Frank has proof of the wedding he must arrange to send me my tocher and I can repay Eli Jenkins."

"Does Eli know about this?"

"Not yet, but he's the only person who could possibly lend me the money. If he can't or won't it's all off anyway."

"I think I understand. Tell me," he demanded and rose to his feet, "aren't you taking rather a lot for granted? Once we are married what's to stop me holding on to all that money?"

"You," said Phemie succinctly.

"And what's to stop me holding on to you?"

Phemie gave him a scornful look.

"I've got a mirror," she told him and just then had a sudden thought which made her feel hot and cold. "Of course if you have . . . I mean you are so anxious not to be tied up to your sister in law . . . if there's someone you really want to marry, of course, there would be no question of . . ."

207

This obvious afterthought made Devayler smile rather grimly.

"There is . . ." he admitted.

"Well, then," said Phemie and tried not to look as downcast as she felt, "there's no more to be said . . ."

"I don't know about that," he observed. "To tell the truth she is not—so far as I can discover—in the same mind as me. It might take some considerable time to . . . press my suit, so to speak."

He smiled as if the thought of her amused him, and Phemie thought, not for the first time, how that rare smile changed his normally dour aspect.

"In the meantime and in consideration of our respective predicaments," he told her, "I would be prepared to consider your suggestion."

When Phemie with a pardonable degree of triumph had told the rest her news she was a little puzzled by their reaction which was a compound of amusement and what seemed to be satisfaction. Before the betrothal could be announced Jenkins was approached about the loan, and, shown Frank's letter, he agreed to lend the sum. The nine hundred dollars was now awaiting Pike's arrival tucked safely inside Phemie's bodice. In Jenkins's safe reposed a note of hand signed by both Phemie and Devayler. With this transaction completed the notice had gone to the paper with the results which Phemie had just read.

Prompt to his time Kellow Pike set out for the hospital. The announcement had convinced both him and his employer that the site was now to be theirs. They had celebrated this discreetly in the back room of the bank. The plans for the Ace of Clubs (this was the name which had captured their fancy) were now far advanced: with the stage that morning had gone orders to warehouses in the East for carpets, furniture and glasses, not to mention a parlour organ of the very latest design. And an order for one hundred cases of high quality whisky accompanied these more exotic requirements. Barstowe in an expansive mood had already approached Janie to see whether she might leave Jenkins and agree to run the 'entertainment' at the Ace.

208

Pike emerged into the first snow of the winter conscious of being on the verge of achieving his life's ambition, to run a high class saloon. He set a somewhat unsteady course for the Lincoln Memorial Hospital and decided to pace out the frontage so as to have some idea of the amount of lumber which would have to be ordered. He then crossed the street and permitted himself to envisage the wood and plaster splendours so soon to replace the workaday little building which stood there. He beamed at the sheepskin wrapped passers by as he visualised them thirstily besieging his pearl among saloons.

At last he recrossed the street and opened the gate. Scipio appeared at one side and Evan at the other; Scipio removed the cigar and Evan removed the hat and they escorted him to the top of the steps where Phemie waited with a pen, ink bottle and receipt form. Pike presented his note and was chagrined unbearably when Phemie drew out nine crisp hundred-dollar bills and counted them out into his hand. He signed the receipt sulkily and was rash enough to speculate on the methods which Phemie and Esther had employed to raise the money: it was not appreciated. He found himself sprawled in the slush of the street, his hat laid in front of his nose containing nine hundred dollars and a smouldering cigar. He scambled to his feet and with a sulphurous expression stumbled back to the bank where he got an unsympathetic reception from Barstowe who now found himself in the unenviable position of suffering defeat and paying for hundreds of dollars' worth of goods he had ordered. He would have been even less sympathetic if he had known that Janie, in gales of laughter, had reported both interviews to Eli Jenkins who struck his knee with his hand and exclaimed:

"That would be what she wanted nine hundred dollars for! I thought it would be for medicines and such. Why in tarnation didn't she say."

"Who?" asked Janie.

"Sister Phemie."

"Uh huh," Janie said, "I do think it's awful romantic her marryin' Captain Lee . . . after him rescuin' her an' all."

"Tell you one person don't think so," Eli confided, and he

jerked his head at the ceiling. "That one. Near enough took another conniption fit when she read the notice this morning."

"Shh!" hissed Janie. "She's comin' downstairs. Wonder what she's at. My, she's elegant, ain't she?"

Violette Devayler cat stepped her way through the slush and went in through the hospital gate. Janie and Eli looked at one another and Janie laughed.

"Wouldn' I like to be a fly on the wall over there! She won't get much change outa Sister Phemie, I lay."

If she could have been on the wall she would have seen the widow knock on the door and ask for Phemie through the folds of a heavy veil. When Esther (rather tartly) told her that Phemie was busy and unable to see anyone for an hour at least, Madame Devayler (as she preferred to be called, the Devaylers being an old French family originally called Duvailleur) replied in a faint voice that surely Sister Witherspoon could spare a few minutes for her unfortunate victim. Esther relayed this message to Phemie who was dressing Millie's stump and consequently in no mood to respond to such fustian stuff.

"Oh, show her into our room and tell her to wait," she said brusquely, ignoring Esther's giggles.

Madame, immured for over forty mintues in a tiny over-crowded room as cold as it was Spartan, found plenty to occupy her. She inspected the contents of the dressing table-cum desk and sought in vain for creams and powders, though she read Phemie's letters with a rapidly fading interest. All those she found were from women. The dresses hanging from nails in one corner were regarded with an incredulous scorn. The trunks, which apart from the table and the two crude cots were the only furniture, were opened and their meagre contents examined. When Phemie, her approach heralded by the clack of her heels on the bare wooden floor, came in, Madame was sitting on a trunk with the air of one hardly treated by the world but sustained by Christian fortitude . . . and her opening gambit was masterly. She gave Phemie a long penetrating stare and then:

"You do not look like a monster," she observed intensely.

Phemie stared and then her sense of humour stirred.

210

"No, ma'am?"

She examined herself anxiously in the scrap of looking glass.

"It could depend on one's point of view of course. I'd agree with you myself, but then I could be prejudiced."

Madame put back her veil.

"Strange," she observed sweetly, "strange how such a commonplace exterior can hide such depths of ingratitude and self ishness."

"Perhaps you wouldn't mind discussing my attributes in the kitchen. It's warmer there."

She led the way across the courtyard and installed Madame in the rocker.

"Now," said Phemie, "how may I help you?"

Madame leaned forward, took both her hands in her own and looked deeply into her eyes.

"How can you return evil for good?" she demanded in richly emotional tones. "You let a man save you from an awful death and repay him by trapping him into a travesty of a marriage. He risks his life to save yours and you repay him by dividing him from the one he loves and who loves him . . . for ever."

"Och, haivers!" responded Phemie briskly. "Away and try your cantrips on some other body. I've neither time nor patience to listen."

She went to the door.

"And it seems to me," she added, "that if you think anyone born of woman could make Lee Devayler do anything he didn't want to do, you don't know him as well as you'd have me believe."

Madame rose and her not inconsiderable bosom heaved with indignation.

"Have you the impertinence to tell me that Lee *wants* to marry you?" she asked in a resonant contralto.

Phemie's mouth twisted as if she had bitten into something sour and she hit back hard.

"The point is that he would prefer not to marry you."

To her surprise, Madame merely laughed at this assertion.

"It is really quite ridiculous," she said indulgently. "You

deceive yourself, my good girl . . . have you no mirror? There can really be no comparison between us. Look!''

She adopted a pose not unlike the professional attitude of some silly show girl which displayed to the full her undoubtedly generous endowments.

''What can *you* offer him?'' she demanded scornfully. ''Look at yourself! Skinny, homely, redhaired . . . and all wrapped up in this nursing work. You don't need a husband . . . and it's just as well . . . my Lee wants a *wife* not a little Sister of the Poor!''

She stretched out her arms to a now white-faced and thinlipped Phemie. It is one thing to know one's limitations, it is another to have them thrust down one's throat.

''I implore you, Miss Witherspoon, release him from this unhappy contract . . . let him have what he needs . . . what he wants . . . a warm and loving help-meet!''

''And who,'' came an acid voice from behind Phemie, ''made you an authority on my wants, Vi?''

Madame looked briefly put about but smoothly relinquished the role of warm, loving help meet and resumed that of the innocent suffering unjustly at the hands of the world.

''Ah, Lee, my dear . . .'' she greeted him in a voice fairly dripping with reasonableness and charity, ''I was only trying to make Miss Witherspoon see her demands on you in their true light.''

Devayler scowled. ''Sister Witherspoon has not . . .''

Phemie intervened. ''If you hadn't come in, Captain, I was going to give Mistress Devayler a reason for your acceding to my demands which even she could understand. Ugly and skinny I may be, but I have something you have not. Look!''

She thrust Frank's letter into the woman's hand.

''I am a wealthy woman, as you can see.''

Lee took a deep and indignant breath but expelled it in a gasp of agony when Phemie tramped hard upon his foot.

''Your dearest Lee is marrying me for my money,'' said Phemie. ''Now put that on your needles and knit it!''

Violette burst into tears and flung the letter on the floor.

212

"Lee, how could you be so mercenary!" she wailed. "And you, miss, how can you stoop to *buy* yourself a husband."

Devayler's protest was stamped on again. Madame, in full rhetorical flow, was suddenly overcome with the injustice of it all.

"And it's not as if you even needed it, Lee . . . it's not fair!"

She ran from the room.

"And that," mentioned Devayler limping ostentatiously to a chair, "is what I was trying to indicate to you. I don't need money. I've got plenty. Why do you think she came here in the first place?"

"Doesn't mean to say you wouldn't take a bit more if you can get it," remarked Phemie. "She thought you would. I had to find a believable reason for your preferring to marry me or she'd never have left me in peace. Now with any luck she'll catch the next stage East."

"And that was the most believable reason that you could find? That I was marrying you for your money?"

"It was more believable than the truth—" she returned, "that I am marrying you for mine."

They stared one another out of countenance for a second and then burst out laughing. Devayler laid his gauntlets on the table and unbuttoned his tunic to produce a scrap of paper.

"I came to tell you I have arranged for the wedding. Eli Jenkins will let us use his small parlour and the Reverend Baker will be there at noon the day after tomorrow. When the election is over."

"Just as well it's not tomorrow . . . I have a feeling we may be busy, one way or another."

She was right. Election Day was certainly eventful. After the first few hours Maggie stationed herself on the porch with bandages and lotion and a bucket of raw beef for the black eyes. In this style she dealt impartially with the victims of political faction who emerged from the Town Hall. Her patients usually staggered back, refreshed, to renew the fray. Phemie's energies were absorbed inside the ward. Millie was suffering from the

213

inevitable post-operative fever and Billy Quinn had had two haemhorrhages since early morning. Scipio patrolled the front of the building trying to keep fire-crackers, comb and-paper bands, horn players, stump orators and other merrymakers away from the vicinty. Evan rode off to make the visits outside the town.

The polls closed at eight o'clock but many people stayed near the Town Hall arguing and drinking and waiting for the results to be announced. Jenkins had his headquarters in the back parlour of the Nugget while Saul Barstowe had his in the bank, but both sides made use of the long bar in the big saloon of the Nugget with results which kept Maggie busy.

At ten o'clock Millie's fever took a turn for the better and she was sleeping naturally. Billy Quinn on the other hand was obviously sinking. Outside it had begun to snow so that both sides crowded into the warm smoky saloon to wait. A beam of yellow light thrust out into the falling flakes from the window and in the quiet ward the sound of laughter and tinkling piano music could be heard.

"Sounds cheerful, don't it?" croaked Billy Quinn when Phemie came to repack his pillows.

At half-past ten the word went round in the mysterious way such things do that the poll was to be announced. The Nugget emptied and so did both headquarters and a noisy drunken crowd converged on the Town Hall.

At quarter to eleven the result was announced: Eli Jenkins had topped the poll by seventeen votes. Not to put too fine a point on it, a riot was let loose at this news. Barstowe's main support lay in the mining population and they were none too pleased. They expressed their displeasure forcibly to those who were leaping in the air and yelling themselves hoarse to welcome the new Mayor by declaring that they intended to find those seventeen voters and tear them into little tiny pieces. The result was a brawl, a mêlée, a collie-shangie memorable even for a Frontier town. It was, so said Mrs Dutton the following day, only by the incalculable mercy of Providence that nobody was killed; though Eli Jenkins's insistence that all firearms be deposited at the desk with his clerk before the bearers could have a drink might have had something to do with it. Drunks had no guns and those who had guns were sober enough not to use them. As it was the noise grew louder and louder . . .

"Sounds real lively, don't it?" said Billy Quinn nostalgically, and died, his head against Phemie's shoulder.

Soon the casualties began to be dragged, carried and assisted in, and the hospital porch swept clear of drifting snow and sheltered by a tarpaulin requisitioned from the livery stable became a casualty ward. It was a noisy, bloody, kaleidoscopic night and as Phemie swabbed and stitched and cursed politicians, politics and all their works, the thought of Billy Quinn under his sheet stayed with her.

About dawn most of her patients had limped off into the freezing darkness to meet retribution in a night cap at home and she had Sandy McHarg face down on the surgery table, in which position he was retained by Maggie holding his feet with all her considerable strength and Evan lying across his shoulders. With probe and forceps she was removing lead pellets from his thighs and calves while Sandy cursed solidly and without repetition. The object of his curses was Elmer Dobbs the Deputy who should, had there been virtue in words, have been withering and fading in the corner. Instead he stood sheepishly admiring Sandy's undoubted range of expression and holding the author of the mishap.

"I tellt ye!" roared his victim. "I tellt ye tae wait on me . . . no tae bleeze away till I won back tae the door . . . Ow!"

Another pellet dropped into the bowl.

It was nearly full daylight when Maggie and Sandy left to return to their frame house. Esther and Evan were clearing up the debris. Outside the snow fell persistently, covering the traces of the night's mêlée. Phemie's legs ached and her back ached and she longed to lie down more than she had ever longed for anything . . . and—she gave a choke of laughter—today was her wedding day.

* * *

Some five hours later she was standing in her one remaining embroidered petticoat and regarding her available wardrobe with a somewhat jaundiced eye. Of the dresses she had brought with her none had been exactly festive and they were all well-worn. She chose a black stuff gown and looked out the lace collar and cuffs which had been her mother's and which she wore for church on Sundays. She took the pins out of her hair and let it fall about her shoulders. Esther had once suggested that she let it out of that perpetual chignon and make a nest of plaits in the nape of her neck. She had never had the time to experiment. The result was not unpleasing.

The first person to receive the benefit of this possible improvement was Eli Jenkins and it goes without saying that he noticed nothing when he came in to find her just before noon. He looked bloodshot and weary.

"Permit me to offer you my congratulations, Mr Mayor."

Jenkins winced.

"Just so long as you don't offer me a drink," he said. "I wanted to catch you before you came over. Don't want you should think there's anything political about this, see, and if I give it you over there . . ." He jerked his head at the Nugget. ". . . folks'll think I'm doin' myself some good."

He pulled the note which she and Devayler had signed out of his vest pocket and tore it into little pieces.

"If I'd done that yesterday it would have been a political bribe. Today's different . . . it's a wedding present if you like. I heard what Saul planned to do. Now I got to get back. Everything's ready. Good luck, girl!"

He patted her shoulder and left, leaving her staring at the scraps of paper with her face like a mask.

Originally the idea had been that no one except the Reverend Baker and the staff of the hospital should know when the wedding took place. It had been considered a diplomatic idea to include Jenkins as a witness . . . just to give him collateral so to speak.

It was therefore something of a surprise to find that the big saloon had suffered a sea-change from a political campaign centre to the 'bower of Hymen' beloved of the *Argus*. An arch of evergreens at the far end framed the figure of the Reverend Baker and Devayler stiff-backed in his best uniform. Mrs Dutton was seated at the piano which only a few hours ago had accompanied Janie in some of her saltier songs and beside it (suitably primed) stood the town's fiddler and his fiddle. The rest of the room was cram full of Argentanians. A number of the menfolk displayed signs of Phemie's handiwork and there was a disreputable sprinkling of black eyes and swollen noses, but for the most part her patients, miners, woodsmen, trappers, traders and farmers were gathered together in their wedding braws to see her married. Mounds of food and drink lurked under tablecloths in the corners.

Mrs Dutton spotted the small black clad figure at the door and struck up The Wedding March from Mendelssohn's *Midsummer Night's Dream*. It was perhaps unfortunate that the fiddler did not see her at exactly the same moment for he remained a bar or two behind. Eli Jenkins had evidently constituted himself 'father of the bride' and in a few seconds she found herself being escorted up a hastily cleared aisle towards the evergreen arch. He halted when they reached Devayler's side but Phemie went straight past and spoke to the Reverend Baker.

"It's not usual . . ." he protested, but Phemie appeared to press her point. "Oh, very well . . . Mrs Dutton, if you would be kind enough to lead the congregation in praise . . ."

Phemie came back to Devayler who raised his eyebrows at her.

"I must speak to you," she said very quitely. "It's important. Not here. We'll go into the office."

Their departure was a source of some surprise to the people in the saloon and ribald comments emerged like spiders from the corners but were chased back by basilisk glares from Mrs Dutton and Mrs Sellars who presided. From the piano came the introductory strains of Hymn number 583 specially chosen for the happy occasion:

The Call to Arms is sounding,

The foemen muster strong,
While Saints beneath the Altar
Are crying, 'Lord how long?'

Once in the office Phemie dropped the scraps of paper on Eli's desk.

"You don't need to do this any more," she told him bluntly. "Jenkins made the hospital a present of the money. He got to hear why we wanted it."

The strains of the hymn filtered through the walls. Phemie turned her back on him.

"Your sister-in law left on the stage yesterday morning. There's no need for this business at all. You can go out that way." She nodded at the unobtrusive door to the backyard in the corner of the office. "I'll explain that I had cold feet at the last moment."

Devayler swept the scraps off the table and put them into the stove as if he was playing for time.

"I'd be a fool to do that," he remarked casually, "and I'll be hung before I'll let you do it either."

"The very perfect gentle knight . . ." remarked Phemie bitterly, "I might almost think that you meant it."

"Oh, I do."

Phemie turned round to face him and her face was very white.

"Look, you don't have to be chivalrous," she begged quietly. "I don't want . . . it was all my doing and now there's no need. Just go quickly . . . no false nonsense. Why should you pretend to want what no one else ever did?"

"Your money, of course," said that very perfect knight, "or had you forgotten?"

The set look on her face relaxed into a reluctant grin.

"I'd forgotten that."

He came across and took her hands in a firm grip.

"Somehow I've got to convince you I've got peculiar tastes," he said. "I like tiny termagants with red hair and tongues like the business end of a hornet. Besides . . . someone's got to be around to haul you out of scrapes."

Phemie tried to wrench her hands away but failed.

"You told me there was someone you wanted to marry . . . you did."

"I imagined that after about twenty years of marriage I might bring you round to my way of thinking. I didn't expect Eli to upset my applecart quite so quickly."

She stopped pulling at her hands and glared at him.

"Do you mean that all that stramash out there is your doing?"

He shrugged. "I mentioned our plans to Mrs Baker . . . that was all. You see I wanted a cloud of witnesses for this wedding even if you didn't."

The hymn rose to a discordant climax.

"You certainly got them."

They both laughed. Devayler's grip on her hands tightened.

"Phemie . . ."

She didn't answer.

"Phemie, I've been wondering . . . do you have odd tastes as well? I mean for bad tempered army officers?"

She looked up at him anxiously at such a question and was given no time to answer because he picked her up and kissed her very soundly. In the meantime the impatient assembly led by Mesdames Dutton and Sellars were exorting one another to,

> Do no sinful action,
>
> Speak no angry word . . .

and they had reached the 'wicked spirit' in the third verse before Lee put her down. She was shaking as if she had a fever and he was white.

"You know," he told her very softly, "Violette was quite wrong about you . . . your hair is beautiful and you aren't all that skinny . . ."

"Lee!"

She tried to pull away from him. He prevented this without difficulty and said wickedly:

"And I have reason to *know* . . ."

Phemie blushed and wrenched herself away.

"You must be out of your mind!" she exclaimed. "Even if, even if . . . I can't leave the hospital yet . . . you *know* that. I won't be any good to you . . . I can't go with you . . ."

"If you can't run me," he observed solemnly, "a quiverful of children, the hospital, the town, probably the Territory as well and run for President in your spare time, you're not the woman I think you are. I'm settling here, buying the freight line. It should be profitable . . . special rates for hospital supplies of course."

He tucked her hand into his arm.

"Come on," he coaxed, "if Mrs Dutton launches them into another ten verser they'll mutiny. I tell you, girl, if we call it off now they'll lynch us."

"You really meant it?"

He looked down at her and smiled.

"I do. Come on, let's get this wedding over and I can prove how much I meant it."

They re-entered the room just in time to save the assembly from

> The ancient Law departs
> And all its terrors cease . . .

. . . and the more observant among them noticed that Phemie's hair was beginning to come down—an unheard-of occurrence.